THE BURNT REMAINS

A PENELOPE PHAIR MYSTERY

ALEX P. BERG

CHAPTER ONE

A cool wind blew as I stopped outside the front steps of the Fifth Street precinct. It was an old building, as most in the city of New Welwic were, but this one was more imposing than most. Four stories high and roughly the shape of a cube, the station looked as if it had been carved from solid granite, though if you looked carefully under the thin coat of grime deposited by decades of coal smoke and dust you'd find fine lines of mortar at the seams keeping the two ton blocks of stone in place. The double doors in front were banded with cast iron, as if they'd been pulled off an ancient castle, and above them hung a massive bas-relief carving of the police department's seal of justice: a soaring eagle clutching a balance scale in its wicked claws.

The rough stone, patinated iron, and eagle's claws all contributed to the building's imposing nature, but they weren't responsible for my throat's constriction. That had more to do with what awaited me within.

I took a deep breath, straightened my uniform, and headed up the steps. A din greeted me as I pulled open the doors.

Despite the early hour, most of the seats in the lobby were full, and not with the usual riffraff. People of all ages congregated before me, many wearing pajamas and fuzzy slippers and with damp hair that suggested they'd just bathed. Behind the information desk, a sea of officers flowed back and forth, the boxy partitions of the cubicles at their backs acting as the stationary coral to their lapping waves. Some led perps by their cuffed hands, others carried cups of coffee and clipboards, all of them with creased brows and tight jaws. I didn't know what caused the mass of people to press into the front of the station, but it wasn't my job to find out. I skirted a group of folks with crossed arms and scowls on their faces and headed for the stairs, taking them two at a time to the third floor.

I followed the edge of the cubicles, retracing my steps from the night before. At the far end, I ducked into the partitions, stopping at a cluster of desks isolated from the rest. Only one chair had a body in it, but that wasn't terribly surprising given I was half an hour early.

Detective Ginger Moss sat at her desk, head bowed over an open manila folder. She was a petite woman with a button nose and slender eyebrows she must've regularly plucked. Her dark blonde hair hung over her shoulder in a tight ponytail, but the variegated cascade rested against a cream blouse rather than the stylish leather jacket I'd come to associate with her. The black piece of cow hide wasn't far off, though. She'd draped it across the back of her chair.

Her head turned as my shadow fell over her. Her amber eyes brightened and a smile split her lips. "Well, look who the cat dragged in."

When I'd started as a patrol officer a week and a half ago, I'd been under the impression detectives were *very serious people*, but Moss had quickly divested me of that opinion. She had an easygoing charm to her, a cool nonchalance that dictated her rebellious clothing choices. I'd only known her for a little over a week, but I felt as if I'd already developed a rapport with her, so I didn't take her greeting the wrong way. Besides, I knew I actually looked pretty good. With my dark brown hair tamed and confined to a bun behind my head, an ample shirt that fit my broad shoulders and simultaneously hid the squishier parts of my midsection, and a tightly-fitting pair of pants that showed off my best asset, I felt I made the department's navy blues look about as good as they could.

"If the cat dragged anyone in, it was the folks in the lobby downstairs," I said with a snort. "Seriously, what happened? Did someone hold up a sauna?"

"Nothing quite so nefarious. As I understand it, some teenagers set off a fire alarm in an apartment building as a prank. The tenants are understandably up in arms. Regardless, it's not anything I have to deal with. Or you for that matter. Speaking of which..." Moss stood and extended a hand. "Let me give you an official welcome to the Fifth's homicide squad. Glad to have you aboard, Phair."

I grasped her hand and shook it. "Thanks for having me, Detective. I think I owe you for that."

Moss waved me off. "It's Moss, not Detective, and I had almost nothing to do with it. It was the report you submitted that convinced Dean, not me."

I still couldn't convince myself I wasn't dreaming. Yesterday I'd been wracked with worry, figuring I'd be reprimanded for submitting a report making my case that one of the NWPD's brightest young minds, Detective Alton Dean, had arrested the wrong man for murder. When Dean himself showed up at the

Williams Street precinct to talk with my captain, I'd figured it was curtains for my career, but instead, as I'd confronted Dean in the parking lot and made an ass of myself, Dean hit me with a curveball that could've banked around a ninety degree turn. He'd offered me a spot on his homicide team. Not as a detective, of course. For the time being, I remained an officer, no more and no less, but with Dean in charge of my training, the path to becoming a detective had been swept clean. Dean hadn't said as much, but it didn't take the world's brightest young detective to see which way the compass was pointed.

I couldn't figure out if I was more excited or terrified by the opportunity.

I swallowed back the lump in my throat and nodded. "Well, I still appreciate your support. If nothing else, you got me out from under Officer Stonefist's thumb. That alone deserves a fruit basket."

Moss's face darkened at the mention of my former training officer. "Nobody deserves to suffer under someone that morally bankrupt for a week, much less a year. The fact that his ilk are being assigned new recruits at all chaps my ass. Makes me think there's something fundamentally wrong with the leadership at some of our precincts." She shook her head. "That's neither here nor there. The important thing is you're part of our team now, ready to rock and roll. You didn't have any issues finding your locker, did you?"

I glanced at my uniform. "If I'm being honest, I wore this here. Given that I didn't accept Detective Dean's offer until last night, I thought there might not be a locker available."

Moss smiled and lifted an eyebrow. "As I understand it, it wasn't an offer so much an order, but regardless, you're underestimating how organized Dean is. Not only do you have a locker ready for you, you've got a desk to boot." Moss shot a thumb over her shoulder at the space next to hers. "It'll be up to you to fill it with photographs and tchotchkes, though."

I took a step past Moss and peered into the indicated partition. Sure enough, a desk bare of everything except a phone and a cup with a few pencils in it sat there. It wasn't even dusty.

"I get my own desk?" I said. "For real? You didn't clear off Detective Justice's stuff, dump it in a box, and tell him to wait around a corner to spring on me as soon as I sit down?"

"As good of a prank as that would be, it wouldn't work given that Justice's desk is over there." Moss pointed to the other side of the cluster where next to Alton Dean's desk was another almost as neatly organized. A dark green potted plant, seemingly of a variety that didn't require much light, was pushed into the far corner, and a golden plate with the name Justice gleamed in the middle, same as Dean's name glimmered from his.

I took another glance at the empty desk. "I don't rate highly enough for a nameplate?"

"You'll get one, but it might take a few days," said Moss. "The engraver doesn't do rush orders. Even Dean's influence has its limits. We did however get you the finest office chair we could steal from the other empty desks on the floor. It's got five wheels and everything."

The chair in question leaned slightly to one side. The pad on the seat was nearly worn through, and the fabric covering it was splotchy and variegated. Something metallic gleamed through one of the cracks in the cushion—hopefully not the sharpened tip of a nail.

I must've hesitated a moment too long, as Moss waved at it with a smile. "Go on. Give it a whirl."

It cried out with a rusty squeal as I sat, reminiscent of a

fork's tines being dragged across a ceramic plate. The armrests wobbled as I set my elbows upon them, and as expected, the seat was more film than cushion. Lucky for me, I had enough natural padding in my derrière to make it a moot point.

The chair creaked again as I put my full weight on it. "I've sat on worse."

Moss clapped me on the shoulder. "That's the spirit. If you keep your expectations low, you'll never be disappointed."

I swiveled in the seat and glanced at my desk. The holder for my name rested against the back partition, empty as a family of ten's pantry. In my mind's eye, I saw my name there, the black letters standing out among the gold. Not Officer Phair, but *Detective*.

My stomach fluttered, and I let out a heavy sigh. "I've got to admit, this feels weird."

Moss shrugged as she returned to her own chair. "Well, you're free to look and see if you can find a better one, but I've got to warn you. If you swap it, make darn sure you're not taking one from an occupied desk. We share a lot of things around here, but chairs aren't one of them. Justice would fight you for his. He might pull a knife."

I smiled and shook my head. "I didn't mean the chair. I meant... *this*. Me being here. A part of your investigative team. Let's be real. Three weeks ago, I was walking across a stage to accept my police academy diploma, and suddenly I'm working homicide? That's not a normal trajectory."

Moss shrugged. "Maybe it should be."

I frowned. "You think every rookie should be promoted within their first month? You're going to run out of chairs real fast."

Moss lifted an eyebrow and gave me an old schoolmarm sort

of glare. "Don't be silly. What I'm saying is the traditional system of pairing every rookie with a patrol officer isn't the best way to train a skilled workforce. Don't get me wrong. You learn a lot on patrol, but if the goal is to have officers knowledgeable in burglary and narcotics and homicide and everything else, then perhaps there should be a system in place to identify those who show promise and pair them with detectives who know what they're doing. That way we're not dependent on random acts of fate like the one that brought you here to identify rising stars."

I blinked. "Excuse me. *What?*"

"You know," said Moss. "A system. Like a standardized test, though something more nuanced would be nice."

"Not that," I said. "You think I'm a *rising star?*"

Moss smiled. "You don't see it yet, do you?"

"See what?"

Moss leaned in. "You're not here by accident, Penelope. Yes, the fact that you got called to the scene of a murder on your first shift was a twist of fate, but everything that followed was up to you. You could've followed your training officer's lead, mentally checked out as soon as you radioed the murder in, and punched out at the end of your day, but you didn't. You were curious. You observed the scene. You took mental notes. You asked questions, even though it was clear you thought you shouldn't have, and you kept thinking about the case long after you should've given up on it. The fact that you were willing to keep searching for the truth after we'd arrested a man proves it. You've earned your right to be here. You possess all the skills you need to succeed. You just have to use them."

I swallowed back a lump in my throat. I'd never been very good with praise, probably because I hadn't gotten a lot of it growing up. Neither of my parents were warm and fuzzy types, and even if they had been, their constant fighting hadn't left much time for interactions with me. My school experience and the handful of waitressing jobs I'd held down during the first half of my twenties hadn't done much to grow my confidence either, so I didn't really know how to respond to Moss. I probably should've thanked her and told her I'd do my best, but there was something about the detective that made me feel like I could trust her.

I spoke softly. "You really think I'll do fine?"

Moss smiled. "Your track record is thin, but I haven't seen anything yet that would make me suspect otherwise." Her eyes flicked up. "What do you think, Dean?"

A strong, steady voice spoke over my shoulder. "If I didn't think Officer Phair was going to be a valuable addition to our team, I wouldn't have asked to have her placed under my tutelage, would I?"

I shot out of my seat and spun to find a handsome elf in a mineral blue sports coat standing a few feet behind me. "Detective Dean!"

"Good morning, Phair." Alton Dean stood tall, his head and shoulders rising above the edge of my desk's partition. Like most dark elves, his skin was more of a dark grey in color than a true brown, though it seemed to me there was a reddish undertone to it that made him look warmer and more vibrant than most. His hair, which he kept short and parted to one side, was so blonde as to appear white, though not quite as white as the brilliant smile he flashed me. "You're early."

The shock of being pounced on from behind momentarily scrambled my thoughts, though it was possible Dean's disarming smile and high cheekbones had something to do with it, too. "I, ah... how long were you standing there?"

Dean's ice blue eyes twinkled. "Long enough to get the gist of the conversation, but not so long that I overheard anything not meant for me, I think. But you didn't answer my question. Why so early? It's quarter till nine, and it seems you've already been here a while."

I shrugged. "I wasn't sure how long the subway would take, plus I wore my uniform from home. Forgot to account for the changing time. Guess I wanted to make sure I wasn't late."

"There's a locker waiting for you downstairs, you know," said Dean.

"We already had this conversation," said Moss. "Phair doubted your ability to prepare for her arrival given the sudden nature of her hire."

"No, I didn't," I sputtered. "I didn't doubt you at all, sir. There was no doubting."

"Relax," said Dean. "I'd rather you arrive early than late. Shows you're cautious and committed. Both good things. And I've already told you, it's Dean from now on, not sir or detective."

A little of the tension bled from my shoulders as I nodded. "Right."

A hint of cigarette smoke wafted my way as Dean peeled off his grayish-blue sports coat and draped it across the back of his chair. He was lean but nonetheless broad in the shoulders, a pleasing body shape that so often went to waste thanks to ill-fitting clothing. Not so with Dean. His crisp white shirt was tailored to his waist, and the sleeves were long enough that they actually covered his wrists, barely revealing the gleam of a silver watch when he bent them.

Dean sat in a chair that was noticeably cleaner and newer than mine, but I remained standing. Despite Dean and Moss's assurances, I couldn't help but feel intimidated by their presence. "So what's the first order of business for today?"

"That's the thing about police work," said Dean. "You never know. Varies from day to day. The only constant is change."

Moss clicked her tongue. "I'm not sure I'd go that far. Paperwork is a constant. But if you want an agenda, Phair, you can start by getting Dean and me each a steaming mug of joe. Break room's in the northeast corner."

I lifted an eyebrow. "You want me to fetch you coffee?"

The smile Moss responded with was more playful than malicious. "Dean might've brought you on to help with investigations, but you're still a rookie. We can't let you get *too* comfortable."

"Don't listen to her," said Dean as his phone rang. "You report to me, not to Detective Moss. You don't have to fetch her anything. Me, on the other hand..." He smiled as he pulled the receiver to his ear. "Dean speaking."

I lowered my voice as I turned to Moss. "Did he just crack a joke?"

"He breaks them out when you least expect them," said Moss. "Though to be fair, I think that one puts him over his monthly quota. I'll have to check my ledger."

I shook my head as I sat back down. Switching from a toxic work environment to one full of good-natured ribbing was a positive change but one I'd still have to get used to. "Just go easy on me. Might take me a while before I'm fully adapted to your comic stylings."

"I'll say," said Moss. "You still haven't fetched Dean his coffee."

I glanced at the dapper dark elf. "You said he was joking."

Once again Moss's eyes twinkled. "Well, it's so hard to

know, isn't it? He's so deadpan on his delivery. Better safe than sorry, I always say."

"Oh, for crying out loud..."

I got out of my chair as Dean set the receiver back on its base with a clack. "No time for that. That was Captain Ellison. Seems like there may have been a murder at the Vernon and Daly Circus. We've been assigned the case."

Moss stood and grabbed her jacket. *"May have been?* Did someone find a body or not?"

Dean stood, too. "From what I heard, a bystander found *something*, but to call it a body might be a stretch. Guess we'll find out when we get there." Dean nodded at me as he slipped back into his coat. "Ready for your first assignment, Phair?"

Nervous excitement tingled in my fingertips. "You bet I am. But to be clear... were you angling for a coffee or weren't you?"

Dean laughed and nodded toward the stairs. "Come on. I'll drive."

CHAPTER TWO

The last time I'd visited the circus, I'd been nine. That was before my parents divorced but not before their feelings of resentment, bitterness, and spite drove a stake between them. My dad had taken me, probably as much to get away from my mother as a bonding opportunity for the two of us. I vaguely remembered snacking on cotton candy and peanuts as I watched the floor show: the jumping acrobats in their multi-colored jumpsuits, the brave trapeze artists spinning from their suspended bars, and of course, I remembered the lion tamer, hopping from platform to platform in his silver and red leotard, cracking his whip and goading his enormous cats into following him. More than anything, I remembered the glamor and spectacle of it all: fire breathers and jugglers at every crook and corner, the tall tents and dense crowds, and the brightly painted sign at the entrance, proudly proclaiming the Vernon and Daly Circus as the "World's Greatest Spectacle!"

As Dean pulled his emerald green Howardson Viper into the Vernon and Daly lot, a few things struck me. For one, the circus didn't seem as gigantic as I remembered it. With the lot included, the grounds stretched a full city block, but the white-washed fence that surrounded it was six feet high at most. Even the billowing triangular flags atop the main tent couldn't have reached more than five stories in the air. None of that surprised me—vistas observed as a child always seem smaller when viewed from an adult vantage—but the state of the circus did. The aforementioned fencing had worn over time, resulting in as much wood showing as whitewash, and the "World's Greatest Spectacle!" sign that hung over the entrance had faded, so much so that the colors barely popped against the sky's clouded backdrop.

Dean parked his Viper next to a trio of police cruisers by the entrance, and we all hopped out. The gates to the grounds were open, and though not a carnie was in sight, a lone cop stood at their side, smoking a cigarette. Other than swilling coffee, smoking seemed to be tied with drinking for the most common addiction of choice among officers and was, as far as I could tell, Detective Dean's only real vice. Then again, if I had as much weight of responsibility on my shoulders as he did, I too might need the occasional chemical pick-me-up to take the edge off.

The officer at the gate tossed his butt to the dirt and ground it out under his shoe as we approached, the smell of the smoke still hanging around him. "Morning, Detectives. You're going to want to head left. Take a right at the covered wagon and follow the trailers that are painted green. You'll find the bird enclosure past the big cat pens."

The officer didn't specify what we'd find there, just as Dean hadn't. Moss asked him on the ride over, but all he'd said was that some remains had been found and it would be up to us to determine whether a crime had been committed. The mention of remains had brought to mind grisly images of bodies torn limb from limb, but neither Dean nor Moss seemed concerned by it, so I figured I should do my best to follow their lead. After all, if I was going to be working homicide cases from now on, it would only be a matter of time until we chanced across something so vile and disgusting that it made me deposit my breakfast across the floor. If fate determined today was that day, at least I'd be vomiting outdoors.

As we passed through the entrance and hooked a left, I found the circus wasn't as deserted as it appeared. To the right of the main tent, laborers stacked poles and coiled guy-wire. On a platform before canvas print advertising the circus's side shows, a shirtless, well-muscled man with a bushy beard practiced lifting an oversized dumbbell over his head in one smooth motion, and not far from him, a pair of dwarves—the tiny human kind, not the race of bearded mountain dwellers—spoke to one of the police officers on the scene. The workers' presence didn't do anything to brighten the circus's appearance, however. If anything, the side show banners were even more faded than the sign over the entrance, the candy apple reds and forest greens long since turned to pink and sea foam. A thin layer of rust coated the chain links of an empty animal enclosure, and weeds grew to knee height to the side of every beaten path.

Not everything visible to the eye had been tarnished by age, though. Posters with ink still glossy from the printer hung between every third set of fence posts, each of them showing the same image of a middle-aged man with a waxed mustache, thick eyebrows, and a bulbous nose. A broad smile graced his lips, and the words "Vote Prosperity, Vote Vernon!" jumped from the bottom of each poster in a bold font.

I pointed to one of them as we reached the covered wagon

mentioned by the officer at the entrance. "Is that the same Vernon who owns the circus?"

Dean glanced at me over his shoulder. "The one and only. You didn't know he was running for office?"

"To be honest, I don't pay much attention to politics."

Dean shrugged. "That's for the best, if you can avoid it. I wouldn't either if my position didn't call for me to do the occasional round of glad-handing. But yes, the greatest showman himself is taking on the fourth district's old incumbent, Maximillian Bumblefoot. I haven't seen any polling, but I'd have to assume Vernon has a shot. He's got name recognition, if nothing else, and he can lay claim to having built a booming entertainment empire from scratch. The rags to riches story always plays well with low-information voters."

"*Booming empire?*" I stared at the peeling paint on the trailers at our side. "Are we looking at the same circus?"

"He owns more than one," said Moss. "As far as I know, there are Vernon and Daly circuses in Eastport, Ravensworth, Port Norell, and Buckhaven, not to mention one that travels internationally. This place might not look like much, but it draws big crowds. I've heard Vernon is a shrewd businessman."

"I think ruthless might be a better word than shrewd," said Dean. "Have you heard the story about how he bought out his former partner Daly? According to Daly, Vernon hired a seductress to break up his marriage, then the home-wrecker in question convinced Daly to sell his half of the company to pay for his divorce and subsequent lavish elopement—after which the mistress immediately ditched him. Of course, it's possible he just got conned by a beautiful young woman and thought his story would play better if he blamed Vernon, but given Vernon's other business ventures, it's plausible."

A pen forged of thick iron bars rose up beyond the trailers to our right. Inside them, behind a large rock and some foliage, I caught a hint of movement. Something orange and striped. "You sure know a lot about this Vernon. Have you crossed paths before?"

Dean shook his head. "Nothing like that. I read in my free time, same as everyone else. History and biographies, more often than not, but I enjoy science and engineering as well. Why? Are you more into fiction?"

I didn't have the heart to tell him most of my free time was wasted nurturing relationships that fizzled out after a few months, at least those that didn't end in spectacular explosions like when I beat up my ex-boyfriend Mick after finding a mostly nude gnome in our closet. I just nodded instead. "Uh... yeah. Mostly fiction."

I saw another flash of orange and black out of the corner of my eyes, so I wasn't completely caught off guard when the beast growled. I may not have jumped, but I nonetheless spun, quickly enough to catch the tiger pawing around the edge of its cage toward us. The animal was huge, with powerful muscles that rippled under its fur. Its teeth flashed in the morning sun as it fought off a debilitating yawn.

Moss shook her head. "Poor thing. I hate seeing animals locked up."

The beast stared at me the same way I might eye a juicy tenderloin filet. "You'd rather that thing be running loose?"

"Not in the city, smarty-pants," said Moss. "But in its natural habitat, sure. Makes me sad to see such a majestic creature locked in a box."

A voice called out from further ahead. "You'll be happy to hear what happened here, then."

Past the edge of the tiger pen, another uniformed officer stood outside a cylindrical cage. This one was fabricated of simple chain links, and instead of a roof, a woven net hung over it from a high pole in the center. In addition, whereas the tiger pen contained a few large rocks, a wooden shack, and had straw strewn across the dirt, this pen was full of foliage. Trees thick with dark green leaves stretched as high as they could underneath the netting. Vines wrapped around the chain links and support beams while bushes pushed past them, their thin branches stretching into the free space beyond in search of sun. Something inside called out with a trill, an undulating avian warble that I couldn't recall ever hearing before. Then again, I'd only ever left New Welwic on day trips. My extent of birdsong knowledge was being able to identify a pigeon's coo.

Dean nodded to the officer standing at the edge of the fencing, a pudgy guy with a weatherbeaten face whose name tag read Wormwood. "Morning, Officer. The remains are inside?"

Wormwood tilted his head toward the entrance, a two-stage thing with a fenced door on the outside and a heavy drape on the innermost gap to keep the birds from flying into the intervening space. "That's right, Detective. My partner, Coldwell, is inside. He can show you where they are if you have any issues finding them."

"What do we know so far?" asked Dean.

Wormwood shrugged. "Not much. Supposedly, the carnies woke this morning to find the outer gate to the enclosure left open. Not sure if it was broken into or what. Either way, some of the animals inside got loose. Nothing dangerous. As I understand it, the only things that live in there are monkeys, birds, and some rodents. The carnies are trying to wrangle up the monkeys, but I guess the birds that got out are gone for good.

Anyway, as one of the crew was returning escaped monkeys to the enclosure, he found the remains and called it in."

I felt that queasy sensation in my stomach again. I glanced into the thick foliage, imagining what lay beyond. "And when you say *remains*...?"

Wormwood shook his head. "It's the damnedest thing. I can't make sense of it, to be honest. You'll have to see for yourself."

That didn't assuage my fears, but if Dean noticed my trepidation, he didn't show it. He nodded toward the entrance. "Time for us to see what we're up against. After you."

I swallowed back the lump in my throat and opened the outer gate.

CHAPTER THREE

Another bird trilled as I pushed past the heavy drape into the dark embrace of the enclosure. The air cooled by several degrees as I passed into the shadow of the trees, but beyond that it smelled cleaner, as if the trees at the perimeter had formed a barrier against the city's soot and fumes. An earthy aroma hung in my nostrils, thankfully free of the distinctive funk of large animal droppings, and I heard the burble of running water, though it must've been from a fountain rather than a stream.

Dean and Moss followed me inside. As they let the drape fall behind them, a small bird with brilliant blue plumage flitted from the low-hanging boughs of a tree in front of us into thicker foliage.

I grunted. "So maybe not *all* the parts of this circus are as run down as they first appear."

"I guess one of the benefits of not having a traveling attraction is that you can put together permanent exhibits." Moss peered into the vaguely tropical environs around us. "Though I still think the animals would be better off elsewhere."

A path snaked through the enclosure. Past a bend, seated on a bench, was the aforementioned Officer Coldwell. Dean nodded and we headed forth. My stomach clenched as I anticipated the grisly scene awaiting me, but I didn't hear the buzzing of flies, nor did I detect the metallic tang of blood or the sour stench of decay in the air. Coldwell stood as he heard us, and then as we rounded a bush, I saw it: not a wrecked mass of human flesh but a disordered pile of bones sticking out from a mound of ash.

Dean stopped a few paces from the pile, his brow furrowed. "Well... that *is* odd."

Dean knelt to get a closer look. I moved around to the other side and did the same, as did Moss. The bones were clearly human. The skull alone made it obvious, but the ribcage was also easily identifiable, as were the femurs and hip. Rather than being an even, bleached white, the bones were varying shades of gray, seemingly covered by a thin layer of soot. That wasn't surprising given the pile of ash in which they sat, but what *was* surprising was how clean they were. To my eye, not a single bit of gristle or meat was attached to any of them. Not that I had any training in forensics, but the bones looked as if they belonged in a catacomb or a mausoleum rather than a crime scene.

"This is a joke, right?" said Moss.

Dean looked up from the burnt remains. "What do you mean?"

"Clearly nobody was murdered here," said Moss. "Look at this. A neat pile of bones stuck in a mound of ash. It's almost comical. As if someone left this here as a prank. People don't spontaneously combust, you know, not even in a circus."

Detective Dean pulled a glove from his coat pocket and drew it onto his right hand. He drew the tip of his index finger along the length of one of the exposed femurs. The soot stuck to the fabric, accumulating on the tip and leaving a trail of clean, white bone behind. "While I won't dismiss your initial hunch, I'd have to disagree. First of all, if you were to prank a coworker, you wouldn't wait until after the police arrived to reveal everything was a joke."

"Unless you were worried about getting busted for something illegal," said Moss. "Or you're a huge ass."

Dean lifted an eyebrow. "More importantly, these bones are the real deal, not porcelain fakes. A prank with fake bones, I could see, but one with real bones? That requires a bigger stretch of the imagination. First you have to get your hands on human remains, which are usually buried or put places where people with sticky fingers aren't likely to slip them into their coats. Even assuming you did find an old set of human remains, they wouldn't be covered with a fine layer of soot like these are. These remains have been freshly cremated, Moss."

Moss rubbed her temple. "So you're suggesting someone cremated a body and dumped the remains in a wild bird enclosure at the circus? That makes more sense than this being a prank?"

"I'm not suggesting anything at this point. I don't have enough data to make an educated guess." Dean turned his ice blue eyes on me. "You're quiet, Phair. What do you think?"

I blinked. The reason I'd been quiet was because I had two brilliant detectives discussing a crime scene that made zero sense to me. Also because I had all the investigative experience of one of the birds trilling above me. "You want *my* opinion?"

"That's what I said, isn't it?" Dean's eyes didn't have any malice in them. It didn't seem as if he was trying to reveal me as a no talent hack, but he must've known I'd defer to him and Moss. Then again, the man seemed to have an overabundance of confidence, all of it of the rational kind. Maybe the thought never crossed his mind that others could be insecure.

I shook my head, trying to banish my feelings of doubt and focus on the evidence. "Well, I don't know how these remains got here, but there was clearly a fire. Look."

I pointed at the ground surrounding the pile of ash. Apart from the mulch on the path, the ground cover in the aviary was a mix of grass and dead leaves, but there was nothing but scorched earth underneath the remains. The blackened soil stretched about a foot and a half from the edge of the ash pile in any given direction, and at the edges where it transitioned into forest ground cover, there were blades of grass and leaves with wispy, ashen edges, as if they'd been exposed to a fire that had fizzled and died.

Dean nodded. "Indeed. There's no question there was a fire. Curious that it didn't spread..."

"It didn't spread because it was a baby fire set to make it look as if someone had been burned at the stake," said Moss. "Seriously. There's no way a fire could've burned anyone here."

"Not necessarily," said a creaky new voice.

I looked up to find two individuals walking along the path toward us. One of them I knew. Detective Ogden Justice, the fourth member of Alton Dean's investigative team, was hard to miss. At six and a half feet tall and tipping the scales somewhere north of three hundred and fifty pounds, he would've made a mountain of a man, but since he was an ogre, he wasn't too far off the median. With buttery smooth, espresso-colored skin, a bright white smile, and dark hair that he kept trimmed almost to the skull, he was quite the looker, although the crisp, three-piece suits he wore certainly contributed to his overall image. All in all, he was a bit brawny for my tastes, but if jokes were any indication of true feelings, Moss had a bit of a thing for him.

The man next to him was everything Justice wasn't. He was barely over five feet tall, rotund, and had a squished face that made him look like a mole. A bit of wispy hair hung over his ears and around the base of his head, but his crown was as bald as an egg. Suspenders stretched and heaved, barely keeping his waistband in place, although one of his shirt tails had somehow broken free and hung over the front of his trousers. Given that Justice's voice was deep and smooth like a professional radio host's, I figured he'd been the one who'd spoken.

Dean stood as the pair approached. "Morning, Cortez. Did Justice drag you out here?"

The mole man shook Dean's hand. "Captain Ellison asked me to come given what he'd heard about the remains. Justice grabbed me as I was walking through the front door."

"And I'd barely been at the station a minute myself," said Justice. "Could've waited for me, you know."

Moss smirked. "We left a note. Not like we'd take one car, anyway. You bottom out the shocks almost by your lonesome."

Dean nodded at me. "Phair, this is Detective Gaspar Cortez; arson. Cortez, this is Officer Penelope Phair. She's joined our investigative team."

Cortez smiled as I shook his hand, which was somewhat limp and spongy. "Finally convinced the captain to spring for a gopher, did you, Dean?"

Given his subterranean appearance, I couldn't help but picture the rodent rather than the demeaning position. Thankfully, I didn't have to defend my own honor.

"She's a little more useful than that, Cortez," said Dean. "She solved our last case. I think she has a bright future in the department."

Cortez put up his hands in supplication, which made him look even more mole-like. "My mistake. Just trying to tickle the old funny bone."

Moss shouldered her way into the circle. "No tickling, Cortez, unless you want to have a long talk with HR. You were saying something about the remains?"

"Right. I heard you say something about the body—" Cortez glanced at the pile of ash and bones. "Err, *remains*—not being able to have burned on site. And while I admit I haven't combed the scene yet, I will say I've seen many a person reduced to ash in fires before. It happens more often than people think."

"But you're talking about house fires, right?" said Moss. "Big blazes with lots of fuel, not small ones set in the middle of a bird enclosure."

Cortez cocked his head and stretched his eyebrows. "Well, people cremated the dead on funeral pyres long before the modern furnace was invented, but those required a lot of wood and oil and were quite large. The flames from a pyre would've spread and charred this entire forest. That said, it's at least *plausible* a body could've been burned here if the proper accelerants were employed. Someone would've had to put serious fire breaks in place to keep the flames from spreading, though. I don't think a metal ring would've done the job."

Moss's lips puckered, and she lifted one of her eyebrows as far as if would go.

Cortez caught the look. "Hey, I'm not saying it's *likely*."

"What kind of accelerants are we talking about?" asked Justice.

"Anything would do," said Cortez. "Most liquid fuels get plenty hot. Propane, butane, gasoline, even ethyl alcohol. Most cremation furnaces only run at about sixteen to eighteen hundred degrees. But you'd need a lot of it, and that stuff ain't light."

"How long would it take to reduce a body to this state?" asked Dean.

Cortez's forehead scrunched as he peered at the pile of ash and bones. "Normally cremation takes anywhere from an hour and a half to four hours, depending on the temperature of the furnace and the size of the individual. Someone like me with a little extra peanut butter and jelly in the middle would take a lot longer than a pinup." Cortez chuckled, but no one else joined him. "Ahh... but in all seriousness, given the condition of the bones, I'd wager we're looking at the lower end of the spectrum. The longer you subject bones to high heat, the more cracking and embrittlement that occurs. Burn a body for four hours, and the resulting remains barely need more than a minute in the ball mill to get to a nice, powdery consistency. These seem like they would take a good bit longer."

Dean rubbed his chin before giving his head a slight shake. "That's too long. It's not plausible to think someone wheeled enough accelerants in to keep a fire going for an hour and a half, failed to char a space more than five feet in diameter, and did so without alerting anyone as to what was going on." A monkey barked in a tree overhead, drawing Dean's attention. Leaves rattled and shook as the thing took off upon being spotted. "Not to mention, I can't imagine the wildlife would've stayed quiet if someone set fire to this place in the middle of the night. Monkeys aren't known for their discretion. We have to presume these remains were dumped here, although why is anyone's guess."

"But if someone left them here," I said, "then why did they try to make it look as if the body was cremated on site? The ground is clearly scorched. There was a fire, though it appears to have been a small one."

Most of our eyes turned toward Cortez. The guy shrugged. "Beats me. In theory, if you deposited recently cremated remains, the latent heat *might* be enough to set a small blaze, but carrying piping hot remains around seems like a logistical nightmare, not to mention a weird thing to do. My guess is someone set the blaze to confuse the issue."

Dean stared at the pile of bones and ash, lightly chewing his lip. "It's a question in need of an answer, but far from the most pressing one. What we need to determine is who placed these remains here, why they did so, and most importantly, whose remains they are. Let's not get too caught up in the oddity of what's before us and forget we're likely dealing with murder."

Dean's pragmatic focus lay a pall over us. We all nodded solemnly, curiosity momentarily overtaken by the grim reality of what might've happened.

Dean continued after a short pause. "Cortez, you should stay here. See if you can find any clues we haven't uncovered, specifically anything that might help identify the deceased. I'm going to track down a facilities manager or overseer, see if they can give me any information about who has access to this enclosure. Justice? Maybe you can track down the circus's fire performance artists. Just because this body didn't burn at our feet doesn't mean someone in the circus isn't responsible. Check stores of accelerants, see if anything is missing. Moss and Phair? I want you to interview whoever found the remains, see what they have to say. Are we all clear?"

I nodded, as did the other detectives.

"Good," said Dean. "Let's get to work."

CHAPTER FOUR

I stood outside the aviary, next to the snake, lizard, and frog house, if its sign could be believed. A cool breeze whipped past, and I wished the sun would make an appearance from behind the clouds.

Moss stood next to me, hands stuffed in the pockets of her leather jacket. "Mr. Radoslaw, please start at the beginning and run us through the morning."

The man who stood before us, Krzysztof Radoslaw, was apparently the circus's chief zookeeper, or at least the one in charge of the bird pen. Finger-length brown hair framed his oval-shaped face, and three day old stubble that was gray in patches covered his chin. He wore a tattered canvas jacket that might've been stitched together before he was born, though it was hard to tell exactly how old the man was. Sallow skin hung loosely from his bones, and dark circles spread underneath his eyes. He could've been anywhere from in his thirties to his sixties, but even if he was on the older end of the spectrum, he still looked terrible.

Radoslaw spoke with a bit of an accent, though I couldn't place it. "I would say it started about five in the morning. At least that is when I woke. I heard the macaques shrieking and squeaking, which they do when they are hungry, but to be honest, they are not the loudest monkeys in the world. I usually do not hear them from my trailer, but when I got out of bed and looked out the window, there were two of them, perched on the edge of my trashcan, fighting over apple cores and watermelon rinds. They had knocked it over, spilling garbage everywhere. It was a mess...

"Anyway, as soon as I saw them, I knew something was wrong. My first thought was that one of them had ripped through the netting, and if that happened, who knows how many birds we would have lost. So I threw on my clothes and ran out to the enclosure. I could not see well so early in the morning, but the problem was obvious. Someone had left the outer gate open. When I got my nephew out of bed, he swore it had not been him, but who knows. He probably would not admit to doing it even if he had.

"The pair of us spent the next two hours trying to lure the macaques into cages so we could take them back into the enclosure. It was not easy. They are smarter than they look, but they have their weaknesses, same as anyone. A dozen bananas and many grapes later, we were pretty sure we had them all, though it was hard to know for certain. We did not hear any more fighting, which made me think we had. We might have lost a couple birds, though. I heard one of the honeycreepers calling at sunrise, and I thought it was coming from the acrobat's pavilion. I am not sure if we will be able to lure those back. They are not as smart as the macaques, but maybe we will get lucky."

"So when did you find the burnt remains?" asked Moss.

Radoslaw coughed into the elbow of his jacket, a wracking, dry cough that shook his whole body. It took him a second to get his breath afterwards. "That was not until later. As my nephew Mateusz and I caught the macaques, we let them into the enclosure one by one. When I could no longer hear them around the grounds, I went into the aviary to see if I could count them, make sure they were inside. That is when I found the bones."

"And that's when you called the police?" said Moss.

"Not at first," said Radoslaw. "I thought I was being tricked. Why would there be human bones in the pen? And I got mad, because I figured whoever was behind it was the one who had left the enclosure open, but none of the other keepers knew what I was talking about when I confronted them. After a bit, Mateusz said we should call the police, so that is what we did."

Moss gave me a sideways glance. "See? I'm not the only one who thought it was a prank."

"I'm not judging you. It's a bizarre thing to find." I turned back to Radoslaw. "The bird enclosure normally stays locked?"

The man cleared his throat noisily. I thought he might go into another coughing fit, but thankfully he didn't. "Locked at night, yes. Not during the day, otherwise the crowds would not be able to get in. It is supposed to stay closed, though. There is a sign on the chain links saying so."

"Did you see any signs of forced entry?" I asked. "Was the lock damaged or any of the chains cut?"

Radoslaw shook his head. "Nothing. At least not at the bird pen."

Moss cocked her head. "What do you mean by that?"

"After we were done with the monkeys, Mateusz discovered one of the supply trailers had been broken into. The window in back had been smashed to bits, and the stuff inside looked as if it had been gone through."

"What do you keep in the trailer?" asked Moss.

"Costumes, mostly," said Radoslaw. "I suppose it could have been one of the macaques who broke the window. They are strong enough, and I have seen them throw rocks before, among other more fragrant things. But I cannot imagine they would break the glass unless they smelled ripe fruit on the other side."

"Was anything missing?" asked Moss.

Radoslaw shrugged. "I do not know. Ask one of the acrobats or the showgirls."

"What about the enclosure?" I said. "Do you think someone intended to rob it, too?"

Radoslaw erupted in another chorus of coughs, but this time he got them under control quickly. He shook his head. "I do not know what you mean by robbing it, but Mateusz and I found the macaques. A few of the birds are missing, but I would bet they flew off. Besides, if someone broke in to steal our birds, why would they leave a dead person behind?"

I glanced at Moss. "You got any ideas?"

She snorted. "If I was that good, I'd be in charge of the team, not Dean. Thanks for your time, Mr. Radoslaw. You're free to go."

The guy dipped his head and shuffled off. In addition to the pallor of his skin, he walked with a limp. I kind of felt bad for him.

"I think that guy needs to see a doctor," I said.

"Undoubtedly, but circus work isn't known for its benefits." Moss stared at the bird enclosure. "Am I the only one getting a setup vibe from this case?"

"How so?"

"We're operating under the assumption that someone was murdered, their remains cremated and subsequently dumped in that pen. We don't know who's dead, but if it's someone with a connection to these carnies, it could easily be a frame job."

My brow furrowed. "If someone was trying to frame someone else for murder, wouldn't they leave the body? As you said, we don't even know who's dead."

"Normally, yes, but ashes are easier to move than a corpse." She massaged her temple. "I don't know. I'm spit-balling. If I'm being honest, I'm not convinced this isn't a prank."

I heard a rattle and turned toward the enclosure. Detective Cortez had opened the outer gate and was looking around.

He waved when he spotted us. "Moss! I found something you should take a look at."

Moss gave me a nod, and we both followed Cortez into the pen. He led us to the pile of ash and bones and knelt next to it, grunting as he shifted his bulk into a comfortable position.

"So I was sifting through the ashes, seeing if there was anything here other than bones, and sure enough, I found something." Cortez wore a rubber glove on his right hand. With his left, he pulled a pencil from his shirt pocket. He used the eraser to point to a couple items he'd dragged from the ashes onto the scorched earth. One was a nebulous blob, and the other looked like a pebble.

"What are we looking at?" asked Moss.

Cortez picked up the oval-shaped blob with his gloved hand. "I'm no metallurgist, but I'm pretty sure this is gold." He dragged the eraser lightly along the top of the blob. The rubber cleaned the soot from the surface, revealing a yellowish gleam. "I don't remember the exact melting temperature of the stuff off the top of my head, but it's in the range of what you'd get from a cremation furnace. And this—" He picked up the pebble and performed the same eraser trick on the surface, revealing a crystalline gleam. "This, Detective, is a diamond. Pretty good sized one, too. Maybe two, three carats."

Moss whistled. "That would fetch a neat crown or two. You think this is from a ring?"

"Engagement would be my guess," said Cortez. "Could be from a brooch, I suppose, but the fact that the gold is in a glob suggests the diamond wasn't hanging from a chain. Likewise, I only found one, so it probably didn't come off earrings, not to mention I've never seen any woman wearing earrings with diamonds that big."

"You're sure the remains belong to a woman?" said Moss.

"Not a hundred percent," said Cortez. "I'm no coroner, but based on the gold and that diamond, as well as the shape of the pelvis? Pretty sure."

Moss patted her jacket a couple times before reaching into an inside pocket and producing a handkerchief. She laid it across her hand and held it out. "Let me see the diamond."

Cortez did as she asked, placing the soot-covered gemstone on the white kerchief. "The strange thing is this was among the remains at all. Mortuaries strip bodies of everything before cremation. Clothes, jewelry. All of it. It suggests whoever cremated this woman didn't know what they were doing."

"And it suggests whoever was responsible wasn't motivated by money." Moss cleaned the soot with the handkerchief, revealing a gleaming stone underneath, seemingly unaffected by the heat and flames. "Not many people would leave something this valuable behind."

"So this was a crime of passion?" I asked.

"Hard to know," said Moss. "We still have no idea how this woman died, whether from murder, manslaughter, or natural causes. What we do have, however, is this." She held up the diamond. "And it might be enough to identify her."

CHAPTER FIVE

Moss and I found Dean crossing the grounds in front of the main tent, headed our way from a cluster of bright red trailers that were less dingy than the green ones we'd passed en route to the aviary. Apparently, Dean located the circus's foreman, but he hadn't known a thing about the circumstances leading to the discovery of the burnt remains. Dean's frustration with the man fled, however, as we told him about the diamond Cortez uncovered. He peered at it intently while we filled him in on our thoughts, agreeing afterwards that it might be our best option for identifying the deceased.

With the diamond wrapped and pocketed, Dean led us in search of Justice. Though they'd split before Justice found his targets, Dean had seen a map of the circus in the foreman's office, so he knew more or less where to look. Indeed, as Dean led us behind the tent, we entered a more industrial section of the grounds. A pile of timbers of equal length and diameter lay on their sides between a quartet of metal posts. Wooden pallets and crates alike had been stacked in tall piles, creating homes for mice if the tiny squeaks and piles of pill-like droppings around them was any indication. Near the back of the space was a rectangular patch of concrete surrounded by chain link fencing. From its general direction rumbled Justice's smooth basso.

"And you're the only ones with a key?" he asked.

"Well, not the only ones," said another masculine voice. "Big Earl—he's in charge of the stage show—he's got one. The foreman, too. Maybe even JT Vernon himself, though I kind of doubt it."

We skirted the edge of the stacked crates and came to the gate at the front of the fencing. Justice stood inside alongside a pair of brown-skinned guys who must've been brothers. Both had long, black hair that hung down their backs in tight braids, as well as matching tribal tattoos that crept along their arms and onto their necks, though it was their nearly identical rounded noses and wide foreheads that confirmed they were related. All of them stood outside another enclosure, this one made of steel mesh and with a solid roof, inside of which were a mixture of tall and short compressed gas cylinders. Next to the men was a cabinet with a steel mesh door that was packed with chemicals, each of the bottles affixed with an assortment of warning and hazard signs.

Dean patted the chain links as we entered, producing a metallic clatter that drew Justice's attention. "Ogden. You get anything?"

Justice gave us a nod. "Hey, guys. This is Langdon Hakka, and that's his brother Lindell. They're the circus's pyrotechnicians."

"I wouldn't go that far," said Langdon, or maybe Lindell. "We're fire breathers, first and foremost."

"Don't sell us short," said the other brother. "We manage all the fire effects. That makes us pyrotechnicians."

"But we don't have any formal training," said Langdon.

"Probably want to stop there," said Justice. "If I don't know about any violations, I don't have to report them to the safety board." The big guy turned to us. "The Hakkas have been showing me the stockpiles of flammable liquids."

"And the gasses," said Lindell, or maybe Langdon. "Don't forget the flammable gasses."

Justice rolled his eyes, suggesting he'd been dealing with this the whole time. "As I was saying, they've been showing me *all* the flammables. Doesn't seem like anything's missing, plus everything was locked up tight when we arrived."

Moss pointed at the mesh enclosure. "You guys need all this for fire breathing?"

Justice gave his head a small shake, but he was too slow. Langdon was already nodding and chuckling. "No. We only use refined paraffin for that. These are for heating the trailers and filling balloons."

Lindell pushed forward. "The propane is for the heating and the helium for the balloons. Not the other way around."

Dean gave the two guys a thumbs up. "Got it."

Lindell kept going. "The stuff in the cabinet, on the other hand, is for the pyrotechnics. Mostly metal powders and nitrates. They can make some really pretty colors when you mix them together. I'd tell you more, but the mixtures are what you'd call a trade secret."

"Well, more of a Hakka family secret," said Langdon. "We're self-taught."

"And yet you still have all your thumbs," said Dean. "Congratulations."

I had to clamp my jaw tight to keep from busting out laughing, but the Hakka brothers didn't seem to get it. They smiled and replied with a gleeful, "Thanks!"

Moss elbowed me in the ribs and gave me a bug eyed look. Dean, meanwhile, continued to show off his incredible composure. "We have everything we need here, right, Justice?"

"And then some," he said.

Dean gave a polite nod to the two performers. "Thanks for your help, gentlemen."

Moss's eyebrows shot up. "Oh. Right. Dean, we should ask them about the diamond before we go."

Justice lifted a thick eyebrow. "Diamond?"

"Cortez found a hefty gemstone among the remains." Dean accepted the handkerchief from Moss and unfolded the corners before holding it toward the fire breathers. "I'm assuming Detective Justice more or less explained the situation in the aviary. We're trying to find out who the remains belong to. Any chance either of you recognize this diamond?"

The guy who I assumed was Lindell whistled. "Hot damn. Now that's a rock! Hey, if you don't want it after this whole business blows over, maybe you can give it to Langdon. He could put it to good use."

His brother shoved him. "Shut up, Lindell."

I wanted to explain to the guy that evidence from murders wasn't first come, first served, but Dean beat me to the punch. "I hesitate to ask, Langdon, but why would you need a diamond?"

Langdon sighed, and for the first time he didn't look effusively jovial. "It's my girlfriend. She keeps dropping not so subtle hints she wants to get married. Getting a diamond like that for free would save me, oh, I don't know, about two hundred years of my salary."

Lindell snorted. "She's constantly badgering him. *When are we going to get married, Langdon?* Telling him about rings she saw other women wearing." He blinked, and a lightbulb burst to life over his head. "Hey... Speaking of, you should ask her about that gem. She really does notice every married woman's ring."

Moss gave me another sideways glance. "That's actually a reasonable suggestion. Who is she?"

"Her name is Elevell," said Langdon. "You can probably find her in the tent limbering up. She's one the contortionists."

Lindell elbowed his brother. "Yeah, she is!"

Langdon shoved him back. "Dude, shut up."

Justice mimed for us to leave, and despite his enormous size, his whisper barely carried. "Quick. Before they start arguing again."

With Justice joining us, we skedaddled and headed to the tent, entering from one of the flaps in the back. As the strip of white fabric fell into place behind us, I had to stop and revisit my assumptions. For one thing, like a fairy home infused with forest magic, the tent seemed bigger within than from the outside. Now that I stood in its midst, I could see my childhood memories of the place weren't total fabrications, what with its multiple circular stages, all surrounded by enough bleachers to sit a couple thousand guests. It did surprise me the structure was so permanent, though. The tentpoles and bleachers were bolted into concrete, not dirt, and based on the various hatches in the concrete itself, I had to assume there was a basement under-neath, some network of tunnels where performers could sneak about and perform tricks on the audience, perhaps. The infrastructure seemed at odds with the tent above, but perhaps the structure underneath had been built in the years after the circus became a permanent attraction. Either that or Vernon decided the tent was nostalgic and attracted fathers with bright eyed youngsters like me in tow where a big cube of bricks and steel wouldn't.

There were several groups on the various stages—laborers on the far left, climbing tall ladders to fiddle with the trapeze, acrobats practicing their tumbling on the right—but it wasn't hard to spot the contortionists. A group of three were on the edge of the stage in front of us, taking part in what to them probably constituted light stretching, though the lazy splits would've had me waddling for a week.

Dean led the way as we approached them. "Excuse me, I'm looking for Elevell?"

The contortionist in the middle of the trio, a cute elven woman who had the wide eyes of one of the forest fae folk, twisted her torso to look up at us, leaving her legs stretched across the floor. "That's me. You are?"

"Detective Alton Dean, NWPD. I understand you're an expert on diamonds."

One of the elf's slender eyebrows rose. "Pardon?"

Moss smiled. "Don't worry. You're not in any trouble. We're trying to find the owner of a diamond that was found on the property. Your boyfriend, Mr. Hakka, said you have a keen eye for other women's rings."

Elevell's other eyebrow rose to meet the first, and her voice frosted. "Did he now?"

"Technically, his brother said it," I offered. "So go easy on him."

The woman gave a sort of piqued *hmm*, but she didn't push the issue. Instead, she pressed her ribcage against the floor and stretched her arms overhead. "What ring are we talking about?"

"Not a ring," said Moss. "Just a diamond. Though we think

it came from a ring initially." Ginger pulled the handkerchief from her pocket, unfolded it, and held it close for Elevell to see.

The elf's eyes stretched wide. "Oh, my. That *is* quite a gem."

The two other contortionists, a dark elf and a human, popped up from their splits and danced over, eager to see.

"Ooooh!"

"Wow, it's huge! It must be worth a fortune!"

"Probably six or seven thousand crowns, I'd wager," rumbled Justice.

We all turned to look at him.

He shrugged. "What? We're detectives. You're telling me you *don't* know the market value of commonly stolen precious metals and gemstones?"

Moss's lips puckered. "We work homicide, Ogden, not burglary. What do you do in your free time, honestly?"

"Let's keep this on track," said Dean. "Miss Elevell? The diamond?"

To her credit, she hadn't been distracted by Moss and Justice's flap. The diamond's glittering core drew her eyes like a moth to a flame. "I, ah... Well, I'm not sure. I feel like I might've seen it before, but I don't know."

"Must've belonged to someone wealthy," said the dark elf contortionist. "Someone glamorous, I bet."

"Maybe the boss's wife," said the second one.

"The foreman's?" said Justice.

Elevell's eyes widened. "No, not his wife. Mr. Vernon's. His wife Stella is here often. Maybe it's hers."

All of us shared a look, and I could tell from Dean's eyes that he didn't like the implications of what he'd heard.

"Thank you very much, Miss," he said to Elevell. "You've

given us a lot to think about. For the rest of us, it's time we track down JT Vernon."

CHAPTER SIX

A s it turned out, JT Vernon lived in Brentford, which didn't surprise me in the least. The swanky neighborhood was home to New Welwic's elite, its lawyers, businessmen, actors, politicians, and all their sundry heirs and heiresses. The neighborhood sat square in the middle of the city, or at least the portion west of the Earl River, and had been there for centuries if the ancient trees that grew from every street corner were any indication. Most of the homes were three or even four stories tall, surrounded by fences of mortared blue-flecked stone or wrought iron topped with intricate fleurs-de-lis. Private security patrolled the streets, rumbling along at twenty miles an hour in their brown and cream cruisers, giving sideways looks to anyone who walked the sidewalks in anything less than a tuxedo and spats.

Barrett's plot looked similar enough to the rest as our car clattered onto his cobblestone drive, but as we passed the six foot-tall hedge that fenced his property and cleared the pines behind them, a few irregularities reared their bizarre heads. For one, the home didn't feature the mortared brick or stone facades so many of the others did, instead exhibiting rounded corners and long horizontal lines. Though the building had different wings, the roofs over each were flat, not sloped, and the white granite blocks of which the home had been built were elegantly carved to achieve a smooth, windswept look. Of course, the house looked plain in comparison to the grounds around it which were populated by a menagerie of topiary animals. Lions, tigers, giraffes, and even a two-story tall elephant posed beside the drive, vibrant green and neatly trimmed. I half expected the leafy cats to bellow out a convincing roar, but it was the mellow tinkle of hidden wind chimes that undulated our way instead.

Dean parked his Viper alongside a burbling fountain containing a half-dozen cherubs spitting water at each other, just outside the reach of a portico that stretched over the home's front entrance. Moss and Justice had stayed at the circus to interface with the coroner and forensics teams, though not by luck of the draw. Dean had specifically told *me* to accompany him to Vernon's, citing his role as my new training officer and my need for practical work experience. He'd made occasional efforts at small talk on the ride over, but I'd been too flustered by the idea of taking a more prominent role in his investigations to give him more than five second responses.

I found my voice as I stared at a lush green lion at the edge of the front steps, rearing on his hind legs with maw stretched wide. "I'd ask if we have the right place, but the gardening speaks for itself. The world's greatest spectacle, indeed."

"If this garden were a feature at his circus, I imagine it would attract big crowds," said Dean, "but then he'd have to come up with an even more ostentatious attraction to set up outside his home. That's the problem with billing yourself as the world's greatest showman."

Together, we got out of the car, headed to the broad front doors, and rang the bell. A melodic chime rang from inside the home, a sing-songy tune that went on indefinitely. Eventually, as the melody died off, the door creaked and opened, revealing... no one at all.

"Can I help you?" said a squeaky voice.

I glanced down to find that, rather than being operated by pulleys and strings, the door had been opened by hand, that of a gnome whose nose reached to the middle of my thighs. His salt and pepper hair curled slightly, framing a too-circular face, but he was dressed to impress, with a prim white shirt, charcoal slacks, a matching vest, and a wide black tie.

Dean pulled a leather wallet from the inside of his jacket and flipped it open, revealing the badge within. "Good morning. I'm Detective Dean with the NWPD. This is my partner, Officer Phair. We're looking for JT Vernon."

I gave Dean a quick glance, but he was focused on the gnome before us. He'd said *partner*, right?

"I believe Mr. Vernon is in his study," said the gnome, who I assumed was the butler. "Can I ask what this is about?"

"We have some questions for him about his wife," said Dean. "I assume she's not around, is she Mr...?"

"Mossbottom," supplied the gnome. "And no, I don't believe so. Please, come in. I'll show you to the parlor while I fetch the master of the house."

We stepped inside, and Mossbottom closed the door behind us. If any part of me thought the inside of the home would be less ostentatious than the exterior, I'd been sorely mistaken. Among the decorations in the foyer alone were a taxidermied grizzly, an antique fortune-telling machine of the kind you might find in a traveling carnival, and a massive oil painting of a man riding a majestic white steed into battle, surrounded by hordes of armor clad minions holding pikes and maces and spiked flails. I didn't know who the man was, but if it was supposed to be Vernon, the fact that he'd commissioned the painting much less hung in his foyer said a certain something about his ego.

Mossbottom ushered us to a sitting room off the entryway, one filled with imported rugs, couches upholstered in purple velvet, and a marble statue of a nude woman whose breasts had apparently never been subjected to gravity. Mossbottom excused himself and hurried off, leaving Dean and me alone.

Dean paused in front of the statue, hands clasped before him. "Vernon seems to have varied and interesting tastes in art."

I glanced at the woman's preternaturally perky breasts. "Although he doesn't care much for realism."

Dean turned my way. "You're talking about that portrait in the foyer?"

"Among other things." I cleared my throat and summoned what inner courage I could find. "Could I ask you about that whole, uh... *partner thing?*"

Dean looked at me blankly. "What partner thing?"

"At the door. You said I was your partner."

Dean nodded. "Yes."

I blinked. How was I the only one confused by this? "When did that happen? Was there a memo I missed?"

Dean smiled, an easygoing grin that transformed his face from a cool, analytical visage to one that was warmer, more human, and dare I say, far more attractive. "I think you're reading too much into this, Phair. You, Justice, Moss. We're all on the same team. We all work toward common goals. You came with me on this call. That makes us partners."

A puff of air escaped my lips, and a bit of tension I hadn't even noticed was there left my shoulders. "Oh. Good. I was concerned there was... more to it."

"Well, of course there is."

I suffered another pang. *"There is?"*

"Sure," said Dean. "Phair, you may not be a detective, but I didn't bring you on board because I needed someone to file paperwork and make phone calls. You've showcased skills that make me think you'd be a good fit alongside me. Your insight. Your intuition. That's what I want to see more of. You don't have to constantly defer all the time."

"Have I been doing that?" I asked.

"You didn't assert yourself much this morning, as far as I could tell," said Dean. "And I get it. You've been thrust into a position where everyone around you has more experience than you, has been at their posts longer than you. It can be intimidating. Only time will make it less so. But you need to fight the urge to blend into the scenery. Your instincts so far have been on point, so if there's a question you want to ask or a clue that's nagging at you, speak up. That's why you're here."

A little voice inside me piped up, telling me I was out of my league, but that was precisely the voice Dean was trying to silence. I may not have felt like I deserved the faith he was putting in me, but I nodded anyway. "Okay. I'll do my best to exhibit the same irrational confidence as the woman depicted in this statue."

Dean chuckled. "Oh, I don't know. It seems her confidence is deserved given her impressive, ah... *lift.*"

I smiled. It wasn't a joke, really. Just an amusing observation about a statue that shouldn't have been in the first room a home's guests were introduced to, but it lessened the tension in my muscles. It seemed Dean wasn't as stiff and formal as he'd appeared from my outsider vantage, and that was helping put me at ease more than any amount of his back-patting or praise could.

CHAPTER SEVEN

D ean had inspected every piece of artwork in the parlor twice and started on his third pass when finally we heard the patter of approaching feet. I'd been sitting so long on one of the velvet-upholstered couches that I feared I might've worn a permanent groove into it, but I was able to get to my feet and claim ignorance of the flattened cushion before JT Vernon strolled around the corner.

Surprisingly, the political posters plastered around his circus hadn't oversold the man. He looked the same as on paper, with a thick head of brown curls, eyebrows as furry as shrews, and a nose that migrating birds could perch upon. Just as in the posters, his mustache had been meticulously curled and waxed, his suit pleated and pressed, and if the brilliant smile he greeted us with was any indication, the man had never lacked for good dentists.

Vernon reached out and began pumping Dean's hand as he spoke. "My most sincere apologies, Detective. When Moss-bottom came to fetch me, I was in the middle of a phone call with my campaign manager, Phillipous. Gods, that conversation stretched *on* and *on*. I told him I had guests as soon as I was able to get a word in edgewise, but did he listen? *Pshaw*. The man's good at his job. I wouldn't trade him for anyone, but he's infamously loquacious. Probably why he insists I pay him by the hour, right?"

Vernon's laugh shook the room as he released Dean's hand and grasped mine, which he sought out and snagged without my having offered it. "And my apologies to you too, Officer. If I'd known I had a lady in waiting, I would've been more curt with Phillipous. Goodness knows he deserves it sometimes."

Instead of shaking my hand vigorously as he had Dean's, he pulled my hand to his mouth and gave it a gentle kiss. I don't know if it was the wetness of his lips or the slight tickle of his mustache, but a shiver ran through me as he kissed it. Thankfully, his grip wasn't so tight that I couldn't slip my hand back out, which I did, hiding it behind my back and wiping it against my pants as I gave the man a perfunctory smile.

"But where are my manners," continued Vernon, his eyes twinkling as his gaze lingered on me. "I'm John Thomas Vernon, but everyone calls me JT. Can I offer either of you a beverage? I'm sure Mossbottom would've done it himself if he'd known how long I would be on the phone. Mossbottom?" Vernon clapped and turned to his butler, who'd followed Vernon and stood by the parlor entrance. "How about a pair of your delectable tropical fruit cocktails? Or a trio, actually. I could go for one, myself."

Dean put up a hand. "That won't be necessary, Mr. Vernon. We're simply here to ask a few questions."

Vernon didn't seem fazed by the rebuff. He nodded, now adopting a look of concern. "Of course. Mossbottom said this had something to do with my wife, Stella?"

"Correct," said Dean. "Do you happen to know her whereabouts?"

"Ah..." Vernon swallowed a mouthful of air, and his eyes drifted in thought. "Well, no to be quite honest. I assume she's out. Mossbottom, is her Pearl Motors Clavelle in the garage?"

The gnome dipped his head. "I believe not, sir."

"Do you know when she left?" asked Dean.

"I have to admit I'm not sure," said Vernon. "At some point this morning, I suppose. You know womenfolk. Always having their hair and nails done." The man gave me another twinkling smile, which turned my stomach. Something about him rubbed me the wrong way.

"You *suppose*..." repeated Dean. "When was the last time you saw your wife?"

Vernon straightened a bit. "That I can answer. Last evening, about an hour after supper. Let's say... eight-thirty. I passed her on my way to my study. She seemed to be heading... well, I'm not sure. Maybe to the second floor living room to listen to a radio serial."

One of my eyebrows crept up. Dean had told me to assert myself when I felt it was appropriate, so I did. "You didn't see your wife later in the evening? Perhaps when you went to bed?"

Vernon didn't sputter and act indignant, but his face drooped. He rubbed his hands together in an idle fashion. "We have... separate bedchambers."

I glanced at Dean. He responded with a slight shake of his head and a stern gaze, as if to say, "It's not our place to ask." And it wasn't, unless it pertained to the case. A lot of people lived in loveless marriages, the wealthy perhaps to a greater degree than most.

Vernon cleared his throat. He seemed to have lost some of

his bluster. "If you don't mind my asking, Detective, what's this about? Is my wife in trouble?"

Dean waved toward one of the sofas. "You might want to have a seat, Mr. Vernon."

"A seat? Why?" Vernon's handwringing intensified, and a nervous edge entered his voice. "What's going on?"

Dean tensed, the tension clear in his shoulders and jaw. I didn't have any experience telling people their loved ones were dead, but I had to imagine it was the hardest part of the job. Even now, despite the off-putting vibe Vernon gave me, I couldn't help but empathize with the man.

"This morning, human remains were found in the aviary at your circus," said Dean. "They've been cremated. We don't yet know how old the remains are, but there are certain pieces of evidence that suggest they're fresh."

Vernon's thick eyebrows furrowed. "And, what? You think they're my *wife's*?"

Dean nodded to me. "Show him the diamond."

Moss had given the handkerchief-wrapped gemstone to me before we left, perhaps figuring a woman would take better care of it than a man. I dug it out of my front pocket, unwrapped it, and held it out. "We recovered this from the remains, Mr. Vernon. We think it might've come from a wedding or engagement ring. Do you recognize the stone?"

Vernon's eyebrows knitted even further, so much so that I feared they might spontaneously braid themselves. "I can't say I do, but I've never paid much attention to jewelry. I buy it for my wife because *she* likes it, not because I do."

"But she wore a diamond ring?" said Dean. "Made of twenty-four karat gold?"

"Her engagement ring, yes," said Vernon. "And I believe so. It's been so long since I purchased it."

"Do you know how many carats the stone was?"

Vernon stared at the stone. His hand-wringing continued, and the corners of his eyes were creased with worry. "You can't think this is my wife's, can you? I mean, she popped out this morning." He turned to his butler. "She did leave this morning, didn't she, Mossbottom?"

The gnome dipped his head. "I'm sorry, sir, but I'm not certain. The last time I saw her was last evening, same as yourself. She must've left before I woke."

"Oh, boy." Vernon started to pace, rubbing his chin as he did so. "I, uh... I just don't understand. This isn't possible. Why...? Why would...?"

Like the seasoned professional he was, Dean took charge of the situation. He placed a firm hand on JT's shoulder, stopping him in his tracks. "Let's take this one step at a time, Mr. Vernon. All we can say at the moment is your wife is missing. Let's not to jump to conclusions."

Vernon breathed heavily, his eyes unfocused. "Right. She's missing, that's all."

"With that said, we need to find her," said Dean. "You said the two of you had separate bedrooms. Perhaps we could take a look inside hers? There might be clues there as to her whereabouts."

Vernon continued to stare into the distance for a second before snapping himself out of it. He gave his head a small shake and composed himself. "Of course. I'll show you the way. Please, follow me."

CHAPTER EIGHT

Vernon flicked the light switch as we walked into the bedroom, but there was enough light streaming through the windows that the glow of the overhead lamps didn't make much of a difference. Right off the bat, it was obvious Stella didn't share the same ostentatious flair as her husband. With a tulle-draped canopy bed, a couple nightstands, an antique vanity, and several dressers and wardrobes, Stella's room looked perfectly normal. No stuffed lions growled from corners, nor did nude portraits of her riding wild animals grace the walls. The room was only notable for two reasons: its size—it could've swallowed my entire apartment—and its disorderliness.

There were clothes *everywhere*: rumpled in piles on the floor, strewn across the bed, over chairs, on the edge of the vanity. One dress was draped across an ottoman, the sleeve folded over the collar in a posture of defeat, as if Stella's ghost had fainted on the spot. Clothes weren't the only source of disorder, though. Bags from department stores slumped against the walls, books lay in piles upon the tops of dressers, and even the trashcans were more full than not, though thankfully not with anything that could decompose based on the vaguely potpourri-like smell in the room.

Dean didn't balk as he entered the space, sweeping his gaze over the piles of clothes and assorted clutter.

Vernon wrung his hands some more as he took a position by a dresser. "I apologize for the mess. Stella suffers the bad habit of never tidying after herself. I didn't realize her room had gotten this bad. Mossbottom, you should've sent the maids up a week ago."

Mossbottom, who stood just inside the door, gave his master a bit of an odd look. "Ah... Of course, sir. I'll be sure they know."

I think Dean caught the look, too. He crossed to a side table that held a phone and an empty notepad. He picked the phone up and held it to his ear for a moment before replacing it. "Can you tell me about your wife's daily routine, Mr. Vernon?"

"Well, I'm not sure she *has* a routine, per se," said the man. "She likes to shop, as you can tell by the clutter. Also spends a good amount of time on her health and appearance. Hair, skin-care treatments, and spa sessions, based on the bills that arrive. She also does a fair amount of reading, but I can't say she has a specific schedule."

Dean picked up a pencil and rubbed the lead across the surface of the notepad, perhaps trying to uncover what had been written on the previous page. He pushed pencil and pad aside when the latter failed to cooperate. "Does she have any haunts? Places she visits without notice?"

"Other than certain stores and a salon or two, I don't think so," said Vernon. "Mossbottom could put a list together for you, but he could as easily call and see if she's there himself."

Dean crossed to the vanity and opened the drawer. He

rifled through the items within. "Might anyone have seen her when she left this morning or late last night?"

Vernon's brow furrowed. "The maids come twice weekly, as well as the gardeners, but none of them were here this morning, were they Mossbottom?"

Vernon looked to his butler, but the gnome shook his head. "I'm afraid not, sir."

Dean spoke over his shoulder as he perused an open jewelry box. "Feel free to jump in, Phair."

I didn't know if Dean meant I should partake in the questioning or the searching of the room, but I felt sheepish either way. He'd just talked me up in the parlor, tried to give me a gentle push of encouragement, and here I was standing next to the door, not doing a damned thing. Part of the problem was that Dean was so mesmerizing. He swept around the room effortlessly, asking questions while he picked up on minutia I never would've noticed, peering past the physical and into the past with his steel blue gaze and cutting quite the striking figure while doing it. Being in his presence made me feel like I was a bumbling idiot. I'd never much lacked for confidence, even if most of it was unwarranted, but then again my previous jobs waitressing and selling cosmetics hadn't required a particularly rare skillset. Still, Moss didn't make me feel the same way. I felt like I could contribute in her presence without looking like a fool, so what was it about Dean that made me clam up? His reputation, or something else?

I swallowed back my trepidation, hoping Vernon hadn't noticed. As I tried to figure out what to ask, I scuttled to a nearby side table and picked up the framed photograph that resided there, one featuring a petite woman with fair shoulder-length hair standing on a beach. She wore a pair of high-waisted shorts with a matching top that showed off a few inches of her midriff, but she wasn't smiling.

"Is this your wife?" I asked, lifting the photo for emphasis.

Vernon nodded. "That's right. I believe that was taken when Stella and I went vacationing on the Beurre Coast."

"Can I ask how old she is?"

"She'll be turning thirty-seven this winter," said Vernon.

I thought it a little strange Stella would have a picture of herself in her room rather than one of her and her husband, but then again, the two didn't share a bedroom. I slid the photograph back into place as I tried to kick my brain into gear. "Has your wife made any new acquaintances recently? Any friends she's started spending a lot of time with?"

"Not to my knowledge," said Vernon. "In fact, I'd almost say it was the opposite. Of late she's become a bit more... reclusive isn't the right word. Antisocial, perhaps."

That perked my interest. "Any thoughts as to why that might be?"

Vernon sighed. "My best guess? She's not fond of my campaign. You know that I'm running for office?"

I nodded. "We saw the posters. She not keen on your electioneering?"

Vernon hesitated. "I think it's getting to be a bit much for her. The attention, the expectations. My focus being elsewhere. It's been difficult for her, in more ways than one."

I caught a slight twitch in Vernon's lips as he said that last part. I wasn't the best at body language, but Mossbottom seemed uneasy, too. "How so?"

Vernon frowned, and he tightened up. "I don't see how my wife's opinions on my campaign have anything to do with this incident at the circus. We're trying to determine if she's missing, not whether she's given me the cold shoulder of late, aren't we?"

I glanced to Dean for assistance, but he wasn't even looking my way, having moved to one of the wardrobes.

I soldiered on. "Speaking of the circus, would your wife have any reason to be there?"

Vernon shrugged, still looking miffed. "She visits it frequently enough, especially since I started campaigning. I think she sees it as a pleasant distraction. Somewhere she can go to get out of my hair and not be bothered by my managers or the newspapers."

Dean ducked into the attached bath. Either he was losing interest in my line of questioning or he thought I was doing well enough that he didn't need to lead me by the bridle. Something told me it wasn't the latter.

I tried not to get distracted. "Does your wife manage any of the circus acts or have any organizational role there?"

Vernon waved me off. "She'd never even been to a circus before I met her. I assure you her presence there is purely a leisure activity."

I heard a clink from the bathroom. What the heck was Dean up to? "You said she'd become antisocial of late. Did she have any friends at the circus? Perhaps that's why she was there more often."

Vernon's jaw tightened, and his cheeks darkened. "Are you insinuating my wife was having an affair? Is that what this is about? Some roundabout police investigation into my personal matters?"

The man's anger pushed me back a step, the sudden outburst reinforcing the bad vibes I'd gotten off him. I held my ground, though. "Not at all, sir. We're just trying to locate your wife and identify the remains found in the aviary. Perhaps instead of worrying about her whereabouts, we could try to eliminate her as a potential victim. If you could point us to the jeweler who sold you her engagement ring, maybe her dentist—"

Vernon scowled. "Her *dentist?*"

I didn't know how to put it gently, so I didn't try. "In cases where remains are beyond recognition, dental x-rays can identify victims."

Vernon swallowed air. Based on the confused look on his face, I could tell the rational part of his brain was having a hard time accepting his wife might truly be dead.

As he gaped, I heard heavy footsteps. Dean emerged from the bath, stomping across the bedroom. His demeanor had completely shifted, his cool, analytical look replaced with ill-hidden rage.

He barely slowed as he reached us. "Mr. Vernon? I think we have all we need. Phair? Let's go."

Dean swept past me into the hall, his furious gale ruffling my collar. I glanced after him, wondering what the heck just happened.

Hurricane Dean had apparently sobered Vernon, as well. His eyebrow shot up. "Is everything all right?"

"Of course," I said with more confidence than I felt. "Thanks for your time. And please call the Fifth Street precinct with those names I asked for. It could really help our investigation."

"Sure thing," said Vernon, but I barely paid attention to him. I was already hustling down the hall, trying to catch up with Detective Dean.

CHAPTER NINE

Dean had pushed through the front doors and almost reached the Viper by the time I got within hailing range. "Dean! Dean, wait up!"

Detective Dean spun as he reached the cruiser, his face contorted with rage. He glared daggers from his ice blue eyes, but not at me. He stared through the molded art deco walls of the home to the meat within. "He knew, Phair. He knew, and he did *nothing!*"

I slowed as I reached him, my heartbeat elevated from the chase. "Who did nothing? What are you talking about?"

Dean ripped something from his pocket. A brown paper envelope, barely bigger than a pack of cards. He whipped it at me without taking his eyes off the house. "I found this at the bottom of the wastebasket in Stella's bathroom. Vernon must've missed it."

The envelope itself was plain, without any writing or marks of any kind. The brads keeping the envelope closed had been pushed back, so I squeezed the sides and popped it open. There wasn't anything within but a bit of white dust that resembled chalk.

I shook my head. "I don't get it."

Dean stabbed a sharp finger toward the envelope. "That powder? It's benzedrine. It comes in tablets. Prescribed to treat narcolepsy and weight loss, but most people use it as an anti-depressant. It's addictive as hell. Vernon knew about it. He knew about it and didn't do a damned thing!"

I may not have known Dean for long, but I'd never seen him angry. Not when I snuck into the police observation room and spied on an interrogation during the case that landed me at his side. Not when I confronted him in the parking lot and yelled and told him to go to hell when I wrongly thought he was retaliating against me for doing the right thing. He'd been miffed during the former and amused during the latter, but now the man veritably shook with rage. The jaw muscles in his lean face bulged, his brows were drawn together, and a vein bulged in his neck. He breathed hard, and fire and brimstone rained down behind the blue shells of his irises.

I held my hands up and spoke gently. "Slow down. What do you mean he knew?"

Dean took a step toward me. His anger burned hot, but it wasn't directed at me. "Don't you find it suspicious how long it took for Vernon to come down and greet us? He said he'd been on the phone, but his ear wasn't red at all as it would be if he'd had a receiver pressed against it for a half hour. So what was he up to? He said Stella was slovenly, but was she? That doesn't seem to track with the woman he described, a woman who took care of herself, who liked to get her hair and nails done. You saw the look Mossbottom gave him when he told us that, same as I did. Stella didn't leave the room in that condition, or at the very least it wasn't entirely her fault. It was Vernon!"

I'd missed the bit about Vernon's ear, but I'd noticed the look between him and Mossbottom. I stared at the envelope in my hands, putting the pieces together. "Vernon tossed his wife's room. He was looking for this. He didn't want us to find it."

Dean plucked the envelope from my hands. "He knew his wife was addicted to benzedrine. He knew, and he didn't do a thing to stop it."

Dean rubbed his free hand across his chin. Beyond the rage, I saw something else in his eyes. Pain or sorrow. Maybe a mixture of the two. He spun away from me and slammed an open palm against the hood of the Viper, producing a resounding clang. *"Damnit!"*

I jumped at the sound. I glanced back to make sure nobody was watching through the windows beside the door, but the panes were empty. It was just the burbling of the cherub fountain, the tinkle of the wind chimes, and us.

I stared at Dean: at the tension in his shoulders, the strain in his arms, his posture, so much like that of a werewolf ready to transform under a full moon's beams.

I took a step toward him. "Dean, is everything all right?"

"Of course everything's not all right," he growled. "That poor woman was addicted to benzedrine. It's dangerous. People die from overuse all the time, and her husband's instinct was to hide it rather than get her help. It makes me furious."

I took another careful step forward, as if I were approaching a caged animal. "That's not what I meant. Are *you* okay?"

Dean didn't say anything.

I often had a hard time reading men, or at least those with

whom I was in a relationship, but it wasn't too hard to guess what ate Dean. "This is personal for you, isn't it?"

Dean sighed, and his shoulders slumped. I wanted to go up to him, to put a gentle hand on his back, but I didn't know him that well. Not yet.

After a moment's silence, he stood and nodded toward the Viper. He spoke softly. "Get in the car."

I'd had angry boyfriends make similar demands of me in the past. Rarely had the results gone in a positive direction, but Dean was different. Not only had I come to admire and trust him in the short period I'd known him, but his voice had lost its edge. He'd let go of the rage.

I got in the cruiser and buckled in. Dean did the same. He pulled the keys from his pocket and stuck them in the ignition, but he didn't turn them. He sat there with his hands on the wheel, eyes staring into the distance.

I didn't say anything. I just sat and waited.

Dean sighed again. "Her name was Arrwyn. We came into the department at about the same time. She was a lot like me, in many respects. She was self-motivated. Had a strong sense of justice. Didn't want to have to climb the rungs of success one at a time, just wanted to hop on a rocket straight to the moon. She was also good at keeping things close to the vest. You might say she was a good liar, but it was more than that. She wasn't an actress, but she could play a role with the best of them. It's no surprise she decided to get into undercover work. Not homicide, though. Narcotics.

"She joined Detective Harmon's team on the streets in plain clothes within two years of joining the force. Took down a few middlemen, but she'd already set her sights higher. Wanted to go after one of the big guns. A major player in the New Welwic distribution scene. So she went in, deep undercover. She could do it. She had the talent, but the problem is when you take on a role like that, some part of you ends up becoming the monster. Too big a part in her case. She started taking benzo tablets. I'm not sure when or how many—she was good at keeping things to herself, after all—but she got addicted. Harmon called her out on it once, toward the end, but she assured him it was part of the role. Maybe he trusted her to know her limits. Regardless, he didn't realize how bad it had gotten. Nobody had, myself most of all.

"It was a little over two years ago that we got the call from the hospital. Arrwyn was in a coma. She'd been brought in by paramedics after having been found outside a slum owned by the guy she was investigating. She was in cardiogenic shock and suffering circulatory collapse from a severe amphetamine over-dose, though they suspected she had a possible cerebral hemor-rhage as well. Ultimately the toxicology report determined she had several drugs in her system, though benzedrine was the primary culprit. The doctors did what they could, but it wasn't enough. She passed away the following morning."

Dean hadn't looked at me throughout the monologue, keeping his gaze fixed firmly on Vernon's garage.

I spoke softly. "I'm sorry to hear that. She was a good friend of yours?"

"She was my fiancée."

Dean turned the keys in the ignition, and the Viper growled to life. He pulled it around the circle drive and headed onto the street. I was too in shock to say a thing, but apparently Dean's soliloquy greased his vocal cords. He spoke again as we turned south along the avenue.

"I blamed myself for a long time for not seeing it, for not

intervening when I had a chance. I guess I still do. Maybe it's easy for me to see the danger in it. I have the benefit of hindsight, if you can call it a benefit. Maybe Vernon doesn't know how dangerous benzedrine is. There are enough quacks in this city who prescribe it like candy. But if I'm right about Vernon tossing Stella's room looking for pills, then he knows. He knows she was a user. He knows she had a problem, enough so that he thought he should hide it. Maybe he thought it would reflect poorly on him. Whatever. The point is he's an enabler, and I can't abide that. Not anymore."

Dean sighed. He glanced at me, his cool blue eyes sorrowful. "I'm sorry I lost my cool. You shouldn't have seen me like that."

I shook my head. "You have nothing to apologize for. There's no shame in expressing sincere emotion."

"No. There isn't," agreed Dean. "But maybe I shouldn't have done so here, with you."

I don't think he meant it as an insult. I think he meant that we didn't know each other that well, though I now knew Alton a whole lot better than I had the night before. He wasn't the robotic, crime-solving machine everyone seemed to think he was. He'd suffered pain and heartbreak like anyone else, myself included. Maybe that's what made him such a great detective.

I swallowed back the lump in my throat, trying to think how I could ease the tension. "Do you think the drugs might've had anything to do with Stella's murder? Assuming it is her remains we found, and that she was indeed murdered."

The Viper rumbled as Dean punched it through a yellow light. "I don't know, but I'll tell you this. Even the city's worst quacks don't distribute benzedrine tablets in unmarked paper envelopes. If Stella Vernon had started visiting the circus more frequently, it could mean she'd found a supplier there to provide her fix. Not that there's any obvious reason why a dealer might've murdered her, but at least looking for a supplier gives us another avenue to pursue. Something for you to look into once I drop you off."

I blinked. "You're not returning with me to the circus?"

Dean shook his head. "I have a meeting with someone at the precinct. You have to remember, this isn't the only case we're working. That's why I brought you on, after all. To shoulder some of the workload Moss and Justice can't handle."

I swallowed back another lump, but this time it was one born of nerves rather than empathy. When I'd agreed to join Dean's team, I'd known I'd be working investigations—but I didn't think I'd be flying solo.

CHAPTER TEN

I breathed a sigh of relief as I approached the aviary at Vernon and Daly's Circus, mostly because of who was there. Moss stood outside the enclosure, chewing on a pencil eraser as she regarded the papers clamped to the clipboard in her hands. Guess I wouldn't be working the case alone after all.

I flushed my nerves as I approached. "Hey, Moss. What have you got there?"

Moss looked up, pulling the pencil from her lips. "Hey, Phair. It's Cortez's report. I'm looking over it, seeing if there's anything he left out. You and Dean are already back from Vernon's, huh?"

"Well, I am. Dean dropped me off. Said he had to take a meeting with someone at the Fifth."

"Oh, right," said Moss. "He mentioned that. Some physicist. An expert in optics, I think. What would you call that anyway? Not an optician. That's reserved for eye doctors. So what then? An opticist? That's not a word, is it?"

"I couldn't tell you. But more importantly, why is Dean

meeting with an, uh... *opticist?* Don't tell me one of his cases requires knowledge of theoretical physics?" It that were the case, I'd really bitten off more than I could chew agreeing to be his protege.

"Maybe, maybe not," said Moss. "Remember when the Tarot Card Killer struck in the park, and you witnessed that strange purple haze, for lack of a better word? Dean's trying to get answers on that, or at least put together a few theories."

Of course. Barely a week ago, as I'd been walking home at night after a shift at the Williams Street precinct, I'd passed through Miller's Creek Park en route to my apartment. The path through the woods had been deserted, but as I'd gotten close to the plaza at the center, I'd suffered the sensation of being watched. I'd peered into the woods, trying to see if I could catch sight of anyone, and I'd noticed a hint of a glow. Something opaque and swirling, deep purple in color and barely discernible from the forest's midnight backdrop. At the time I'd thought it might've been a firework even though I hadn't heard one go off, but I'd since questioned that supposition. A firework would provide an initial burst of light and leave colored smoke lingering in the air, but the smoke itself wouldn't glow, meaning the glow I'd seen was... what? A mirage? A reflection? Or something less easily explained?

Honestly, I'd tried to push the experience from my head. The idea of being so close to the Tarot Card Killer had rattled me, whether I wanted to admit it or not, but as the lead investigator on the case, Dean didn't have the same luxury. More importantly, I don't think he *wanted* to let it go. By his own account, he'd become obsessed with the murders, which he'd been investigating for almost two months. It was because of his singular focus on them that he'd missed clues on the New Age Alchemical case and brought me in to assist.

"Anyway," said Moss. "Did you get a positive identification on that diamond from Mr. Vernon?"

I blinked away the fog of memories. "Unfortunately not. At least, not definitively. According to Vernon, the diamond is roughly the right size, and his wife's engagement ring was yellow gold, same as the glob Cortez found, but he couldn't be sure it was Stella's. Doesn't pay much attention to gemstones, he said."

"I don't find that surprising." Moss tapped the pencil against her clipboard. "But he didn't know the whereabouts of his wife, either?"

I shook my head. "He couldn't account for her. Neither he nor his butler had seen her since last night. And on top of that, Dean found this in her bedroom."

I plucked the brown paper envelope from my pocket and held it to Moss. She frowned as she took it, but her face dropped as she opened it and saw what was inside. *"Oh, shit."*

"Don't worry," I said. "Dean told me about Arrwyn."

Moss cocked her head. "He did?"

"Well, not unprompted," I said, taking back the envelope. "He blew up after we got out of Vernon's hair. Was boiling over with rage, to the point where I knew it wasn't about what he found but something far more personal. I gave him a gentle push and he opened up to me in the car."

Moss lifted an eyebrow. "I'm surprised to hear that. He doesn't like to talk about it, for obvious reasons. You don't know Alton that well, but he doesn't like to express weakness, emotional weakness in particular."

"That was apparent, too," I said. "But I think he felt obligated to tell me given the circumstances. Call me crazy, but I think he felt better having shared it. It might've been cathartic, even if he didn't want to remember the incident in the first place. And as frightening and confusing as his outburst was, I didn't mind hearing him out. It was kind of nice, actually. Not the story. That was incredibly sad, but it's comforting when someone is willing to share a piece of their true self with you. That's not easy for people to do." And I knew, because I suffered the same problem.

Moss returned the pencil eraser to her mouth. "Yeah. I agree."

She stood there for a moment, staring at me curiously, the eraser pressing into her plump lower lip. She'd said she was surprised to hear Dean was willing to share with me, but her look suggested it was *me* she was surprised by.

Somewhere inside the enclosure, I heard soft voices. That same mysterious bird from the morning trilled, and Moss gave her head a bit of a shake. She returned her pencil to her clipboard, tapping it. "So Mrs. Stella Vernon might've been hooked on benzedrine. That's interesting, but I'm not sure how it ties into her murder."

I nodded, shoving aside Moss's pensive looks. "That's what Dean said. But Mr. Vernon noted she'd been coming to the circus more of late. Dean hypothesized her dealer might've been one of the carnies."

Moss snorted. "Well, sure, but how are we going to find out?"

"Ask around?" I gave Moss a hopeful smile.

Ginger pursed her lips. "Come on. You're not that naive."

I sighed. "Of course not. Nobody would admit they're a

dealer to a cop. But I've got to figure something out. Dean told me to look into it when he dropped me off."

Moss rolled her eyes. "Okay, far be it from me to countermand an order given to you by your new training officer, but I have to assume what Dean wanted was for you to use the drug angle to progress the case, not specifically to track down Stella's dealer. After all, proving she was an addict doesn't in and of itself help us figure out who might've wanted to kill her. The question we need to ask ourselves is how might've Stella's addiction provided a motive for someone to commit murder?"

"Maybe she owed her dealer money?"

"If so, that would be a terrible reason for someone to murder her," said Moss. "I know it's one of the most stereotypical gangster moves to threaten to kill someone who owes you money, but have you ever tried to collect from a corpse? Doesn't work too well."

"Unless they weren't trying to collect from her," I said. "What if they were trying to collect from her wealthy husband?"

Moss's brow scrunched. "Possible, but again, when you commit murder, you use your lone bargaining chip. It's not really a tactic in debt collection."

"Maybe it's the other way around. Maybe someone killed her so Vernon *wouldn't* have to pay a debt."

Moss snorted. "Slow down. Are you suggesting JT Vernon had his wife murdered to avoid paying off a dope dealer? That's out there, even for me. Did you see or hear anything while you talked to him to suggest that was the case?"

My shoulders slumped, and once again I felt like the rookie I was. "Sorry. Dean said I should be more open to contributing.

I'm thinking out loud. And no, I didn't get any sort of murderer vibe from the man—although he did strike me as creepy."

I think Moss realized she'd gone a little far, as her face softened. "No. Thinking outside the box is good. Ideas that seem crazy at first often contain nuggets of truth. Don't let my disbelief stop you from spitballing. But going back to Vernon, creepy how?"

I shrugged, still feeling dejected despite Moss's reassurances. "I can't say for sure. Don't you ever get a bad vibe from some guys? Like a feeling that if you're ever stuck alone with them, they might tie you up and throw you in their basement?"

"Interesting way to put it," said Moss. "But I know what you're talking about. If I end up interacting with JT Vernon, I'll let you know if I get the same bad juju. But we're getting off track. If Stella Vernon was using benzos recreationally, it probably means she was self-medicating for depression. That's the most common usage, as far as I know. Someone who's depressed makes poor choices, potentially takes more risks and puts themselves in more dangerous situations than someone who doesn't. That's something concrete we didn't know earlier this morning."

"But it doesn't put us anywhere closer to determining who murdered her, if indeed she's even the one who's dead."

"No, but there are other avenues to pursue." Moss waved toward the enclosure. "I say we track the remains."

"Are you talking about dental records?" I said. "Because I already asked Mr. Vernon to put us in touch with his wife's dentist."

"That might give us a positive ID on the bones, which would be useful," said Moss. "But no, I mean we should track where the remains came from. We're assuming the body was cremated and dumped here, so why not visit a few nearby crematoriums and see if any of them experienced break-ins overnight?"

That seemed like a logical enough course of action. "You think Dean'll be fine with that?"

"Dean wants to solve the case by any means necessary, I assure you," said Moss. "Besides, everything here is under control. Cortez and the coroner are finishing up. We've got officers canvassing the grounds. All we need is to track down Justice."

"Yeah, I imagine he'd be pretty miffed if we left him behind."

Moss smiled. "There's that. Plus he's the only one of us who drove here. Come on. I think I know where he is."

CHAPTER ELEVEN

Justice parked his matte black Howardson Phantom outside the doors to Fogel and Sons Crematorium. It was the third such business Justice, Moss, and I had visited, so by now I knew what to expect: a fancy storefront where the owners sold expensive caskets and funeral packages to grieving families and tucked behind it, the guts of the building, where the furnaces and ball mills were hidden.

Fogel and Sons apparently hadn't gotten the memo about the fancy storefront, though. The building looked like a warehouse, with a corrugated metal roof pockmarked by hail damage and built of speckled brown bricks that might've been cream once upon a time. The name that hung across the facade was big enough to be easily seen from the roadway, but up close, the paint was peeling and the letters were rusted at the edges.

I clambered out of the back seat—Justice's Phantom was more boat than car—and shut the door with a clang.

Moss eyed the sign with the same distaste I felt as she climbed out of the front seat. "I don't think Fogel and Sons are going to sell a lot of premium headstones with a sign like that."

Justice grunted as he walked around the car's mile long hood. "Not everybody can cater to the rich. You think most people can afford granite mausoleums and aged redwood caskets? Most folks die penniless, and it falls onto their kids to foot the bill. Besides, who cares what happens after you die. You could get burned in a fruit crate and it wouldn't make a difference."

Moss smirked. "Good to know that when I die in the line of duty, Ogden, you'll make sure my corpse gets laid to rest in the finest cardboard money can buy."

Justice shook his head as he pulled the door open for us. The shopkeeper's bell rang as we stepped into the lobby. True to form, the front room was filled with samples, same as the others we'd visited, but Justice had sniffed the place out. There wasn't a luxury material to be found amid the displays, and the prices were roughly a quarter of what I'd seen at the other crematoriums.

A shopkeeper with a salt-and-pepper goatee and similarly colored hair that fell to his shoulders sat behind a desk at the far side of the room, his face buried in a ledger that was so large it could've served as ballast on a tanker. He looked up at the sound of the bell.

"Good morning." He stood and glanced at a wall-mounted clock above the casket displays. "Err... afternoon. What can I help you with today?"

The man had probably figured out we were cops based on my uniform, but Moss nonetheless dug her badge out of her pocket. "Detective Moss, NWPD. This is Detective Justice and Officer Phair. Are you in charge?"

"Indeed, I am. Harvey Fogel, at your service." He skirted the desk and met us at the floor samples. "What seems to be the problem?"

"I've got a bit of an odd question for you, Mr. Fogel." Moss returned her badge to her pocket. "Have you had any remains go missing recently?"

The man blinked. "Pardon me?"

Justice had split from Moss and me, opting to wander the isles and thumb through the merchandise, but his smooth voice carried over. "We found some cremated remains. We're trying to determine if they were stolen."

"Cremated remains?" said the man. "Nearby?"

Moss shook her head. "Not exactly. At the Vernon and Daly Circus. We think someone might've broken into a crematorium and swiped them, though I couldn't tell you why."

Fogel's brow furrowed. "Huh..."

Moss lifted an eyebrow and leaned in. "Is that a *that's curious,* huh, or a *this explains everything,* huh?"

Fogel focused back on Moss. "What? Oh, no. Sorry. We haven't had anyone's remains go missing, I can assure you. And yet..."

"And yet what?"

Fogel's eyebrows hadn't uncoiled themselves. "Well, you said you thought someone might've broken into a crematorium, and although I don't have any reason to believe someone's done that to my business, I did find our back door unlocked when I arrived this morning. It's happened several times over the past month."

"Several times?" Moss shot me a sideways glance. "Has anything gone missing?"

"Nothing," said Fogel. "I would've called to report a burglary if that were the case. I'd chalked it up to careless employees until now."

I snorted and shook my head. "Can't even trust your sons, huh?"

Fogel's face scrunched up. *"What?* Oh. No, I'm not Fogel. I mean, I am Fogel, but the Fogel and Sons refers to my dad. I'm one of the sons. I hire help now, though. My brothers moved on to other endeavors long ago."

Justice joined us from the adjoining aisle. "So to be clear, you haven't found any evidence to suggest anyone's broken into your shop?"

"Not exactly, but... bear with me." Fogel held up a finger as he retreated to his desk. He grabbed a piece of paper and hustled back with it. "I got our gas bill this morning, and it's high. A *lot* high. Twenty percent higher than normal, at least. That might not sound like a lot, but given the fact that we run furnaces all day long, gas is one of our bigger monthly expenses. This business doesn't exactly have high margins, you know. I was going to call the utility to complain, but I was checking our records to make sure I hadn't overlooked a dozen cremations over the past month. Thought I might be going crazy."

"A *dozen?*" said Moss. "How big a discrepancy between your estimated and billed gas usage is there?"

"In terms of furnace hours?" said Fogel. "Thirty-five, maybe forty hours. Like I said. *A lot.*"

I looked at Moss. "Cortez said it takes about an hour and a half to four hours to cremate someone. That *could* add up to a dozen people."

Moss lifted an eyebrow. "There's no way a dozen people have been murdered and cremated over the past month without us hearing about it."

"What? *Murdered?*" Fogel took a step back. "You didn't say anything about murder."

"We're homicide detectives." Justice turned to Moss. "Something doesn't add up."

"I agree," she said. "Mr. Fogel? Could you show us your furnaces? We'd like to take a look at them."

The man bobbed his head nervously. "Uh... of course. Anything to help."

Fogel headed into the hallway behind his desk, and the three of us followed. We passed a few doors that led to offices and storage closets before punching through the heavy steel door at the end of the hall. That led into a high-ceilinged room that felt as much like a garage as a mortuary. There was a ten-foot tall door on rolling shutters against the west wall, probably to allow trucks to back up to the three hulking furnaces along the back wall. Each of them were built out of dull gray fire bricks and had thick steel doors with long levers on the end through which they could be locked shut. A half dozen gurneys had been parked at their sides, all of them currently empty of any dead.

There were a few living souls in the room, however. A quartet of four-foot tall green goblins sat at a round table, holding cards and with a pile of chips on the table between them. One of them spotted us and pointed, causing all of them to spring from their seats. One of them even grabbed a nearby white sheet and threw it over the table, obscuring their illicit poker game from view. A little too late for that, though...

Fogel smiled nervously as he led us down a few steps to the concrete floor. "Heh... My apologies. They play for fun, not for keeps. I have to admit I let them when business is slow. Good help is hard to find, you know, especially when you run a funeral home."

"No worries," said Moss, shooting the help a quick glance.

"We're here to see the furnaces, not to bust anyone for gambling."

The goblins breathed a sigh of relief. Some of them returned to their chairs, though they left the sheet in place.

Fogel led us to the nearest of the furnaces. He slapped the bricks as he turned to us. "Here they are. They're nothing special, but they do the trick. My dad built them himself when I was a toddler. Fire bricks, Sherman gas burners, and some doors he had cast special from a local foundry. Exhaust flues in back. The gurneys were modified for the task, too. They tilt to allow us to slide folks in and out. The gas controls are on the side, and we use a thermocouple to keep track of temperature. That's all there is to it. Oh, and the ball mills are over there."

Fogel pointed to the far side of the room to a couple metal cylinders that looked like raffle drums. The metal seemed thicker, though, and there was a power cord coming out one end.

Moss nodded to the furnaces. "You're not cremating anyone now, are you?"

Fogel shook his head. "Last time we used one was yesterday, midday."

"You mind opening one?"

"Guys?" Fogel waved at the goblins, and they hopped to it. A pair came over, setting a stool next to the furnace door. One jumped up and cranked on the lever, which gave a rusty groan as it unlocked, and the other grunted as he pulled the door open.

Moss moved in as the goblins stepped aside, peering into the dark mouth of the furnace. "Phair? Can you get in here with your flashlight?"

I pulled the torch off my belt and clicked it on as I joined her. I half expected to be greeted by a foul stench of death, but the aroma was more subdued. The furnace smelled of ash and char, of old stone and centuries old death, but it lacked that pleasant aroma of a campfire.

I cast about the inside of the furnace with my flashlight's beam. A thin layer of ash covered every surface, and the odd fragment of bone gleamed as the light caught its edge, but the tomb was otherwise empty. "Looks picked clean."

Moss turned to Fogel. "You empty these after each use?"

Fogel nodded. "We sweep them clean and take the remains to the mills. Run those for ten to fifteen minutes to reduce the bones to a nice powdery consistency. Then we bag the powder and put it in a vase, if the clients purchased one. Sometimes the families don't want the ashes. In those cases, we toss them in the dumpster out back."

"I don't suppose there's any way for you to tell when the last time one of these was used, is there?"

"Like I said, my dad built these by hand," said Fogel. "There aren't any fancy sensors or printouts. I can control the gas flow. That's about it."

"And you don't have a night watchman?"

Fogel snorted. "Are you kidding? There's nothing here worth stealing."

Moss chewed on her lip as she stared into the furnace's yawning maw.

I gave her a nudge. "What are you thinking?"

She shot me a sideways glance. "I'm thinking this doesn't help us much, but maybe Emmett can make sense of it."

"*Emmett?*"

"Emmett Jowynn. Our coroner. One of them anyway. He was helping Cortez at the scene." Moss turned toward the owner. "Mr. Fogel, I'm going to need you to sweep these three furnaces again, bag any bits that might've been missed during the last cleaning. With any luck, our coroner can match the bone fragments to the remains we found."

"Of course." Fogel waved to the goblins, and the quartet got to work.

Justice came over, shaking his head. "You know this isn't going to tell us who's behind this. At best, we'll get a match on Mrs. Vernon's remains."

"That would be better than nothing," said Moss. "At least it would let us put a timeline together on this homicide. Plus it could lead to a positive ID on a suspect. We can canvass the other businesses in the area. This place might've not been open at night, but someone might've seen something."

Justice rubbed his chin. "I don't know. That's a lot of legwork for our lone rookie."

"She can handle it. Can't you, Phair?" Moss clapped me on the shoulder.

"Sure," I said. "Give me a few hours."

Moss laughed. "I like you. You don't say no. But I'm pulling your leg. Once we get these remains from Fogel, it's time to head out."

"So... no canvassing?"

"We'll order some patrol officers to do it," said Moss. "Besides, we've got more important things to do, like get Justice some lunch. He's starving. Haven't you noticed?"

I looked at the big guy, who stood there with his hands in his pockets and a neutral look on his face. "If I say no, is that a strike against me when I try to make detective?"

"All it means is you haven't spent the last few years at my side," said Justice. "I get quiet and broody when I'm hungry. Better than quick-tempered and aggressive, though."

Justice shot a finger toward Moss, which produced a playful sneer from her in turn, but luckily Fogel came over at that moment with a small bag of remains in hand, ending the spat. Moss waved us toward the exit, and we headed out.

CHAPTER TWELVE

As Justice and I walked to our workstations on the third floor of the Fifth Street precinct, we found Detective Dean hunched over his desk. A pair of books were open before him, and there were several stacks of documents strewn about, though all were contained to neat piles in the fashion I'd come to expect from him.

Dean gave us a quick glance as we reached our chairs. "You two ditched Moss?"

"She's delivering remains to the morgue," said Justice.

Dean set his pen down and spun around. "I thought the remains were already here."

Justice's chair groaned as he settled into it. "Not the remains from the aviary. We visited a few crematoriums. Tried to see if any had been broken into and used overnight. Seems like we found one, so we had the owner sweep the furnaces and give us what was left inside. With luck, we'll match something to the bones from Vernon and Daly's."

My chair sank as I put my weight on it. Part of me thought the thing might give entirely if I lifted my feet off the ground.

Was this really the best chair Moss had been able to find, or was it part of some initiation prank?

Dean glanced at me as I tried not to break any government property. "And was this before or after the... I'm going to say *burgers and fries?*"

I squinted as I returned the man's glance. "How did you know what we had for lunch?"

Justice snorted. "This is Dean we're talking about. You think he flips his detective switch on and off for cases? He's always like this. Chances are he smelled the char-grilled meat stink on us, or maybe I have something stuck in my incisors. You'd tell me if I did, wouldn't you?" The well-dressed ogre sucked on his teeth preemptively.

Dean smiled. "I would, and no, my sense of smell isn't that acute. I just notice things. Specifically, Phair..." He mimed pinching his cuffs.

I looked down. Sure enough, there was a red stain at the tip of my sleeve. I'd probably dunked it while dragging my fries through ketchup. It probably wouldn't have happened if we'd eaten inside, but since Justice had wanted to get back to work, we'd visited the drive through and taken the meal in the car. Then again, given my penchant for acquiring stains, if we'd sat down for lunch, I probably would've traded a ketchup-covered sleeve for a lap full of milkshake or something equally embarrassing.

I sighed. "Thanks. You don't have any napkins, do you?"

Dean held out a box of tissues, and I plucked one. As I fruitlessly dabbed at the spot, Dean turned to Justice. "Did you get any physical evidence of a break-in at this funeral home?"

"Just the owner's word," said Justice. "Said he'd found the

door unlocked several times over the past month, and his gas bill suggests someone's been the using the place after hours."

Dean lifted an eyebrow. "Did you also find men in black robes digging an unlicensed mass grave behind this funeral home?"

Justice smirked. "Trust me, I don't think it adds up, either. But maybe one of the bone fragments will match the remains from the circus. Even if they don't, might be worth keeping an eye on the place. The words *after-hours* and *crematorium* don't exactly mix."

Dean nodded. "Agreed. Phair? Any progress on the drug front?"

I looked up from my thoroughly ineffective de-staining efforts. Moss had argued Dean didn't want me to ask each carnie at the circus if they were dealing benzos on the side, yet here I was, looking the fool even apart from my ketchup-covered sleeve.

I cleared my throat as I gathered my nerve. "No. Moss and I talked it over, and it seemed to us that if anyone at Vernon and Daly's was dealing, or buying for that matter, they'd keep it under wraps. But we instructed the patrol officers to ask around to see if anyone caught sight of Mrs. Vernon last night."

Dean gave a small shrug. "Fair enough. For what it's worth, I called Detective Harmon and asked him if he knew of anyone at the circus who was selling dope. He didn't, so it's probably not worth putting the bulk of our efforts into that avenue. Anything else you've learned?"

Given Dean's demeanor, I hadn't expected to be yelled at, berated, or ordered to scrub his car with a toothbrush for failing to execute his suggestion to the letter, but I'd nonetheless expected some pushback. To have him consider my point of view and consider my decision reasonable was, while rational, a complete departure from the rage-fueled culture of compliance of my former TO.

I shook my head. "Moss and I were tossing some theories back and forth, but nothing concrete. Can't say we've gotten any new leads other than the crematorium."

"Well, let's find some, then," said Dean. "First things first, we need to get a positive ID on the remains. Phair, call the Vernon residence. Get the name of that jeweler and Mrs. Vernon's dentist, then follow up with both of them. You can also file a missing persons report. I already called in a BOLO for Stella Vernon's car. If we find that, we might uncover more evidence about her whereabouts last evening. Justice, I'm still wrapping things for another homicide. Maybe you can get started on the case file? Pull arrest records, if any, for Stella Vernon, JT Vernon, and any of the folks at the circus who work in the aviary, for starters. Call the DMV for Mrs. Vernon's photo. That sort of thing."

Justice nodded. "Can do."

Dean turned to his desk and picked up his pen, but a voice inside me, the voice Dean had encouraged not to be silent, poked its inquisitive head out and waved furiously.

I cleared my throat again. "Dean?"

He turned back around. "Yes?"

"I was curious about that meeting you had this morning. Moss said it was with a scientist regarding the tarot card murders."

Dean tapped the butt of his pen against his armrest. "That's right. A physicist. I wasn't sure how much to involve you given your proximity to the case."

Justice had already pulled his chair into his desk, but he

spoke over his shoulder. "She might be the closest thing to a witness we have, but in terms of proximity, you're as close to the case as they get, Dean. She's part of the team now. Anything you'd share with us, you can share with her, I'd think."

Dean nodded. "Fair enough. We'll need to bring you up to speed, but I'll focus on that when we don't have another murder sucking up the oxygen. What about the meeting did you want to know?"

I shrugged. "Moss said you were talking about the strange purple glow I saw in the park. I'm as curious to know what it was as you are."

Dean hesitated for a moment, keeping my gaze as he did so. "Well, the short of it is my expert couldn't provide a logical physical explanation for what you saw."

I blinked. "I don't understand."

Dean leaned back in his chair. "He walked me through a number of atmospheric optical phenomena that could produce a purple halo or glow similar to what you witnessed, from auroral light to airglow to something called the Alexander's band, which is essentially the darkened region between two rainbows. There are a few issues that rule out all of them, however. For one, the phenomena you observed occurred at ground level, not in the atmosphere. For another, it occurred at night and under a forest's protective canopy. That suggests moonlight probably wasn't responsible. Also out are any phenomena reliant upon dew, including sylvanshine and some other one with a complicated name I can't remember. The evening you walked through the park was dry, and the temperature hadn't dropped enough for dew to form until the wee hours of the morning. That leaves us with a few other possibilities. One is that you witnessed some sort of chemi or bioluminescence. Are you familiar with will-o-wisps?"

I lifted an eyebrow. "You're talking about ghosts?"

"I'm talking about the flickering light that for centuries people *attributed* to ghosts. Thanks to science, we now know those strange flickering lights are the result of chemiluminescence from the oxidation of marsh gasses like phosphine and methane. That's why people always witnessed them over marshes and bogs."

My brow remained furrowed. "But there's no bog in Miller's Creek Park."

Dean tipped his head. "Indeed. And while the professor I spoke with perhaps isn't the world's foremost expert on luminescence, he was quick to point out there aren't any living organisms or natural chemical processes that occur in the parks of our urban environment that could produce the purple glow you saw. The limited research I've done suggests he's right. At the very least, no one else has reported a similar phenomenon that I've been able to find."

"So where does that leave us in regards to the glow?" I asked.

Dean shrugged. "There are two possibilities, neither of which are particularly satisfying. The first one the professor offered is that you're misremembering the experience."

I stiffened, even though I knew it wasn't a personal attack. "I know what I saw."

Dean held up a hand. "And I believe you. While traumatic events can create mental blocks that prevent individuals from accessing memories, more often the opposite occurs. The events imprint themselves on your mind, and you can recall them clearly long after the incident. The fact that you recall such a precise detail from the encounter leads me to believe your experience conforms to the latter. Rarely do traumatic events cause anyone to imagine something that specific, after all. Which leads me to the professor's second option: that what you saw has no physical explanation."

I frowned. "I'm still confused. You're talking about a biological or chemical explanation? So the will-o'-wisps?"

Dean shook his head. "No. What I mean is that there may not be a natural explanation for what you saw. To make sense of it, we might need to consider the *super*natural."

I was silent for a second before scoffing. "You're kidding, right?"

Dean didn't laugh or smile. "I'm not. I told you yesterday. Not everything in this world makes sense. Not everything that can be known is known, and sometimes the unknowable works its way into our cases. If you want to solve the impossible, then you have to reconsider everything you consider to be such first. Isn't that right, Justice?"

The ogre nodded over his shoulder. "I won't go into specifics, but I've seen some weird stuff sitting behind this desk. So has Dean. You have to keep an open mind, otherwise reality opens it for you."

As I sat there in my seat, with a slack jaw and a stupefied look on my face, Moss popped around the corner.

"Hey, guys. Dropped off the sample with Emmett. He said not to expect anything for a day or two." She stripped off her coat and draped it across the back of her chair, but she paused as she saw the look on my face. "Did I miss something? Phair looks like someone told her a secret she'd only shared with a friend who died back in sixth grade."

Now Dean smiled. "Nothing that dramatic. I'm simply expanding Phair's horizons."

"Well, stop it," said Moss. "She doesn't need her mind blown right before she talks to the captain."

I blinked. "The captain?"

"He caught me on his way up from the basement," said Moss. "That's why it took me so long to get back. He asked how it was going, and as we were shooting the breeze, he asked to meet you. You should probably head down to his office. He doesn't like to be kept waiting."

I swallowed hard and nodded. If my previous experiences with police captains were any indication, meetings such as this one were never about getting to know each other.

CHAPTER THIRTEEN

The office was on the first floor, encased in glass and positioned so the entirety of the main floor could be seen from the desk inside. The blinds had all been pulled up, and the door stood open. I nonetheless stopped short of the office's heart, pausing at the door as I knocked. "Excuse me? Sir?"

The man behind the desk was in that nebulous range known as middle age, but regardless of the true number of years under his belt, he carried them well. His hair, though graying, was thick and had a waviness to it that gave him a rakish flair. Though there were a number of creases in his brow, the skin at his neck and his chin was tight. He wore a black tie over a crisp white shirt, one with curved dress pocket flaps and epaulets that held fours stars over each shoulder. A portrait of him hung on the wall with his full name, Henry Herbert Ellison, engraved on a bronze plaque underneath it. In it he looked about ten years younger than he did in real life.

He looked up at the sound of my voice, smiling as much

with his warm brown eyes as with his teeth. "Officer Phair. Come in."

I nodded as I stepped across the threshold into his office, though I paused after the first step. "Should I close the door?"

"That won't be necessary." He stood and extended a hand. "I'm Captain Ellison."

I took the man's hand, giving it a single firm shake. "Penelope Phair, sir. What can I do for you?"

"You can take a seat and tell me about yourself," said Ellison as he returned to his chair. "I like to get to know everyone in my precinct, and given the unusual conditions of your hire, we never had the pleasure of being introduced. I had to take Detective Dean's word on your abilities."

A pair of plush chairs upholstered with a pale blue fabric were positioned at matching angles to his desk. Either of them would've won a boxing match against the half-dead one Moss found for me upstairs in half a round, but I figured asking if I could drag one upstairs would be a major faux pas.

I sat. "What would you like to know, sir?"

"Anything you'd care to share," said Ellison with a smile. "What got you into police work? What drives you? And most importantly, how did you come to draw my star detective's eye?"

I snorted. "Are you sure you have that much time?"

Ellison kept his smile in place, but there was a stiffness to it that suggested it wasn't as genial as advertised. "The condensed version, then."

I took a deep breath. "I don't know if you've read my file, but I'm new to the force. Just graduated from the academy a few weeks ago. I can't say I always dreamed of being an officer, but I grew up in a household that respected the law. My great-grandfather was a detective, and my great-grandmother was one too.

At least, she was until she became captain. Right here at the Fifth, no less. Shay Daggers."

I pointed to the hall where her portrait hung before realized how foolish that was. "I'm, ah... sure you're familiar with her. Anyway, she put the bug into my head about serving others, and I decided I'd give it a shot. Which isn't to say I'm not serious about it. By give it a shot I simply meant I'd see if I could cut it."

Ellison didn't say anything, but he gave me a nod of encouragement.

I appreciated it. Despite his outwardly kind demeanor, my stomach was flipping like a flapjack. "Anyway, my partner and I answered a murder call my very first shift. Detectives Dean, Moss, and Justice showed up to investigate, and I did my best to help. Detective Moss gave me a ride back to the precinct after my TO was, ah... called away." Actually, he ditched me because it was the end of his shift, but I didn't need to throw him under the bus. Ellison probably didn't even know who he was. "From there, Moss called me to provide backup a couple times, and if I'm being honest, I may have gotten more invested in the investigation than I should've. Long story short, I kept thinking about the case after Detective Dean made an arrest, and I came to the conclusion the wrong man had been pinned for murder. I submitted a statement regarding my conclusions, and I suppose you know the rest."

Captain Ellison nodded. "Captain McGuire at the Williams Street precinct sent it over. Dean wasn't happy reading it, but not because of your efforts. He holds himself to a high standard, and to have missed the conclusions you drew bothered him deeply."

"I could imagine so, sir, but that was never my intent. I only wanted to make sure justice was served."

Ellison waved idly as he leaned back in his chair. "No one thinks otherwise. Anyone familiar with Dean wouldn't voluntarily pit themselves against the man. You weren't familiar with the detective's work before you met him at the scene of the crime, were you?"

My lips puckered. "No. I'd never heard of him, honestly."

Ellison steepled his fingers before him. "So it was the luck of the draw that put you at New Age Alchemical when Dean arrived, and simple curiosity that kept you emotionally invested, not some attachment to our well-respected detective?"

My brow furrowed. I thought I'd known more or less where the conversation was going, but now I found myself at a loss. "No, sir. It was chance, nothing more. I know some people think my great-grandmother pulled strings for me to get a position, but she's been retired for decades. I doubt most people in the department would know who she is even if they had her official portrait as a reference."

Ellison rubbed his fingertips together, continuing as if I hadn't spoken. "It's happened before, you see, for people in all walks of life. People who see a long set of coat tails and think they can ride them to the promised land. Individuals have already tried with Dean, but he sees them coming a mile away. Not you, though. He sees something in you. Potential. Talent. Shades of himself, perhaps. I'm not sure."

I felt a little of the anger that tended to boil out of me at inopportune times churn within, but I kept it under control. "Sir, I assure you, I'm not here to ride anyone's coattails. I didn't ask to be added to his team. I wasn't even consulted. To be honest, after hearing he'd requested my transfer, I thought he'd sent me to some god-forsaken corner of the city as punishment."

Ellison waved a couple fingers. "I believe you, Officer. I

don't think this is part of a greater scheme. I think you're precisely who you appear to be, which might be exactly what Dean needs. More importantly, it's exactly what *I* need."

Once again, I felt as if I'd lost the thread of the conversation. *"Sir?"*

Captain Ellison turned slightly in his chair. He met my gaze, eyes narrowing. "Alton Dean is an excellent detective. The best in my precinct. Perhaps the best in the entire department. In most cases, an intellect like his is accompanied by an equally impressive ego. While he might be the exception to the rule, he doesn't break all the stereotypes. When working cases, his focus is singular. He does his best to solve the mysteries placed in front of him, no matter the barriers. When those barriers are due to a lack of information, his drive works in his favor. When the barriers are institutional or procedural, less so."

I lifted an eyebrow. "Are you saying he's not above breaking the rules to solve cases?"

"What I'm saying, Officer, is that he's willing to ruffle feathers and ignore orders if it gets him results, which is a trait you seem to share if your file is representative. It might be why he asked to hire you. I'm not sure. But that's not why I agreed to bring you aboard."

The captain didn't provide a follow-up, so after I moment I gave into his prompt. "So, why *was* I transferred here, sir?"

Ellison smiled. "I need someone to keep an eye on Dean. Someone who will grow to have his ear and make him listen to reason. Someone who will report to me and follow orders I give to the letter. Someone I can trust."

My stomach fluttered. I understood the power dynamic at play. I knew exactly what the captain was asking of me, but there was information I was missing. "Sir, I know I haven't been in the force long, but I can assure you, I'm not a troublemaker. I don't make a habit of breaking rules. That said, if you think I'm cut from the same cloth as Detective Dean, then what makes you think I'm someone you can trust?"

The Captain's smile widened. "Oh, that's simple. It's all about self-preservation. Because of his talent, Detective Dean is nigh untouchable." The smile disappeared. "You, on the other hand, are anything but."

I swallowed hard, and Ellison's smile returned. "But don't worry. Be smart. Play by the rules—*my* rules—and we won't have any problems. Understood, Officer?"

Oh, I understood him. But I wasn't sure I believed him.

CHAPTER FOURTEEN

I sat at my desk, my phone's receiver pressed against the side of my head. Blood rushed in my ear. It felt hot and sweaty, the byproduct of hours spent making calls in search of information.

I'd started with the low hanging fruit. I'd placed a call to JT Vernon's home which had been answered by Mossbottom. After a lengthy search, the gnome provided me with the name of the jeweler from which Vernon purchased his wife's engagement ring, as well as her dentist. I'd called the dentist first, figuring it was the best avenue to achieve a positive identification on the remains, but in what would turn out to be a portent for the rest of the afternoon, I wasn't able to speak with him. Instead, I reached the man's receptionist. She told me Dr. Ernoost was busy performing a root canal but that she would pass along my request to pull Stella Vernon's x-rays. Supposedly, they'd be ready by end of day. Similarly, when I called VanBuren Jewelers, I spent fifteen minutes being passed from salesperson to manager before ultimately discovering that Aivars VanBuren, who sold the ring to Mr. Vernon, wasn't in and wouldn't be until tomorrow. The manager informed me we could drop the diamond off and Mr. VanBuren would authenticate it first thing, but I told him we couldn't leave evidence with them overnight, no matter how secure their safes. Instead, I instructed him to ask VanBuren to drop by the precinct the next day.

That left me with an endless series of phone calls to the rest of the city's precincts. Currently I was on the phone with the Marguerite Avenue precinct on the east side of the River Earl. The line buzzed, as if the connection wasn't very good. In the background I heard the heavy clomps of frustrated officers walking by, the indignant cries of those being arrested, and the occasional wail of a siren.

I pulled the receiver from my ear to wipe away the sweat. As I did so the speaker crackled. "Officer Phair?"

I quickly pressed the thing back against my head. "I'm here."

"No Stella Vernon in custody," said Officer Barkley, who'd introduced himself when I first called the front desk. "I also checked with our Missing Persons division. No reports of her there, either."

I made a note on the pad in front of me. "Thanks. What about the cremated remains?"

Barkley's voice crackled. "I checked with homicide. None of those have been reported or found by our officers."

Moss didn't think it was likely that a dozen people had been murdered and cremated at Fogel and Sons over the past month, but it was worth investigating. "Alright. I appreciate your time, Officer. Have a good day."

"You, too."

The phone clicked, and I put it down. I leaned back in my chair, which produced a pained squeak, and sighed.

From across the partition, I heard Moss's voice. "Cheer up, Phair. You know what they say. Seventeenth time's the charm."

I snorted as I rubbed my tender earlobe. "Technically, that was the fourteenth precinct I called."

Moss pushed back in her chair and smiled at me. "Then you have nothing to complain about! See? Isn't homicide investigation riveting?"

I smiled back. "I know you're trying to goad me into complaining—which I wasn't doing, for the record—but I'm not going to take the bait. Even if *all* I got to do as a part of this team was work the phones, that would still beat the emotional torment of patrol with my former TO."

"Fair enough," said Moss. "But don't let Dean hear you say that."

Dean and Justice had headed off to pull files for another case, leaving Moss and me alone at our desks. "Why not? He doesn't seem like the type to take advantage of my willingness to be a team player."

"Of course not. He's the cool and aloof type. But you don't want to seem too eager. Too thirsty."

I shrugged, recalling how Dean opened up to me in the car. "I don't know. He doesn't seem that detached to me. He comes across as warm and genuine."

Moss gave me another one of her sideways glances, but whatever she might've had on her mind was preempted by the arrival of an officer.

"Excuse me," he said. "Detective Moss?"

Moss turned to the young man. "Yes?"

"Officer Marks, from the circus," he said. "Wanted to let

you know we finished canvassing the area, and we found a tan Pearl Motors Clavelle parked in a lot less than a block from the northeast corner of the property. Checked the license plate. It's registered to JT Vernon."

Moss perked. "Any signs of forced entry?"

The officer shook his head. "No, ma'am. Doors were locked. No one inside the vehicle. No blood or signs of a struggle that I could see through the windows."

"Do you have an address on the lot?" asked Moss.

"Sure do. It's in the report." The officer held forth the folder in his hands. "Also in there are the notes we took from talking to the carnies, plus the owners of the businesses near that lot with the Clavelle."

Moss took the folder and flipped it open. "Anything specific we should know about?"

"No one at the circus admitted to seeing Mrs. Vernon there last night, but we did find a vagrant who claimed to have seen something."

"A *vagrant?*" Moss whistled. "Okay, I'm listening."

The officer nodded in agreement. "The guy said he was walking along the north side of Eleventh, across the street from the circus, when he spotted a woman running from that lot with the car to the white fencing that surrounds Vernon and Daly's. Said she hopped the fence and disappeared inside, but get this. The guy said she was *naked*."

"Did he?" said Moss. "And did this vagrant have a distinct aroma of cheap booze on his breath?"

The officer smirked. "Not so much an aroma as a kick to the nostrils."

"Right," said Moss. "I don't suppose he got a look at this naked woman's face, did he?"

The officer shook his head. "No, ma'am. Seems as if he wasn't focused on anything above the neck. Called her a *skinny piece of ass*, though."

"And he didn't know what time she ran across the street?"

Another shake of the head. "I don't think the guy even knew what time it was when we interviewed him."

Moss closed the folder. "Alright. I appreciate the help, Officer. Dismissed."

The young man bobbed his head and headed out. Moss swiveled in her chair to face me, a look of curiosity on her face. "That was interesting."

"I'll say," I agreed. "Do you believe the homeless guy's testimony?"

"I'm going to leave that alone for the time being," said Moss. "I want to focus on Stella's car. The fact it's there lends credence to our theory that her remains were the ones found at the scene. My question is: *should* the car be there?"

I frowned. "What do you mean?"

Moss tossed the folder on her desk. "Let's assume Stella Vernon was murdered, and her remains left in the aviary. The presence of her car might suggest she was murdered at the circus, and yet nothing we've uncovered so far suggests Stella was actually murdered *in the aviary*. I know you were gone with Dean, but Coroner Jowynn didn't find any blood at the scene, nor did the CSU techs."

I pursed my lips. "I don't know if I see it that way. To me, the car might suggest precisely the opposite."

"How so?" said Moss.

I leaned forward in my chair. "You said it yourself. There's nothing about the crime scene that suggests anyone was murdered there. Moreover, there doesn't seem to be any way

Mrs. Vernon could've been cremated on site. She was murdered elsewhere, cremated elsewhere, and her remains dumped. If her car is at the circus, she couldn't have been the one who drove it there. Perhaps someone she knew murdered her, stuffed her in the trunk of her car, drove her to a crematorium, and then took the remains to the aviary."

Moss nodded slowly. "Could be. If so, there would be evidence in the trunk. Blood. Hair. There might also be physical evidence from her attacker in the front. Either way, we need to tow that thing and sweep it."

Moss pulled her phone off her receiver and held it to her ear. "Operator? This is Detective Moss. Get me CSU."

I scooted my chair around the edge of Moss's partition to get closer. "The problem with my theory, of course, is that beggar's testimony."

Moss held up a finger. "CSU? Officer Moss. I've got a car that needs to be towed and evidence collected." She gave them the car's make and model and the address and hung up. "You're talking about the possibility of the vagrant having seen Mrs. Vernon as opposed to some other naked woman or having imagined the whole thing while blitzed on malt liquor."

"Exactly," I said. "If he saw Stella, my theory goes out the window, or at the very least it suggests she was murdered at the circus after all, if not necessarily in the bird enclosure. But the fact that she was naked could imply there was another component to this case."

Moss rubbed her chin. "She might've been sexually assaulted. Can't imagine why else she would've been naked. Of course, I also can't imagine why she would've been running from her car to the circus." She shook her head. "Or the bum is just nuts. That's a real possibility."

"Not that I wish mental illness upon anyone, but that would certainly clear things up." I cast an uneasy glance at the clock on the wall, its hour hand already past six. "Does this mean I need to call the precincts back and ask if any of them got reports of a naked woman running around last night?"

Moss snickered. "Not today. It's getting late. In fact..." She nodded as Dean and Justice appeared from around the edge of the cubicles.

Dean must've caught Moss's look or at least overheard the tail end of our conversation. He cast a curious look her way as he approached his desk. "Are we walking into something not meant for our ears?'

"You know me," said Moss. "Pair me with a gal pal, and I can't stop gossiping."

Justice lifted an eyebrow and scrunched his face up. "Really? *You?*"

"I'm kidding, Ogden. Lighten up... which you could do by agreeing to my plans for the evening."

Dean dropped a file on his desk. "You have plans?"

"Call it a fit of inspiration," said Moss. "I thought we might go out. Have a team building exercise to get to know Phair better."

A smile spread across Justice's face. "And by team building exercise, you mean consuming food and the occasional cold beverage?"

Moss clicked her tongue and shot him with a finger gun. "Can't pull one over on you, big guy. What do you say, Alton?"

Dean rifled through the piles of his desk, coming up with a new folder. "I say it sounds lovely. You guys'll have a great time, but I have too much to do to join you. Maybe next time."

He clapped Justice on the shoulder as he headed back out.

Moss sighed as he left. "Same thing every time."

Justice shrugged. "Honestly, I'm not sure why you ask. Ever heard that the definition of insanity is doing the same thing over and over and expecting different results?"

Moss smiled, but the rest of her face revealed it was a forced mirth. "Guess I'm a little crazy, then. But mostly hopeful. I'd hate not to offer and have him want to join us for once." Moss brightened and slapped me on the shoulder. "Whatever. Ready to get out of here?"

In an absolute sense, I was. The day hadn't been the most demanding, not from a physical perspective, but a nervous energy had smoldered inside me from the moment I'd awoken, an energy I'd mostly spent trying to avoid making a fool of myself. I'd tried not to focus on it, but keeping a veneer of confidence up had taken more out of me than I'd cared to admit. Emotionally-speaking, I felt exhausted, and I could only blame so much of that on getting up before the rise of the sun.

The mental exhaustion probably should've been reason enough for me to head home, even before considering that my boyfriend Cliff, whose shift ended at two, was most likely waiting on me for dinner. Still, Moss hadn't posed my joining her as a request, and failing to take up my co-workers on an opportunity to bond after our first day at work was probably the worst career move I could make.

Besides, it sounded fun. I just wished Dean would've agreed to come with.

I nodded. "Ready when you are. Though as I said this morning, I didn't bring a change of clothes."

Moss stood and grabbed her jacket. "You won't be the first uniformed officer to tip back a drink or two, nor the last. Besides, the place we're going to is used to us. We're sort of an institution."

I stood and pushed my chair in, too. "You specifically, or cops in general?"

Moss shrugged. "More of the latter than the former. Trust me, this place is a landmark."

CHAPTER FIFTEEN

As I stood outside the Jjade Palace's front stoop, a few thoughts crossed my mind. First and foremost was that Moss hadn't lied. The place was definitely a landmark—a historical one, to be specific. The rectangular pile of sooty, cracked bricks looked as if it had been slapped together back when soldiers carried spears and were paid in salt rather than legal tender. To appear older than your neighbors in a city like New Welwic that was built on the bones of twelve previous civilizations was quite the achievement, but like a centenarian eating a whole apple, the Jjade Palace pulled it off with gumption and resilience.

The other thing I noticed was that the name on the sign was misspelled. Given how ratty the storefront looked, I figured the owners bought the thing from a fly-by-night craftsman who either didn't offer returns or went broke before the owners could collect. Then again, no one in their right mind might've considered the place a palace either, not even at the bar's grand opening. Perhaps the name was something ironic. New Welwic suffered from an infestation of such places.

Moss noticed the look on my face, which couldn't have been hard. I probably would've looked less apprehensive if I'd been asked to dive headfirst into a wolverine's den. She laughed as she hopped up the steps and opened the door. "Take my word on this place, Phair. You'll dig it."

If I did any digging around Jjade's Palace, I might destabilize the foundation, resulting in the whole place collapsing and crushing me to death, but I kept that thought to myself as I headed inside.

There, I paused again, probably with as much confusion on my face as before. I'd expected a hole in the wall with liquored-up derelicts passed out on the floor, but instead I was greeting with old-world charm. The outward facing walls were brick, same as they appeared from the outside, but everything else, from the booths to the tables to the bar itself, was made of wood, dark and rich and worn smooth from age. The booths were upholstered in leather, and thick drapes hung over the windows, letting the mellow glow from vintage bulbs that hung over every table control the mood. A bit of cigarette smoke hung in the air, as did a greasiness from a fryer, but neither smell was overpowering. Groups stood in clusters and sat at tables, drinking and eating and chatting at a level that stopped a dozen decibels short of ear-splitting.

The front door clunked shut. I felt a presence over my shoulder before I heard Moss's voice in my ear. "See? First impressions can be deceiving."

That much was true—I was walking proof—but rarely were pubs the exception to the rule. As I continued to gape, Justice shouldered his way forward, clearing a path to a free table that he must've seen thanks to his height. We'd barely taken our seats before a waitress stopped by. I thought she might give me a side-

ways look because of my uniform, but I might as well have been
wearing sweatpants and a T-shirt for all the attention she gave
me. Moss asked if I drank beer, and after confirming that I did,
she ordered a pitcher for the table and a few assorted appetizers.

I guess the look of surprise still hadn't fled my face, as
Justice gave me a sympathetic glance. "Don't feel bad. I didn't
trust this place at first either, but it's got a reputation in the
department for a reason. Good food, good drinks, all reasonably
priced. And they don't mind cops, which is kind of important.
Depending on who you believe, the men and women in blue
have been coming here for over a century."

"And they're quick, too," said Moss as our waitress returned.

The young woman deposited our pitcher and a trio of
glasses before scuttling off. Moss separated the glasses and
Justice poured, delivering Moss's and my pint before filling
his own.

Moss held out her glass as Justice finished. "To a successful
first day from the newest member of our team. May she have
many more and continue to learn and grow."

"And not royally screw things up like our last one," added
Justice as we clinked.

"Wait... last one?" I paused with my glass held high. *"Royally screwed up?"*

"Ogden!" Moss smacked the ogre across the arm. "We've
alternated between three and four members in the past. The last
guy who came around was a brown-noser with as much deductive ability as a cheese sandwich. Don't worry about it, Penelope. Can I call you that off-duty?"

I recalled what Captain Ellison had said about others who'd
attached themselves to Detective Dean, but the knowledge that

they'd failed didn't put me at ease. "I go by Nell. And I'm glad you think it was a successful first day. To be honest, I felt out of my element more often than not."

"It's to be expected," said Moss. "You're in a new situation. Don't sweat it. You'll adjust. But I'd rather not focus on work when I have a drink in my hand." Moss tipped her beer back for emphasis.

"Agreed," said Justice, a massive mitt wrapped around his glass. "So tell us about yourself, Phair—I mean, Nell. What's your story?"

Moss grunted as she set her glass back down. "Please. Haven't you ever been on a date, Ogden? You can't expect someone to lay their life bare. You've got to give them prompts. Offer up specific topics of conversation."

Ogden snorted. "I've been on dates..."

I didn't know why Moss mentioned dates. Hopefully she wasn't trying to set me up with Justice. "I don't mind talking about myself. That's why we're here, isn't it?"

"We're here to have fun," said Moss. "And we can learn about each other in more creative ways. Have you ever played never have I ever?"

Ogden groaned. "A drinking game? You realize we have to report to work tomorrow, right?"

Moss smacked him on the arm again. "Like you have anything to worry about, Og. You could probably chug an entire keg and barely feel it. Now as penance for your surly attitude, you can get us started."

Justice scowled, but there was a hint of mirth in his frown. "Fine. Never have I ever... misfiled paperwork and had a prisoner transferred to a meatpacking plant."

"Ugh. You louse." Moss took a drink. "For the record, I tran-scribed the address incorrectly. The real fault belonged to the driver of the paddy wagon who couldn't tell a poultry factory from a prison. But you're forgetting something, Ogden. It's not supposed to be work related stuff."

"Why not?" he said.

"Because work stuff is boring, and I'd rather not revisit all the dead people we've tripped over through the years," Moss said. "I'd rather list personal stuff. Experiences that show who we are. Things you and I don't even know about each other."

Justice rolled his eyes. "Alright…"

"Here. Let me give you an example. Never have I ever… made out with a lawyer in a courthouse." Moss grinned devil-ishly and took a sip of her beer.

My mouth opened. "You didn't."

"You'd be surprised the number of people Ginger's kissed," said Justice. "Few careers remain untouched. But lawyer isn't really a surprise. She dated one for a long time."

"I actually wasn't talking about Javier," said Moss. "We never made out in a court-house. This was a guy I never saw again."

Justice shot a thumb Moss's way as he looked at me. "See what I mean?"

"Well, you can't leave it at that," I said. "Who was this mystery lawyer you dated?"

Moss waved a hand, but there was a mistiness in her eyes I hadn't seen throughout the day. "That's a story for another time. Besides, it slows down the drinking game if you expound on everything, you know?"

"Speaking of which," said Justice. "Am I supposed to sit

here with my hands in my lap? Knowing you, I'll never touch my lager."

"You do you, big guy. Nell. You're up."

I knew how to play the game, but I also wasn't entirely sure how far to take it. Moss had shared something mildly scandalous, though, and I figured the whole point was to share experiences that were somewhat embarrassing or incriminating. "Okay. Here goes. Never have I ever... driven my dad's car into the Earl River." I cringed as I took a drink.

Moss's eyes widened. "Really? And *I* got a funny look for making out in a courthouse?"

Justice looked at me sideways. "You drove it *into the river?* And you passed the driving course at the academy?"

I set my glass down and wiped my lip. "It was the canalized portion of the river, near Jameson Avenue where the guardrail is almost nonexistent. But... yeah. The front half got pretty wet." I gave him a sly grin.

Justice erupted in laughter, either at the look on my face or the story itself. "Well, I'll be. She just raised us, Ginger."

"You know what that means, Ogden. You've got to raise back. Give us something tawdry. Something salacious." Moss's eyes twinkled.

Ogden rolled his eyes again. "I'm not talking relationships if that's what you're getting at. But I do have something that's coming to mind. Not an incident I'm proud of, mind you. Never have I ever... accidentally sat on a pixie and sent her to the hospital."

Justice drank. I sputtered in my beer, and Moss gasped. "No!"

The ogre shrugged. "You think I have side mirrors on this

big body? I've got blind spots, woman. How was I supposed to know she was there?"

We all laughed, and the rounds continued apace. Appetizers came and went, and the pitcher was taken and refilled. I learned Moss's appetite for men was bigger than my own, and based on the situations she'd put herself in, she wasn't too concerned with what other people thought of it. I learned that Justice, for all his dapper attire and professionalism, was someone I never wanted to mess with. More importantly, I got the impression it bothered him that he had to constantly suppress his baser, more emotional side for people to take him seriously, though he never came out and said it in so many words. In return, I think I did a good job conveying to Moss and Justice that I'd been quite the screwup as recently as a few months ago but that I was doing my best to turn over a new leaf, and both of them seemed okay with that. Maybe it was part of being in homicide. They'd seen so much that was beyond the pale that my occasional indiscretions were amusing rather than concerning.

More than anything though, I laughed and drank and had a good time, which was something I hadn't done in a long while, not even alongside Cliff. Sure, we'd gone out and had dinner and drinks on occasion, but I couldn't recall a single instance with him where I'd even had a good belly laugh, never mind been wracked so hard with laughter that my stomach ached. Once again I wished Dean had made the time to join us, because if anyone needed the sweet release of laughter, it seemed as if it was him. Perhaps it was his fiancée's death that still bothered him, or maybe it was the weight of expectations he'd placed on his own shoulders, but even I knew most problems couldn't be solved by working harder until they went away.

Moss set down her empty pint glass as an epic burp erupted from her lips. Her eyes widened in surprise, and she patted her chest. "Whoa. Pardon me. I guess that's what I get for downing three pints in two hours."

"Pretty sure that was four," said Justice. "And it's been closer to three hours."

Ginger glanced at her wristwatch. "Holy harvest. You're right. About the time, if not the beer. We should wrap this up. If one of us is hung over tomorrow, Dean might find it funny, but all three of us would rub him the wrong way."

"As you already said, that's more of a you problem than a me problem," said Justice as he lifted his glass again. "But that's what you get for having such a low body mass."

"Oh, really?" said Moss with a smirk. "Are you suggesting you'd like me better if I was shaped more like you?"

Justice shook his head. "Wouldn't bother me one bit, Ginger. You know that's not what I like about you."

"Well, it should be. 'Cause I look *damned* good." Moss got up from her chair and gave a little wiggle, which given her small waist and ample bosom was something worth looking at. "You want to hit the bathroom, Nell?"

I waved her off. "I'm doing okay."

"Suit yourself. I'll flag down our waitress if I see her." She shot a playful wink in Justice's direction before heading off through the crowd.

She must not have gotten all her wiggles out, or she was feeling the effects of the beers, because she had a decent strut going as she left, even if her back end wasn't as full and round as my own. It was enough to captivate me, and yet I don't think Justice gave her a second glance.

I leaned over. "You know she likes you, right?"

"Ginger?" Justice raised an eyebrow. "We're friends. She might like me, but not like that."

"Oh, yes indeed like that," I said. "And you might just be friends now, but I guarantee you she'd be willing to steer that car into a new lane if you waved her over."

Justice set his glass down. "Look, Nell, don't get me wrong. I love Ginger, I really do, but not that way. She's like a little sister to me. I'd put my life on the line for her, and I have once or twice, but that's it. She's not my type, and even if she was, we work together. I wouldn't cross that line. It's too risky, know what I mean?"

I thought about my relationship with Cliff, who worked patrol at the Williams Street precinct. I'd been concerned about our supervisors finding out we were dating, but now that I'd moved to the Fifth that probably wasn't an issue anymore. Then again, there might be more pressing concerns for our relationship. We'd talked about my transfer, though not yet in depth. The fact that Dean had picked me up, even without having made me any promises of future success or granting me any favors, might not sit well with him. He was very much a by the books kind of guy.

I brushed my concerns aside. "So if Moss's small and busty thing doesn't work for you, what *is* your type?"

For the first time since we'd ordered our pitcher, Justice stiffened. He gave me a glare that wasn't entirely playful. "My type is none of your business, same as it isn't Ginger's." He shot a thumb toward the exit. "Go on. You can head out if you'd like. Moss and I will take care of the bill."

I lifted a slightly beer-soaked eyebrow. "You sure?"

"We make more than you do. Not a *lot* more, but enough to treat you this once."

A smile returned to his lips as he said it, enough for me to know I wasn't in the doghouse for pressing him on his romantic tastes. With a quick glance at my watch, I told him to give my regards to Ginger and headed out.

CHAPTER SIXTEEN

The lonely glow of a floor lamp greeted me as I stepped into my apartment, a simple one bedroom with a common space in the front and a half height wall separating the living room from the kitchen. Other than the muted warble of a neighbor's radio, the space was quiet and still.

"Cliff?" I said in a low voice. "You still up?"

He didn't respond, so I latched the door shut and took off my shoes. I flicked a switch as I headed into the kitchen, but Cliff wasn't hiding in the gloom like a brooding father, ready to confront me after breaking curfew. There was a piece of lined paper resting upon the counter however.

I picked it up. The note was in Cliff's messy script.

NELL,

I got takeout. Chicken stir fry with noodles. I don't know when you'll be home, so I left it in the fridge. Hope your first day at the Fifth went well.

Love,
Cliff

THE MESSAGE WAS SHORT AND SWEET, BUT I BLINKED AS I read the valediction one more time. *Love, Cliff.* We'd been living together for over two months, and yet I couldn't recall ever having told Cliff I loved him. Surely I must've said it in passing? It seemed like the sort of thing I'd randomly utter as he headed off to work or while lying in his arms, playing with his chest hair after sex, but I couldn't remember having uttered the words, nor could I remember him saying them to me before. Yet here they were, staring me in the face from a note on the counter about chicken lo mein. Had he done it on purpose? Was it a message, or had he scrawled it on his way to bed, not even thinking it over?

I set the note down, thinking I might need another drink to help me understand the implications of it, but as my stomach growled in frustration, I realized I might need the stir fry instead. For as many beers as I'd tipped back at the Jjade Palace, I'd only eaten a few potato skins and soft pretzels, which constituted more of a snack than a true meal.

I pulled open our fridge and searched inside for the leftovers, which wasn't a tall order given the appliance's perpetual state of emptiness. With the waxed paperboard box in hand, I pulled a fork from a drawer and tested the contents. The noodles and chicken had cooled, but they weren't stone cold either, which was the only bar they had to clear for me in my inebriated state.

I cast a glance at Cliff's note as I stuck a forkful of sauce-slathered noodles into my maw. Clearly, Cliff's amorous intent would have to be carefully considered, but I was in no condition to do it now. More importantly, I didn't want to, so I folded the piece of paper in half and tossed it to the side before retiring to the sofa chair in the living room.

My mind remained pleasantly empty as I shoveled cubed chicken and oily noodles down my gullet, but I could only sit for so long in the quiet before my mind wandered off in search of more intriguing surroundings. Luckily for me, those environs weren't hypothetical fantasies of Cliff's and my future but rather the Vernon and Daly aviary.

Not that I was a seasoned expert in the detective game, but it seemed to me as if Dean, Moss, Justice and I had spent far too long trying to identify the remains rather than answering the far more pressing question of why anyone would've dumped remains there in the first place. Don't get me wrong. I understood the value in identifying the bones. Without knowledge of who'd been murdered, we couldn't speculate as to a motive for murder, but gosh darn it if the motive for leaving the remains in the aviary wasn't the real head scratcher.

The fact that the ground underneath the ash and bones had been scorched suggested someone had placed the remains there on purpose, intentionally setting fire to the ground cover to make the scene look realistic. I could only assume the intent was to frame someone for murder, but who? Krzysztof Radoslaw, the zookeeper with the sallow skin and the bags under his eyes, or one of the other attendants? Why would anyone come after them? As carnies, they wouldn't have financial assets to speak of, so maybe the frame was personal. If the bones belonged to Stella Vernon as we suspected, perhaps the motive for her murder was related to something salacious. According to JT, she largely led her own life. She was often out and about. If her drug use was any indication, she was depressed, and Vernon's statements made it seem as if she was disaffected with her life. It wouldn't be crazy to think she was having an affair. Maybe her husband even knew about it, but he wouldn't murder her over it, would he? If she'd been the one committing infidelities, he could divorce her without having to worry about giving her a portion of his assets, and that's assuming someone like JT Vernon would divorce her at all. Given his political campaign, he might choose to keep such behavior close to his vest, at least until after the election. So who then might have a motive to off Stella? Someone at the circus who loved her from afar?

Then again, maybe the remains weren't left in the aviary on purpose. After all, if the murderer intended to frame someone, they'd done a terrible job at it. There was no murder weapon at the scene, no witnesses, no body, and no physical evidence. If not for the diamond recovered from the ash, we wouldn't have anything tying the bones to Stella Vernon, though I'm sure we would've made the connection eventually after a missing persons report was filed. Maybe the remains were left there on accident. As Cortez mentioned, it was possible that recently cremated remains could've scorched the earth under them, but that presented an even more implausible situation than a poor frame—that someone had been carrying Stella Vernon's hot remains in a thermos or cooler, been spooked, dropped them, and abandoned them.

It all came back to the same thorny question: why were the remains in the aviary?

I dug around in the bottom of my paperboard container, searching for the last of the noodles. Maybe the drug angle Dean uncovered was more important than he'd realized.

Perhaps it wasn't Stella's dealer who murdered her but a fellow user. After all, someone would have to be high out of their mind to carry their friend's cremated remains around, stumble into an aviary, and accidentally lose them. But what explanation made more sense?

I hopped out of my seat and headed back to the kitchen, licking the sauce from my fork as I considered my hypothesis. I didn't know much about benzedrine, but from what Dean told me, it was a dangerous drug. I didn't know if it could cause paranoia or psychosis that could turn an otherwise normal individual into a crazed killer, but we didn't know for sure that Stella Vernon or her friends were only using benzedrine. If they were hooked on one kind of pill, that made them more likely to be abusing other drugs as well, or so my high school health teacher would have me believe.

Of course, if the case turned as much into a narcotics investigation as a homicide one, how would that affect Dean? He'd taken it hard learning that Stella was an addict, and though he'd composed himself in short order, I had to assume being confronted with the same drugs that killed his fiancée time and time again wouldn't be easy for him.

I shook my head as I tossed the paperboard container into the trash and the fork into the sink. Even thinking about what happened to his fiancée made my heart ache for him. While I couldn't relate exactly to what he'd gone through, I had an inkling. My father was still alive, but alcoholism had irrevocably changed him, taking from me the man I'd loved and killing him as effectively as an overdose might've.

Still, seeing Dean in that moment of weakness, seeing him stripped down to his raw emotional core and laid bare, he'd seemed so much more human. It wasn't that I didn't like his cool, analytical side. His intellect and drive, while intimidating from a professional standpoint, were eminently attractive, but the humanity he'd shown me in the car was even more so.

Actually, if I was being honest with myself, there were a *number* of things about Dean I found attractive.

I chewed on that fact as well as my lip, glancing at Cliff's folded note. I shook my head and sighed, wondering what I was doing as I headed toward our bedroom. I opened the door slowly, slipping inside without a sound. Once there, I worked quickly, stripping off my uniform, brushing my teeth, and emptying my bladder in the attached bath, all before sliding into bed next to Cliff. He shifted and groaned, turning onto his side and preemptively putting a stop to any cuddling that might've happened.

I settled my head into my pillow, my gaze on Cliff's broad back. "Sorry," I whispered as I closed my eyes. "I'll be home earlier tomorrow. Promise."

But even though he was asleep, I didn't say *I love you*.

CHAPTER SEVENTEEN

Only Justice was in his chair when I arrived at my desk the following morning. He tipped his head at me as I entered our cluster. "Morning, Phair."

I gave the ogre a small wave as I passed him. "Morning, Justice."

I must not have responded with enough verve, as a knowing smile spread across his lips. "Feeling alright this morning, Officer?"

I sat down gingerly, setting my mug of coffee beside me. I spoke with more conviction than I felt. "I don't know what you're talking about, Detective."

Justice snorted. "Sure you don't. But I appreciate your willingness to tough it out. That's one thing you'll learn about us. Do whatever you please in your own time. So long as it doesn't affect performance, none of us will give a darn about it."

I took a long draught from my mug, filling my nostrils with the brew's vaguely earthy aroma. Truth be told, I wasn't in bad shape. I'd woken up with a headache and a dry mouth, but of nausea I had none, nor had I barfed up my noodles. I would've appreciated a few more hours of sleep, but when wasn't that the case? "I'll keep that in mind."

Justice turned to the materials on his desk, but I wasn't quite ready to get back to work. Wasn't that one of the perks of being a detective, after all? Getting to waste the first half hour of the day over a mug of joe?

"I had fun last night, for what it's worth," I said. "It was nice getting to know another side of you."

Justice turned back around, his chair complaining. "Me, too. But that was last night, and now we're on the clock. The socializing is best kept for after hours."

So much for my delusions of a slow morning. "Got it. So where's everyone else?"

Justice lifted one of his thick eyebrows. "You're telling me your early arrival is an accident and not a plan to show how much of an eager beaver you are?"

I took another sip of coffee to hide my reaction. "Um... no. Clearly I'm trying to prove how dedicated I am."

Justice snorted and gave me a toothless smile. "Fact of the matter is, I'm not sure where the others are. Moss doesn't always get the worm, if you catch my drift, but Dean practically lives here. I'm surprised I beat him, much less you. Although... Speak of the devil."

Justice tipped his head in the direction of the aisle. A moment later, Dean rounded the corner, once again dressed in a crisp white shirt and grey slacks, but this time wearing a sports coat that was not quite maroon and yet too muddy to be pink. He held a folder in his hands, giving us a nod as he headed to his desk. "Morning, Justice. Phair."

"Morning, Dean," said Justice. "I was just telling Phair how out of the ordinary it is for you not to be the first one in the office."

"Could be that there's a reason for that, hmm?" Dean fanned himself with the folder as he picked up his phone's receiver and held it to his ear. "Operator? Any messages?"

Justice rolled his eyes. "Fair enough. Let's see it."

Dean handed the folder over, which Justice opened as Dean responded on the phone. "Alright. Thank you."

Justice pulled a page of translucent film from the folder and held it to the light. I wasn't a radiographer, but even I could tell it was an image of teeth.

"Stella Vernon's dental x-rays?" asked Justice.

Dean nodded as he returned his phone to the base. "I stopped by her dentist's on my way in. I don't suppose either of you want to accompany me downstairs to see what the coroner has to say about these?"

He didn't have to ask twice. Justice and I both popped up, me a tad slower than he thanks to my hangover, and we all headed to the stairwell.

I'd been in the Fifth's basement once, a couple days ago when Dean took me to the records room to have me judge his career on its merits, but I'd never been to the morgue. In fact, I'd never been to *any* morgue, not counting the crematoriums I'd visited the day before. With that in mind, I couldn't comment on whether the Fifth's was representative of them all, but compared to Fogel and Sons, the station's mortuary was down-right clinical. The tile floors had been recently mopped and treated with a lemon-scented cleaner, the stainless steel cadaver vaults along the far wall gleamed, and the half dozen examination tables that were evenly spaced throughout the rectangular room had been cleared and dusted, all except for two. One had a white sheet draped over it and the suggestive shape of a body protruding from beneath, and atop the other, a seemingly complete skeleton had been arranged in painstaking detail.

In the corner, sandwiched between a pair of filing cabinets and a glass-doored chemical cabinet, was a stainless steel desk. A young elf in a white lab coat sat there, clacking away at a typewriter as he stared at the clipboard next to him, the pages bent over and folded underneath the clip at the top.

Dean called out as we approached. "Morning, Emmett."

The elf startled and popped up, turning to meet us. "Ah. Detective Dean. Good morning. To you too, Detective Justice. And, ah..." The elf's brow furrowed over his square-rimmed glasses as he set eyes on me, as if he was having a hard time remembering who I was.

Dean got the gist of the expression, too. "This is Officer Penelope Phair, Emmett. She joined our team yesterday. Phair? Emmett Jowynn, our coroner."

Jowynn stuck up a finger. "Well, ah, one of them. There's also Emily Carruthers and Milton Heel. We split the schedule, though it's mostly Emily and I. Milton's more of a night owl, though he takes emergency shifts, too. Anyway. Pleasure to meet you, Officer."

The coroner had a shock of unruly brown hair atop his head, which seemed to go with his nervous nature and glasses, but he was kind of cute despite his stammering. "Nice to meet you, Emmett." I figured if Dean called him by his first name, I should too, though why police naming conventions didn't extend to the folks poking and prodding the dead bodies, I couldn't say.

Dean pointed toward the exam table with the bones atop it.

"Are those the remains from the circus?"

Emmett bobbed his head. "Indeed, Detective. I have my notes about them right here." He picked up his clipboard. "It's quite a complete skeleton. Do you need to take another look at it?"

"The opposite. I need *you* to." Dean held the folder out.

Emmett placed it over his clipboard and opened it. His eyes widened as he spotted the film prints. "Ah. X-rays. Excellent."

Dean nodded. "How long do you think it'll take to see if those are a match?"

Emmett cocked his head. "That depends. If I find a definitive matching feature, maybe only a few minutes. It might be a few hours if I have to do a deeper dive. Do you need results now?"

"I'd rather not waste the morning if I don't have to."

"Of course," said Emmett. "Detective Justice? Could you grab the skull and the mandible, and all of you join me at the light box?"

Jowynn waved for us to follow him as he headed to where the aforementioned light box hung over another exam table. He pulled the x-rays from the folder and clipped them into place before clicking the switch on the side of the box. Justice arrived as the thing burst to life, the skull and mandible looking small in his massive mitts.

"Thank you." Jowynn plucked rubber gloves from a drawer. "You can set them on the tabletop."

Justice did so while Jowynn pulled the gloves onto his hands. Jowynn flicked the switch on a table lamp, one with a magnifying glass attached to it. He pulled on the swivel arm to bring the thing to a comfortable height and picked up the mandible. He peered at it through the lens, then leaned closer to the light box. After a couple rounds of that, I couldn't tell if he was being meticulous or it his eyesight was that bad.

"I meant to ask you," said Dean. "Did you find anything of note while cataloging the remains? Anything that contradicted Cortez's findings?"

Emmett blinked and looked away from the mandible, his brow scrunched. "I'm sorry, what?"

To his credit, Dean didn't show the slightest hint of annoyance. "I asked if you found anything else of note during your investigation, but if I'm distracting you, I can stay quiet until you finish."

"No, it's not a problem." Jowynn tilted the mandible back and forth under the light. "Overall, I agree with Detective Cortez. Victim was an adult female, about five foot four. I would guess in early adulthood to middle age, as I didn't observe any signs of bone density loss women see post menopause, but it's hard to tell because of the cremation. And the body was certainly cremated. I would assume at high heat for a short period of time, though I couldn't give you specifics."

"Why high heat?" I asked. "Does that affect the process?"

Emmett blinked at me, a look of mild surprise on his face. I wasn't sure if it was because I was asking questions at all or because he'd forgotten I was there.

He recovered quickly and gave me a shy smile, which made me think it was more the latter. "Uh... it does, actually. The cremation process calcifies bones, which leads to embrittlement. The longer you expose bones to high heat, the more calcification occurs. Heck, if you heat a corpse long enough, the bones will decompose into tiny fragments on their own, but most cremato-riums don't do that. Takes too long, and it's more efficient to turn the last bits of bone to powder by hand or with a mill. The remains recovered from the aviary aren't that brittle, however. They're quite clean though, which to me suggests high heat and a short exposure time. Of course, what really clinched it was the bit of molten steel in the ashes."

"Molten steel?" said Dean.

Jowynn lifted an eyebrow as he set the mandible down and picked up the skull. "Did Cortez not tell you? As we were trans-ferring the ashes into a container, we found it at the bottom of the pile, half melted into the dirt. A globule of steel. I'd say it prob-ably was from a belt buckle, button, or key. Easy to miss, not like that diamond and the lump of gold, but steel also melts at a higher temperature than gold. Quite a bit higher, in fact, depending on the composition. That's what confirms to me the heat."

"Hold on," I said. "The steel was *melted into the earth*? That would suggest the body was cremated on site, doesn't it?"

"It might." Dean lifted an inquisitive eyebrow and turned it toward Emmett.

The young coroner hemmed and hawed. "Well, ah, perhaps that was a poor choice of words. We found it stuck in the dirt, not necessarily *melted* into the dirt. It could've gotten stepped on. I wouldn't necessarily draw any conclusions from it, although you're free to examine the globule if you want. It's on the exam table with the rest of the remains."

Justice frowned. "Are cremation furnaces powerful enough to melt steel?"

Dean gave his head a slight shake. "I couldn't tell you. We'll have to research it."

Everyone grew quiet, which seemed to bother Jowynn more than anyone else. He chuckled nervously. "Sorry. Didn't meant to throw a wrench into your investigation. But I do have good news."

Dean waved his hand. "Go on."

"It's the remains. See this stretch of bone that's darker in color?" Emmett held the skull under the magnifying lamp, pointing to a thin striation I could barely see. "That's a sign of stress from an old injury. Not necessarily a fracture, but perhaps a bruise from a fall. You can see the same discoloration in the x-ray image here." Jowynn pointed it out.

I think Dean had as hard a time making it out as I did. He squinted. "You're sure that's the same contusion?"

Emmett nodded. "Absolutely. Not to mention there's a slight chip on the right maxillary central incisor that's present in the specimen as well as the x-rays." He held the skull forward. "You have yourselves an identification, Detectives."

Dean let out a deep breath. "Stella Vernon it is, then. Given what we know about her sudden disappearance, that officially makes this a murder investigation."

I didn't want to make my ignorance known, but I also wanted to know what that meant. "How does that impact our investigation?"

"In a lot of ways," said Dean. "First and foremost, it provides us more judicial muscle. We can more easily procure warrants to search her home and pull the financial records for her assets. It lets us clear a lot of procedural hurdles. And it means we have to deliver the bad news to Mr. Vernon."

Justice grunted. "You want me to come with you?"

"I'll probably take Moss, if she gets in soon," said Dean. "No offense, but she's better at delivering that news than you are. You and Phair can get started on the finances."

Justice snorted. "Pulling records. My favorite."

Jowynn piped up, the skull still in his hands. "If you don't mind, I have one more thing for you before you go."

"Shoot," said Dean.

Emmett waved us toward the exam table with the remains. "You know those scraps from the crematorium you dropped off?"

"From Fogel and Sons," said Justice. "Were you able to match them to the bones?"

"Unfortunately, no. As I mentioned before, the remains from the circus—Mrs. Vernon's remains, I suppose—are in incredible shape given the heat they must've been exposed to. I didn't find any chips or cracks in them, nor was I able to match any of the bone fragments from the crematorium to them. But I did find this."

Jowynn replaced the skull on the table and reached into a metal tin. From it, he pinched something between his fingers, placing it on his open palm. I wasn't sure what it was, but it appeared to be a black pebble, about the size of a pea.

"Is that obsidian?" asked Dean.

"It certainly looks like it," said Jowynn. "To be honest, I'm not sure. I want to do more research before I give you any information that might lead you down the wrong path, but for the record, that's not the only chip I found. I was able to separate six smaller ones from the ash."

"Did you find those in the ashes at the circus, too, or only from the ones at Fogel and Sons?" I asked.

Emmett waggled his finger at me, as if I'd hammered the

nail on the head. "Just the latter. It's probably nothing, but I figured I'd let you know all the same."

"Thanks, Emmett. We appreciate your efforts." Dean nodded to me and Justice. "Guys? Time to get to work. We have a murder to solve."

CHAPTER EIGHTEEN

Moss was at her desk when we returned to the third floor, so Dean plucked her and headed to Vernon's. I didn't envy her, to be honest. I hadn't enjoyed Vernon's company the first time, and I'd never been good at delivering bad news. Given that Moss had assured me she'd be on the lookout for any skeevy behavior on Vernon's part, I didn't have any reason to return to the man's mansion.

Of course, after thirty minutes of serving as Justice's mule, I wished I'd fought harder for Moss's spot after all. Not that Justice abused me—he worked as hard as I did—but there was a lot to do. While he called the Captain to arrange for warrants, he tasked me with obtaining the necessary forms. I figured picking them up from the office would be the easy part, but given my intricate knowledge of the case, I made quick work of the papers—or at least as quick as my cramping hand would allow. When I was about three quarters done, Justice ripped them away from me, telling me he'd fill in the remainder on his way to the judge. As he left, he yelled at me to call the banks to find out which one served the Vernons.

With the help of the station's operator, I started calling the likely suspects. While all of them initially refused to let me know if the Vernons were even clients, they became more cooperative once I told them we had a warrant for the information. I felt a little odd saying as much given I didn't have the official piece of paper in my hands, but Justice had assured me it was a formality. I figured it would be easier for me to call Vernon's home and bother Mossbottom for the information, but even with a warrant in hand, we couldn't compel him or his master to tell us. Besides, there were only so many banks in the city a man such as Vernon would bother soliciting.

I located the bank in question before Justice returned, earning myself a coffee break, but as soon as the big ogre arrived and I filled him in, we headed to the parking garage, hopped in his Phantom, and drove off in search of the branch of New Welwic Bancorp closest to the Vernon's estate.

It wasn't too far, closer to the circus than to Brentford, in a part of the city that wasn't technically downtown but was close enough not to make any difference. As we stepped through the bank's heavy bronze doors into the lobby within, one with marble floors and a high, arched ceiling whose detailed mural would've been more at home in a church than a financial establishment, Justice took a quick look around to get his bearings before heading to the nearest teller.

The young woman behind the counter smiled as we approached. "Good morning. How can I help you?"

Justice pulled his badge from his pocket. "I'm Detective Justice with the NWPD. Officer Phair here spoke with a Mr. White on the phone about some account records."

The woman nodded. "I see. Mr. White's desk is on your right. I'll see if I can locate him for you."

Justice thanked her, and she headed into the back. Meanwhile, Justice and I retreated to the desk the teller had pointed us to, upon which White's name shone from a gold plaque. Justice didn't sit, so I didn't either. I simply stood there, biding my time, wondering if Justice was going to open his mouth to do anything other than breathe. He hadn't said much on our ride over, and I'd started to think I'd imagined the fun-loving jokester I'd gotten to know over drinks the night before. Then again, Moss had insinuated on more than one occasion that Justice was the consummate professional. Perhaps I should've taken her at her word.

Still, I figured work-related small talk wasn't off limits, even if everything else was. "Does Dean always assign you all the grunt work?"

Justice lifted a thick eyebrow. "What do you mean?"

I shrugged. "You made an off-hand comment while we were in the morgue. Made me think you got stuck pulling records more often than not."

"I was giving Dean a hard time," said Justice. "He doesn't play favorites. We're all as likely to end up filling out paperwork as we are to be kicking down doors. Just depends who's available and what needs to be done."

"Do you think that's going to change now that I'm around?"

Justice snorted. "If Dean needed a lackey, he could've plucked one from our own precinct. Instead, he went out of his way to bring you aboard. What does that tell you?"

It told me that he saw something in me, that my ability to solve the New Age Alchemical case impressed him and suggested to him that I had real talent, but I still couldn't convince myself of it, not when I'd spent most of my morning on the phone, pretending as if I were a real detective and hoping no one would call me on my bluster.

I'm not sure Justice wanted me to share my insecurities, but fate dictated I shouldn't have to. A lilting voice carried across the lobby. "Ogden? What are you doing here?"

Justice and I both turned to find a dapper man in a purple silk shirt and tight trousers approaching. He was shorter than Justice and me, an inch over five and a half feet at most, though his expertly coifed pompadour granted him another couple inches. A pair of mirrored glasses hid his eyes, but the rest of his face was blemish free, as if he regularly treated it with rich lotions and exfoliating creams. His faint aroma of bergamot orange further suggested he did.

Justice's brow creased. "Marion?"

The man pulled his glasses from his face and tucked them daintily into his front shirt pocket. "Well, isn't this a delight?"

He opened his arms as he stepped forward, as if he was going to hug Justice, but he stopped short as Justice stuck out a hand. He eyed it with a hint of disdain before giving it a single shake. "Hmm. Yes. Well, how are you? I feel as if I haven't seen you in ages."

"I'm fine," said Justice, "but I can't talk. We're on duty."

Marion held his hands up apologetically, his mouth making a delicate little circle. "*Oh.* My apologies. I won't keep you. Just saw you and wanted to say hi. But you really must introduce me to your ravishing little friend here."

"Ravishing?" I said. "*Little?*"

"Yes, dear," said Marion, reaching out and touching me lightly on the arm with delicate fingers. "You look fantastic. Strong. Powerful. The prototypical image of a modern woman in uniform. I love it."

"Uhh... thank you?"

Justice's jaw tightened, and his nostrils flared. "Marion, this is Officer Phair. She recently joined our team. Marion is an acquaintance of mine, Phair."

"Indeed. I'm an *acquaintance*." Marion gave Justice a squinty eye, puckered lip sort of look while holding a hand against his chest. "We live in the same neighborhood. Have run into each other a few times, though not recently enough for my liking. Anywho, I can see I'm interrupting, so I'll leave you to it. Keep the city safe and whatnot. Toodles!"

Marion gave Justice a bit of a wave with his fingertips as he turned and headed toward one of the open tellers.

It took me a moment to gather myself. "He seems... friendly."

Justice turned his back on the lobby, choosing to stare at the wall over White's desk. "He's a neighbor, as he said. He's nice enough."

Justice's ramrod straight posture, the tightness in his jaw, and eyes that were currently tunneling through the wall all suggested he had nothing more to say on the subject, and given my general instincts for self-preservation, I wasn't about to push him. Then again, I wasn't sure I needed to. Marion's behavior had spoken for itself. *Loudly*.

As I stood there contemplating the banter between Justice and Moss last night at the Jjade Palace, considering it in a whole new light, a balding man in a gray suit approached from the side of the room, a folder in hand.

"I'm terribly sorry for the wait, Detective. Jeremiah White, at your service. Mr. and Mrs. Vernon have several accounts with us, and I wanted to make sure I pulled the statements from all of them."

Justice nodded, though his usually smooth, deep voice was strained. "I appreciate the thoroughness." He held out a hand.

The banker hesitated. "If I could see the warrant?"

Ogden pulled it from his jacket. White gave it a once over before handing it and the folder over. "Thank you so much. Is that all I can do for you?"

"For now. Phair?" Justice nodded to me and stormed toward the exit. He burst out the front doors, barreled down the street, and lurched into his Phantom, tossing the folder onto the dash as he got behind the wheel.

I had to hustle to keep up. I'd barely closed the door when he turned the key in the ignition, gunned the engine, and pulled the car onto the main thoroughfare. His lead foot pushed me into my seat as I buckled in, and in a short few seconds we'd reached cruising speed.

Justice's eyes were riveted to the road. I got the impression that if I said the wrong thing—or rather, mentioned the wrong person—mine might be the next homicide the team wound up investigating.

I couldn't go without speaking to Justice for the rest of my career, but I'd need to tread carefully until he determined I wasn't a threat. "Mind if I take a look at the statements?"

His voice came out in a growl. "Knock yourself out."

I brought the folder into my lap and opened it. After getting over the initial shock of how much money Vernon had, I moved on to the deposits and withdrawals. Even though most of the transactions were abbreviated, I got the general gist of things. Vernon was making regular payments to cleaning staff, gardeners, Mossbottom, utilities, department stores, various organizations that seemed to be affiliated with his campaign, plus assorted other small transactions. Incoming money was mostly from the circus, although there seemed to be a handful of investment services that made regular deposits into his accounts.

What struck me as odd, however, were the cash withdrawals.

Justice hadn't bitten my head off the first time I'd spoken, so I gave it another go. "Question. Does a fifty thousand crown withdrawal seem like a large sum to you?"

Justice pulled his eyes off the road long enough to glance at me. "Vernon did that?"

"He did it twice. Within the past month. Same amount each time."

Justice pursed his lips before picking up the two-way radio in the center console. "Dispatch, this is Detective Justice. I need to get ahold of Alton Dean."

CHAPTER NINETEEN

"To be clear then, Mr. Vernon," said Dean. "You're claiming these withdrawals were to pay down debts on behalf of the circus?"

Dean, Justice, Moss and I were in JT Vernon's office on the top floor of his mansion. The room was about three times the size of any study I'd been in, but it needed to be to accommodate Vernon's bizarre curios and collectibles. There was a tribal headdress full of vibrant white feathers, opals, and bone fragments on display, supposedly from the Orwannee tribe of mountain elves in the far northern lands. A glass display case contained a size thirty-seven shoe that was roughly the size of my torso. The inscription engraved at the base claimed it belonged to Guzz Crumley, the largest giant who ever lived. Next to it stood another case, but rather than containing Crumley's necktie or the shoe of the world's tiniest pixie, it contained a taxidermied black rooster, albeit one of considerable size and with a plumage that glimmered green and gold in the right light.

The study contained all the room's traditional trappings as well, or at least those that fit the tastes of an eccentric circus owner: built-in shelves packed with books and adorned with the occasional shadow box, antique stained-glass lamps, sofa chairs upholstered in gold brocade, and at the far end, a rosewood desk whose size suggested it had been built on site. I didn't see how anyone could've gotten it through the doors, otherwise.

Vernon sat behind the desk, wearing a striped black vest over a puffy white shirt with ruffled cuffs that I suspected he'd bought off a pirate. "I know it may be hard to believe in this era of limited partnerships and charters and corporations, but my circus is structured as a proprietorship, Detective. Has been ever since I got full ownership of it from Daly. Is it risky? Certainly. But it gives me sole control. No investors. No stocks, no dividends. Just me and the company, and as I'm sure you know, it's perfectly legal for me as the proprietor to pay business expenses from my personal accounts. These withdrawals you're talking about were used to pay creditors."

Dean stood behind one of the golden chairs while Moss sat in the one to his right. Shortly after Justice called dispatch, we got word that Dean and Moss had left Vernon's but were turning around to meet us there. We met the pair on the street corner outside his estate as we shared the information we'd found. Dean hadn't been pleased to learn about the sums being withdrawn from Vernon's account, but his displeasure was nothing compared to the look of disgust Mossbottom gave us when he opened the door to find the four of us waiting under the portico. The gnome currently stood by the door to the hall, outwardly patient but looking as if he'd eaten nothing but lemons all day.

"You took out two identical fifty thousand crown lump sums three weeks apart to pay creditors?" said Dean. "In cash?"

Vernon shrugged. "For as large as my business is, not all my suppliers and subcontractors can boast the same. Some people I do business with don't even have bank accounts. Cash is king, as they say."

"What businesses did you pay using this cash?" asked Dean.

"Well, there are a number of them," said Vernon. "As I said, they're smaller creditors. It's hard to remember them all."

"Name one," said Dean.

Vernon hesitated, but only for a moment. "Ah... Northridge Printing. They produce some of the merchandise I sell at the circus."

Moss produced a notepad from her leather jacket. "Do you have an address or a phone number?"

JT's hesitation was more pronounced this time. "I'll have to look it up. Or perhaps Mossbottom can. Mossbottom, could you get that information for the detectives while we wait?"

Dean cast a withering glance at the butler. "And I don't suppose while Mossbottom is off acquiring that address that he might pause to phone Northridge and remind them that you stopped by to pay them in cash, something they would surely remember on their own if they want to retain your patronage?"

Mossbottom's face turned even more prune-like, and Vernon scoffed. "Listen, Detective, if you're insinuating I was—"

"You listen, Mr. Vernon," said Dean, his voice as sharp as a knife. "I understand you've had a difficult couple days, and I'm terribly sorry we had to deliver the news of your wife's passing this morning. It's a hard thing to accept under the best circumstances, but in case you hadn't realized it, her death puts your actions under a microscope." Dean reached into his jacket and produced the warrants Justice had given him. "While you've welcomed us into your home twice this morning, these documents make it so your consent isn't required. We have a right to search your property for any clues that might provide insight into her death. We already know about her drug use, and all we've done is skim the surface. What else do you suppose we'll find once we start digging? And keep in mind that if it turns out you're misleading us about these payments, we can charge you with making false statements and obstruction, among other things. So I'll ask again. What were the fifty thousand crowns for?"

Vernon's eyes met Dean's. There was a dullness to them that hadn't been there a moment before. The man sighed a heavy sigh and waved at his butler. "Mossbottom? If you could leave us, please?"

The butler stuck his lip out in displeasure, but he nonetheless nodded and left, closing the door behind him.

Vernon reached into one of his desk drawers and pulled out a glass and a bottle of Montvue special reserve whiskey. He popped the stopper and paused with the bottle's mouth above his glass. "Can I offer any of you a drink?"

"Answer the question, Mr. Vernon," said Dean.

"I'll take that as a no." Vernon poured himself a couple fingers of the amber liquid, put the stopper back, and set it down. He took a draught from his glass and let out another sigh. "I didn't use those withdrawals to pay creditors."

Justice, who stood by the larger than life chicken with his arms crossed, snorted. "You don't say."

Dean gave the man a moment, but not more than that. "What was the money for?"

Vernon took another sip from his glass before setting it down with a clatter. "This isn't easy for me to discuss, Detective, and even more difficult now knowing..." He paused to take a slow breath, and a glimmer shone in his eyes. "Knowing what happened to Stella. But know that my instinct to hide this information wasn't to deceive you but to protect myself. I'm being blackmailed."

"Over what?" asked Moss.

Vernon drew his finger along the rim of his glass. "This can't leave the room. My political career could be over before it starts."

"Mr. Vernon, all of us here are professionals," said Dean. "If we leak anything, not only does that put our investigation at risk, but we put our careers on the line. We may have to share knowledge with other officers and detectives in the course of our investigation, but I assure you, none of us will treat your confidential information as anything but."

Vernon eyed the glass, licking his lips with the tip of his tongue. Without saying a word, he stood and crossed to a portrait of himself behind his desk. He pulled on the edge, and it swing out on hinges. Behind it, a black safe with a steel combination dial glimmered in the light streaming through the windows. Vernon gave the dial a few quick turns, cranked on the handle, and opened it. From it, he pulled a crinkled manilla envelope, which he tossed on the desk. He nodded to it, but he didn't say anything more.

Dean motioned for me and Justice to come as he sat in the golden chair next to Moss. He unfolded the brads keeping the envelope shut and tipped it up. Several eight by ten glossy photographs slid onto the desk. I leaned over Dean's shoulder to get a better look, but I didn't have to look too hard to figure out what they were. In the top photograph, a woman with shoulder length blonde hair lay on a bed. She wore stockings, suspenders, a garter belt, and not a scrap else. She thrust her chest out, displaying her small, pert breasts to the best of her ability while chewing her lip seductively as she stared at the camera.

I stated the obvious. "These are pictures of your wife, Stella."

Vernon stood against the wall, his arms crossed over his chest. He nodded.

Dean spread the images across the desk. There were five in total, but they only became more pornographic after the first. Stella Vernon was the only one in them, but the remainder showed her with her legs spread or playing with her privates in sexually suggestive ways.

Dean picked up the envelope and flipped it over. "Were these mailed to you?"

"Yes," said Vernon. "Not in that envelope. It was inside another."

"Do you still have that one?" asked Dean.

Vernon shook his head. "I threw it away without thinking. Is it important?"

"Probably not, but it would've given us one more piece of evidence to consider." Dean collected the photos and slid them back into the envelope. "Walk us through the events. When you got the parcel, what instructions it came with, how you followed them."

Vernon turned back to the safe. This time he emerged with a folded piece of paper, which he handed over. "The package came about a month ago. It included that note, which demanded fifty thousand crowns in payment otherwise the photos would be leaked to the press. As you can see, a drop location was given. I followed the instructions, but clearly it wasn't enough. A little over a week ago, another letter arrived asking for another fifty thousand crowns. I had no choice. I paid that, too."

"But you didn't contact the police?" asked Moss.

Vernon sighed again. He'd yet to make eye contact since handing over the photos. "As I said, I couldn't risk them getting out. Not with the election coming up."

"Are the photos recent?" I asked.

That finally brought Vernon's head up. "I assume so, but I don't know for sure. Why do you ask?"

Moss and Justice looked at me inquisitively, causing me to second guess whether I should've opened my mouth, but Dean had told me to trust my instincts. "If they were old photos, something Stella had taken part in before you married, for example, that might explain why she participated in the shoot, even if it might not free you from scrutiny in the public eye." Although I'd argue that anything Stella did shouldn't reflect negatively upon Vernon, or vice versa. "But if the photos are recent, she would've had to have been complicit in the blackmail against you, wouldn't she? Why take the photos otherwise?"

Vernon stretched his eyebrows. "Ah. Well, as to that... she claimed that she didn't."

"Didn't what?" asked Dean.

"Take the photos," said Vernon. "When I confronted her about it, she was adamant she'd never do such a thing. That she'd never taken her clothes off and allowed herself to be photographed in such a manner. At first I assumed she was lying, and I won't mince words. I got angry, and I nearly struck her. But after demanding that she leave my presence, I thought things over. I realized she probably didn't remember. It's the drugs she took, which you already seem to know about."

Dean stiffened at the mention of the narcotics, but he didn't lose it like he had the day before. "Benzedrine doesn't cause walking blackouts, Mr. Vernon."

The showman shrugged. "Perhaps not, but I don't know what other recreational drugs Stella might've been taking. In retrospect, perhaps there's a lot I didn't know about her..." His eyes got misty, and they drifted toward the window.

Moss cleared her throat. "Do you think one of your wife's dealers might've been behind this?"

Vernon turned his attention toward us again. Gone was the wistful longing, and in its place was an ill-contained rage. "No. As far as I'm concerned, there's only one man who could be behind these, though I doubt you'll ever prove it."

"Who might that be?" asked Dean.

The midmorning sun glinted off Vernon's eyes. "My political rival, of course. The man who's held New Welwic's congressional seat for two decades. The man I'm beating in the polls. *Maximillian Bumblefoot.*"

CHAPTER TWENTY

Dean pulled his Viper into a free street spot on the corner of Grandview and 1st, one that was listed as fifteen minute parking, but I suppose the designation didn't apply to police officers. The building in front of which he'd parked was four stories tall, made of heavy gray stone blocks on the first floor and a tan-colored stone on the floors above. There were thick columns at the front holding up a triangular pediment at the top, one with gods and goddesses carved into the stone. The building was designed to look as if it were thousands of years old, but despite New Welwic's pedigree, it couldn't have been more than a tenth of that. The architects of yore didn't know how to make any building that tall with windows.

A sign over the front doors listed the building as the City of New Welwic Executive Offices. I got out of the car and closed the door behind me, staring at the building from the sidewalk. "For what it's worth, I'm not buying that this Bumblefoot guy is the blackmailer."

Dean crossed from the driver's side and joined me on the

sidewalk. Moss and Justice had stayed at Vernon's to help with the CSU sweep of Stella's room, as well as to make sure they'd gathered all the evidence they could on the blackmail. I'd figured Moss would stick by Dean's side after the morning, but he'd insisted I come instead.

Dean stuck his hands in his pockets. "And what leads you to that conclusion?"

"Bumblefoot is one of New Welwic's representatives, right?" I said. "Let's take Vernon's accusation at face value and assume Bumblefoot somehow coerced his wife into taking pornographic photos while she was high out of her mind. Wouldn't it be in his best interests to release the photos to the press rather than blackmail Vernon with them? I mean, for one thing, there's the legal ramifications of getting busted for black-mail, but more importantly, releasing the photos would probably do precisely what Vernon suggests they would: hurt him with voters, or at least with those who think a woman doesn't have a right to do whatever she wants with her body."

Dean lifted an eyebrow at that last part. "Ignoring the black-mail, you do realize it's illegal to produce pornographic material for sale or distribution, don't you?"

I shrugged. "It's a sexist law, but that's besides the point. You can't honestly think Bumblefoot is behind this?"

"We have no evidence to suggest he is," said Dean. "I suppose it's possible, though. If he's behind the photos, he could be trying to extract money from Vernon before releasing them to the press, but that seems like an incredibly high risk strategy for anyone, much less a public figure like Bumblefoot. And yet... here we are."

Dean gave me a bit of a smile, one I couldn't quite decipher. "Don't look at me. You're the one who chose to come here."

Dean snorted. "I was trying to nudge you into figuring out why we made the trip. Apparently I was too subtle."

"Oh." I chewed on my lip as I looked back at the building. "Well, I suppose it could be in the name of thoroughness. Follow every lead, cross every t, dot every i."

Dean's lower lip jutted out a touch, and he nodded. "Could be."

He didn't seem convinced, so I tried again. "Or could be that the blackmailer is working multiple angles. They might be demanding money from Vernon while simultaneously shopping the photos to his opponent. I mean, it's incredibly scummy, but we're talking about a blackmailer who took pornographic photos of a drugged woman who likely didn't even know what was happening."

Dean's smile reappeared, this time a little wider. "Not bad."

The smile looked good on him. "Thanks. But is that *really* why we're here?"

Dean chortled. "You've got to trust your instincts, Phair. Believe in yourself. In fact..." He pointed at the building. "I want you to take the lead on this round of questions."

I cocked an eyebrow at him. "What? *Me?*"

"No, the magically shrunken version of Detective Justice you stashed in your pocket. Of course you."

I might've been more appreciative of Dean's attempts at humor if I wasn't feeling an oncoming butterfly hurricane in my stomach. "You know what I mean. You want me to take point on interviewing a *legislator* of all people?"

"Why not?" said Dean. "As I said, your deductive instincts are in the right place, you just need experience. Searching crime scenes, questioning witnesses, piecing together evidence. I know you're new, but this is a great learning opportunity. Why waste it?"

I didn't know Dean well enough to know if he had any tells, but it felt to me as if there was something he wasn't saying. "Are you planning on leaving?"

He cocked his head. "Leaving where?"

"Us. It feels like you're grooming me. Like you've got another position lined up and you need a replacement, quick."

Dean snorted and shook his head. "Dang. You *are* good."

"You *are* leaving?"

"No. I'm not going anywhere. I just..." Dean hesitated. "The department isn't a meritocracy. There are always people jostling for position, fighting for jobs. You may not have noticed, but there are people who aren't happy you got placed on our team. A rookie who didn't finish her year on patrol before being reassigned? It's not normal."

"If this is a pep talk, it's not working."

"Motivational speaking isn't my strongest suit," said Dean. "But I want to be frank with you. I think you deserve your spot here. Certainly, you deserve a shot to prove it. Not everyone else believes the same."

I thought back to when I was called away the day before. "You're talking about Captain Ellison. About what he said to me yesterday."

Dean shook his head. "I wasn't there."

"No, but you must've guessed part of the reason he wanted to see me. He's the one who approved my hire. And he didn't do it because he believes in my ability, but because he wanted to use me against you."

"*Use you?*" said Dean.

"He didn't use those exact words," I said. "But he made it

clear that if I wanted to stick around, I needed to be on his side, not your side. You knew, didn't you?"

Dean held up a finger. "I suspected. There's a difference."

I felt as if a weight had been placed across my shoulders. "So what am I supposed to do? Tiptoe the line between doing exactly as the captain says, not making any enemies, and yet progressing as an investigator at an unprecedented pace? As a rookie?"

Dean put a hand on my shoulder. "Don't worry about Ellison. He's tough and a bit of a megalomaniac, but push comes to shove, he's fair. Work hard, learn the job, and he won't be able to get rid of you."

I sighed. So all I had to do was make myself indispensable before the captain realized I wasn't his stool pigeon? Easy as pie.

CHAPTER TWENTY-ONE

I stood in a spacious front office that was as refined as it was bland. It had all the traditional trappings of luxury—a white marble floor with grains of grey that swept through the stone as if from a drunken painter's brush, wainscoting along every wall, a fireplace with logs that had never been lit carefully stacked in the firebox—but it lacked even a hint of anything personal. No photographs graced the desk. No artwork adorned the walls. No curios joined the leather-bound spines of the books stacked on the bookcases. The only effects that even came close to personal were a wilting shrub in the corner and the framed picture of Congressman Bumblefoot that hung above the desk.

The intercom buzzed, and a static-tinged voice punched through. "Send them in, Moira."

The middle-aged woman who sat at the desk gave us a nod. "Go ahead. He's ready for you."

Dean waved toward the door at the far side of the room. As I pushed it open, I found myself in an office that was nearly a clone of the first, except the desk was bigger and there was actually a view, a snippet of the leafy elms that lined 1st. A pear-shaped guy with more hair sprouting from his cheeks than remained on the top of his head sat behind the desk, the smoldering stub of a cigar clenched in his right hand.

He smashed the cigar into an ashtray already overflowing with remains before standing and rounding the desk. "Sorry to keep you waiting, officers. Congressman Maximillian Bumblefoot, at your service." He stuck out his hand.

Bumblefoot's musky scent of sweet tobacco nearly bowled me over, ten times stronger than the worst whiff I'd ever gotten off Dean, but I could forgive his cigar addiction. His handshake was another matter. While some men approached a handshake as a test of their manhood and tried to crush your metacarpals into dust, Bumblefoot took the opposite approach. His hand was limp and clammy as he grasped my own, and I had to force myself not to grimace as he shook it.

"Officer Phair, sir." It felt odd to take the lead on the introductions, but Dean had insisted. "This is Detective Alton Dean. We're with the Fifth Street precinct."

Either Dean didn't mind the cool, invertebrate handshake, or he hid his displeasure masterfully. "Pleasure to meet you, Congressman."

Bumblefoot smiled as he clasped his hands before him, a practiced political grin that wasn't reflected in his eyes. "Can Moira fetch you anything? Water? Coffee?"

I glanced at Dean, but he gave his head a shake. "No thank you, Congressman."

"Well then, please, have a seat." He waved to the chairs in front of his desk as he wove back around to his. "Tell me what brings you to my office. Is it the upcoming appropriations bill? Because I assure you I'm working to ensure city funding gets increased by at least four percent and to have language included in the bill that mandates the police department receives that same minimum. There won't be any bureaucrats rerouting those funds into parks and recreation this year, I assure you."

I shook my head. "We're not here because of any legislation, sir. We're conducting an investigation."

"Into my tireless pursuit of lower taxes for the citizens of New Welwic?" Bumblefoot flashed his unctuous grin again. "You've got me, Officer. Guilty as charged."

As oily as he was, I was surprised the man hadn't slipped and fallen off his chair. "No, sir. We're investigating an incident of blackmail." *A homicide, too,* I thought, but there was no reason to reveal that yet.

The congressman's grin disappeared, and his eyes flashed toward Dean. "You are?"

Dean nodded. "We are."

"But... not me, obviously," said Bumblefoot. "If I was being blackmailed, I think I'd know. Assuming the blackmailer wasn't a bumbling incompetent."

I'd thought interviewing Bumblefoot on my own would be intimidating. The man was a congressman, after all, but his unpleasant nature made it easy for me to go on the offensive. To ask the tough questions without worrying about his reactions.

"The blackmailer isn't coming after you, Congressman," I said. "They've targeted your political opponent. They're smearing JT Vernon."

Bumblefoot snorted, and a look of disdain twisted his face. "*Vernon.* He doesn't need a blackmailer's help. That man smears himself."

I lifted an eyebrow. "Pardon?"

Bumblefoot waved his hand. "Nothing. A poor attempt at

toilet humor. My point is Vernon doesn't need a blackmailer airing his dirty laundry to make him look like a buffoon. He does that on his own. The man's all bluster. He's a charlatan more than a showman, and he's certainly not a politician. He sticks his foot in his mouth as often as he opens it."

It seemed to me someone who was a charlatan and a showman would make the perfect politician, but I kept that to myself. "Nonetheless, someone has been blackmailing him for the past month with embarrassing photographs. Photographs Vernon believes would hurt his campaign and that the blackmailer has threatened to release to the press."

Bumblefoot shrugged. "I'm sure that would be terrible for him."

"Vernon believes you're behind them," I said.

Bumblefoot laughed, but his eyes remained void of emotion. "Are you serious? Is that why you're here? You think *I'm* blackmailing Vernon?"

"Vernon believes it," I clarified. "We're simply here to take your statement."

Bumblefoot's eyes narrowed. "Well then let me state plainly for the record: I'm not blackmailing JT Vernon. I didn't take or obtain salacious photographs of the man, nor do I know about the existence of any. More importantly, I have no need to blackmail him. As I've already told you, the man's an incompetent clown. I'm going to beat him like a drum come election time, same as I have many other challengers over the years."

"That's not what the polls suggest," said Dean.

Bumblefoot turned his ireful gaze onto the detective. "Polls are worth less than the paper they're printed on. What matters are votes, and I guarantee you when the citizens of New Welwic step into their voting booths in two months time, only two things will be on their minds: my name, which carries more weight than a shameless self-promoter's like Vernon, and the long, illustrious record I have of making their lives healthier, safer, and more profitable. My history of helping them. Vernon, on the other hand, can't even help his own employees—or he chooses not to."

I lifted an eyebrow. "I thought you said you had no need to smear Vernon."

Bumblefoot held up a finger, and his smile turned devilish. "It's not a smear when it's true. I've done my opposition research. Vernon has a long history of shady behavior. He underpays his employees. Subjects them to poor working conditions and refuses to offer them the barest of benefits. Heck, I've heard tell of his carnies passing out in broad daylight from dehydration. And that's before we get into the unsanitary conditions in the snack carts inside his circus or the inhumane treatment of the animals in his care. Tell me, how is someone who can't be trusted to take care of his own be entrusted with the care of hundreds of thousands?"

Dean smirked. "It seems to me there's a fine line between blackmail and opposition research, Congressman."

This time Bumblefoot's smile was genuine. "The difference, Detective, beyond the information being damaging but not salacious, is that I'm not demanding payment in exchange for my silence. On the contrary, I plan to bring up all the above and more when Vernon and I debate before a live audience in a month's time."

And right there, Bumblefoot admitted it. The same thing I'd said to Dean—that if he had dirt on Vernon, he'd be happy to lay it in the open for others to gaze upon. I didn't put it above the man to use pornographic photos of his opponent's wife to win a campaign, but if he had them, he wouldn't be hiding them.

Still, there were a few questions yet to be answered. "So for the record, you have no knowledge of any blackmail attempts against JT Vernon?"

Bumblefoot's brow furrowed, and some of the disdain returned. "I already stated I don't."

"You haven't been approached by a third party looking to sell you blackmail on Vernon?"

The furrows deepened. "Absolutely not."

"And I don't suppose you know anything about the movements of Stella Vernon two nights ago?"

"*Stella Vernon?*" said Bumblefoot. "Vernon's wife? Why on earth would I?"

I looked to Dean for guidance, seeing as I didn't know how far to take it. He kept his attention on Bumblefoot as he spoke. "We wouldn't expect you to, Congressman, but seeing as she's been murdered, we had to ask."

Bumblefoot's eyes opened wide. *"Murdered?"*

"Yes," said Dean. "I'm a homicide detective. Did I fail to mention that?"

Bumblefoot leaned back in his chair. His mouth hung open in shock, and he blinked a few times. "Murdered..."

Dean stood. "We won't take up any more of your time, Congressman. We appreciate your assistance with the investigation. Phair?" He gestured toward the exit.

I took the hint and headed out. As we reached the hall, I gave Dean a prod. "Do you always do that?"

"Do what?" he said.

"Drop a bomb on people and walk out. That's practically a war crime."

Dean snorted and smiled. "It's called knowing how to make an exit. But in all seriousness, no. It was obvious from Bumble-foot's reaction that the news caught him by surprise. Despite all the practice they get at lying, politicians aren't any better at dealing with shock than anyone else. Given we have no reason to suspect his involvement with Stella's murder, I didn't think it was necessary to question him any further."

"Hopefully you don't think I went too far," I said. "Asking him about Stella Vernon, I mean."

"On the contrary," said Dean. "I would've asked if you hadn't. Her murder and the blackmail are likely intertwined. It only makes sense to investigate them together. Overall, you did great."

"Really?" If I was being honest, I felt as if I'd done a good job, but given my inexperience, I wasn't the best judge of my own work.

"Trust me, I would've stepped in if I felt like you were cocking up the investigation," said Dean, "just as I would've spoken up if there was anything I thought you missed. If anything, you might've done too good of a job."

I knew when I was having smoke blown up my hind quarters, but I played along. "There is such a thing?"

Dean's smile spread. "Not really, but it means you might have to do it more often going forward. Hopefully that won't be a problem."

I snorted and shook my head. As little as half an hour ago, it might've been, but now? The prospect didn't seem particularly intimidating.

CHAPTER TWENTY-TWO

I strolled the Vernon and Daly Circus between the whitewashed fence and some of the painted green trailers that served as homes and storage for the carnies. We'd stopped by the circus on our way back from the offices of Maximillian Bumblefoot, in part to check that Stella Vernon's car had been towed but mostly because Alton wanted to speak to the overseer again regarding some of the new revelations in the case. Dean told me I could tag along if I liked but that he'd lead the questioning this time seeing as he already had a rapport with the man.

I'd opted out, choosing instead to take another look around to see if I could catch anything we'd missed the first time. I'd started at the northeast corner of the property because our drive-by of the parking lot from which Stella's car had been towed reminded me of the hobo's testimony. He'd told the officers who questioned him that he saw a naked woman run from the lot, cross the street, and scramble over the fence into the circus.

Honestly, I didn't know if the testimony could be believed.

Even if it could be, there was no reason to think the naked woman had been Stella Vernon, and yet... might not it make sense for it to have been? Alongside Moss, I'd hypothesized that a friend of Stella's had murdered her, stuffed her in the trunk of her car, driven her to a crematorium, and returned to the circus with her ashes. If Stella were in an intimate relationship with one of the carnies, it might provide a motive. Say, for example, that Stella had been romantically involved with one of Vernon's employees. Given her drug use and depression, it wouldn't be too hard to imagine. But Vernon was in the middle of a political campaign, and suddenly pornographic photos of his wife arrive in the mail. Stella might've claimed not to remember taking the photos, but what if she did and refused to admit as much to her husband? What if, after being threatened and berated by her husband, she told her paramour that she was ending the relationship, causing him to react poorly? After all, Stella may have been this man's source of income, either as a sugar momma or via the blackmail. Perhaps upon informing her kept man that their relationship was over, he attacked her and she escaped, running naked into the night, after which the man caught up to her and murdered her.

I paused at the edge of one of the trailers as I considered the yarn I'd spun. It was a good story, but the evidence suggested it was just that. For one thing, an encounter such as the one I'd pieced together in my head would be violent, unplanned, and almost certainly loud. There would be shouting and yelling, not to mention blows aimed at one another before Stella's murder. The trailers were only parked a half-dozen paces away from each other, and the walls couldn't have been more than a single board thick. People would've heard the shouts and cries, and based on the testimonies collected thus far, none had. More importantly, it would be hard to hide such a relationship in the first place. If a young, handsome carny was having an affair with the boss's wife, the rumor would've spread to every corner of the circus within days. It was possible the carnival folk would band together and refuse to tell us about the affair in hopes of protecting whomever was involved, but would they do the same with a murder on the line? Folks were less willing to protect each other from a felony than a marital indiscretion.

Not to mention, the hobo's testimony still didn't fit. According to him, Stella had run from the lot to the circus. If she feared for her life and was fleeing attack, wouldn't she have run the other way? Certainly she would've if she'd had her car keys. Maybe that's why she returned. She'd forgotten them in a rush to get away, and her return to the circus had been in an unsuccessful attempt to retrieve them.

I shook my head as I kept walking. No, that didn't quite work either. If she'd been stark naked, she would've known she didn't have her keys on her. She must've run to the car for some other reason. Or perhaps I was barking up the wrong tree. Maybe there *was* another naked woman. Perhaps Stella had been involved in a love triangle. Maybe she'd found her paramour in the arms of another woman. Maybe she ran her off and attacked her lover, but while trying to protect himself he accidentally killed her. Maybe then, in a panic, the paramour enlisted the help of his new side-piece, loaded Stella in her car, and cremated her remains to hide everything.

But then why leave the remains in the bird enclosure where they were sure to be found? I snorted in frustration, but I didn't expect anyone to hear me.

"Rough morning, Officer?"

I looked up from the ground at my feet to find I'd made it

back to the aviary. Not far outside it was the same brown-haired zookeeper I'd interviewed yesterday morning, Krzysztof Radoslaw. He stood outside the entrance to the enclosure, broom in hand, wearing the same tattered canvas jacket I'd seen him in the day before. If anything, the circles underneath his eyes were even darker than I remembered them.

I shrugged as I closed the last of the distance between us. "Just trying to wrap my head around things, Mr. Radoslaw. Precious little about this investigation makes sense."

Radoslaw looked at the aviary, his skin waxy in the midday sun. "Not every day you encounter a dead man's remains in an animal pen, that is for certain."

"Dead woman," I corrected.

One of Radoslaw's eyebrows inched up. "You know who died, then?"

I figured it would only be a matter of time before the entire circus knew given Dean was speaking with the foreman. "Stella Vernon. Mr. Vernon's wife."

Radoslaw shook his head, his eyes downturned. I got the impression there was something he wanted to share, but he broke into a violent fit of coughing, causing him cram his mouth into the crook of his elbow.

I gave him a moment before pushing forth. "I don't suppose you saw Mrs. Vernon the night of her death."

Radoslaw wiped his mouth on his sleeve and cleared his throat. "No. The last time I saw her was maybe a week ago, while I was refilling the feeder for the cotingas. I said hello, and she responded. She was a nice woman, but not very talkative."

"What are cotingas?" I asked.

"Small bird, brilliant blue plumage. They are easy to spot

once you know what to look for. I can show you if you would like." Radoslaw shot a thumb toward the aviary.

My brow furrowed. "You last saw Mrs. Vernon *in the aviary?*"

Radoslaw nodded. "She liked to spend time with all the animals, but it is easier to be alone and unsupervised there than with the tigers. I think she found a special bond with the birds, though. She was particularly fond of our scarlet aracanga. It is a beautiful bird, with feathers like the setting sun. Sadly, it escaped the night of the murder. I have not been able to find it."

"So Stella spent time in the aviary often?"

Radoslaw started coughing again, but he nodded his assent.

I mulled that over as I allowed the man to gain his breath. "Do you know if Mrs. Vernon was... seeing anyone at the circus? Romantically-speaking, I mean."

Radoslaw shook his head as he took a deep breath. "If she was, I did not know about it."

"Did you hear any screams or shouting the night before you discovered the remains? Not necessarily from the aviary but inside the circus in general?"

"I did not," said Radoslaw. "I am sorry."

"Did you see a naked woman running loose?"

The man surprised me by not saying anything lewd. "No. Was there a nude woman here that night?"

"There might've been," I said. "We have an unreliable witness who says he spotted one."

Radoslaw's brow scrunched in thought, but before he could say anything the coughs overtook him again. His body shook from the force of his coughing, and he doubled over, hanging onto his broom for support. I gave him another moment to recover, but this time he just kept going and going.

I started to get concerned. "Are you okay, Mr. Radoslaw? Should I find a medic?"

Perhaps the mention of medical attention was anathema, as it was enough to slow the coughing enough for him to get a few words out. "No. ... I do not need a doctor. ... It is chronic. Cannot be helped."

"Are you sure?" The man still hadn't straightened.

Radoslaw nodded as he pushed himself up using the broom. He took a few deep breaths before speaking. "It is what it is. I am sorry, Officer, but I really should get back to work. It takes me longer to finish my tasks these days, and I am already behind."

There were things I still wanted to ask him—how the recovery of his animals was going, for one—but none of it was critical to the case. I couldn't justify taking more of his time for smalltalk, or any talk given his propensity to coughing.

I thanked the man for his time as he hobbled off before heading out in search of Dean.

CHAPTER TWENTY-THREE

I was sitting at my desk eating a corned beef reuben with coleslaw in place of the sauerkraut when I heard Moss's chipper voice behind me. "See. She got lunch. Don't paint me as the villain."

I wiped thousand island dressing off my chin with one of the five hundred napkins the sandwich place had stuffed in my bag as I swiveled around. Moss and Justice were tossing their jackets onto their chairs. Moss had a mischievous look on her face, while Justice looked aggrieved.

The big ogre rolled his eyes. "No one's attacking you, Ginger. Though I might accuse you of being a drama queen..."

I tossed the used napkin onto a pile of three or four others I'd already gone though. While I wouldn't need the whole stack, the sandwich was one of the messier ones I'd eaten. Good thing I hadn't taken a crack at it in Dean's Viper. "What's going on?"

Moss gave me a playful smirk. "Justice was whining because we didn't pick you up anything when we stopped at Quickie Dogs on our way back from Vernon's. I told him you're a big girl and you could fend for yourself, but apparently he's going soft on me, even if his exterior is rock hard."

Moss followed that last bit with a mischievous grin, but if what I'd witnessed in the bank was any indication of Justice's leanings, no amount of pouting lips and arched eyebrows would sway his interests, regardless of his professionalism.

Justice snorted. "In my defense, Dean often works through lunch. When he's got a serious case on the brain, his bodily needs go totally ignored. You can't fault me for thinking he might forget what time it is and that he's got a flesh and blood human tagging along with him. Back me up, Dean."

Dean didn't turn from his chair, but he held up a finger. "He's partially right. I do hyper focus. I don't forget what time it is, though. I make conscious choices about how to allocate my time, including on meals. Sometimes I need them, other times I don't. This time, I chose to eat, taking into consideration Phair's needs as well."

Dean hadn't mentioned any of that while in the car. He'd simply driven to the nearest Loaders franchise outside the circus and asked what I wanted, ordering a grilled ham and cheese for himself. I hadn't realized he might've skipped lunch if not for me. On the one hand, it bothered me that he might skip meals at all. As svelte as he was, there was no need for it, but it did bring a smile to my face to know he was thinking of me. I should thank him, but I figured I might keep that for a moment when we were alone. I didn't want to come across as a doe-eyed fawn in front of the others.

Moss threw up her hands as she settled into her chair. "Fine. Apparently, I'm the jerk for not caring enough. Sorry, Phair."

"Don't apologize to me," I said. "I got a sandwich. If

anything, I was worried for you. It's almost two. I figured you were still stuck at Vernon's with CSU."

"Well, we were stuck there for a long time. A lot longer than I wanted to be, if you catch my drift."

I scrunched my face. "I don't, actually."

"Vernon," said Moss. "Remember how you told me he gave you a weird vibe and you wanted me to see if I felt the same? Well, sound the alarm, girl. That guy's a creep."

Justice had sat down, but he hadn't turned to his desk yet. "He is?"

"Absolutely," said Moss. "I'm surprised you didn't notice. Actually, I'm not. You're a guy. You're not attuned to that sort of thing. But he's a grade-A creeper."

Dean turned around, his brow bunched in concern. "Did he harass you?"

Moss shook her head. "He didn't do anything illegal, or even say anything particularly crude or offensive. It's just something about the way he behaved. His smiles were too toothy when he spoke to me, his tone of voice too fawning, and from the way he looked at me, I got the impression he wished he had x-ray vision, if you know what I mean. I don't know. It's hard to explain other than to say I wouldn't want to be left alone with him, and I certainly wouldn't drink any beverage I didn't closely watch him make."

"You think he'd drug you?" said Justice. "Because if you have evidence to suggest he might, that could be significant. We're operating on the assumption Stella was drugged during that pornographic shoot, after all."

"Just a turn of phrase, Ogden," said Moss. "I'm saying I trust him as far as I can throw him."

The half-eaten reuben on my desk called my name, but the

case was niggling at my mind. Perhaps that was how Dean felt when he skipped meals in the name of criminal justice. "Speaking of Vernon, do you guys think he was telling the truth about his wife?"

"In what sense?" asked Dean.

"Well, he claimed she didn't remember taking part in the nude photoshoot when he confronted her, and maybe that's what she told him. But it seems odd to me that she wouldn't remember any of it. It's one thing to be drugged and pass out. It's another to be drugged enough not to remember anything afterwards but still lucid enough to be able to follow directions and make an attempt to look sexually receptive."

Justice rubbed his chin. "If she remembered the encounter, that suggests... what? That she was in on the blackmail attempt?"

"I suppose that's one possibility," I said. "From what we know about her, Stella was depressed. Potentially trapped in a loveless marriage. Maybe she wanted to get divorced but Vernon refused. The lewd photos could've been a roundabout way to force the issue. The other option is that she was in on the photos but not the blackmail. If she was having an affair, the photos could've been intended for her paramour who then used them to blackmail Vernon. Stella would've assuredly disavowed knowledge of the photos' existence in that case. Easier to claim you've been drugged and exploited than to admit you're having an affair."

Dean nodded, his eyebrows furrowed in thought, as his phone rang. He turned to answer it while Moss leaned in.

The beautiful blonde lowered her voice. "You're presuming that last part, I assume."

I smirked. "My love life is not nearly as salacious as you seem to think it is, Detective."

Dean sighed and spoke into the receiver. "Yes, sir. I'll get right on it."

"What was that about?" asked Justice as the phone clacked back onto the base.

"That was the captain," said Dean as he stood. "Apparently, our operators received an anonymous tip about the third of the Tarot Card Killer murders."

A cold ripple shot up my spine at the mention of it. That was the murder I'd been in close proximity to, after all.

Justice perked. "They did?"

Dean pulled his coat off his chair and shrugged into it. "Don't get your hopes up. Based off what the captain told me, I'd wager there's a ninety-five percent chance of this being a load of bull. Still, a five percent chance of a lead is better than none. Want to come with?"

"Sure." Justice hopped up and grabbed his coat, too.

Dean gave the rest of us a nod. "Moss. Phair. Hold down the fort."

Moss gave the men a wave as they headed out. "I'll grab my spear."

I turned back to my sandwich, trying to banish thoughts of the Tarot Card Killer from my mind as I took another bite of toasted bread and corned beef. I didn't even have it halfway chewed before I heard Moss's voice in my ear. "So... what's next, champ?"

I swallowed and looked over my shoulder to find Moss hanging on the edge of our partition. "Champ?"

"Justice is big guy or handsome, for obvious reasons. Dean isn't particularly fond of nicknames, but sometimes I call him boss, which he tolerates. I'm still working on your pet name. So as I said, what's next?"

I took another bite and spoke around it. "You mean after I finish this sandwich?"

"With the case, Miss Literal."

I swallowed another half-chewed chunk of slaw and meat. "Why are you asking me? Did Dean circulate a memo before I arrived instructing everyone to be as encouraging as possible as a means of building up my confidence?"

"Depends. Is it working?" Moss smiled.

"More than I'd like to admit." I set my remaining sandwich back on its square of waxed paper, grabbed another couple napkins, and stood. "Are you and I in agreement that the black-mail attempt against JT Vernon is tied to his wife's death?"

Moss didn't get up. "I'd give it at least even odds that the blackmailer killed Stella or knows who did."

I finished wiping my fingers and plucked the envelope with the pornographic images from Dean's desk. "In that case, these nude photos are our best lead into solving her murder. How well did you look at them in Vernon's study?"

Moss smiled. "You're asking me how well I ogled the naked lady?"

I dropped the envelope into Moss's lap. "I played more sports than I can remember growing up, and spent as much time in as many locker rooms. You're not going to get a rise out of me by referencing nipples and pink bits. My point is, you've spent a fair amount of time in Vernon's home. Do those pictures look like they were taken there?"

Moss emptied the photographs onto her desk. "I can answer that with an emphatic no. These were clearly taken in a seedy hotel."

"That's my guess, too," I said as I came to a stop behind Moss's chair. "If we can figure out which hotel, maybe we can figure out when Stella was there or even who took the photos."

"That's a big if," said Moss. "Have you been to many seedy hotels? They all look like this. They're all shitholes with decades old mattresses that are as loaded down with dust mites as they are semen stains. Trying to pick one out from another based on the décor is a fool's errand."

"There's got to be something we can glean from them." I leaned over Moss and spread the images across her desk, focusing not on Stella Vernon's nude form but on everything else. True to Moss's description, there wasn't much of note in the room around her. The sheets on the bed were plain and light in color, the headboard simply carved and worn smooth from age. The nightstand next to the bed could've come from any number of cheap mass producers. There was something, however...

I tapped the nearest photo. "There. Above the headboard. See that lens flare? It's in all the photos. You know what that means, right?"

Moss's eyebrows rose. "That there was a mirror above the bed." She pulled open one of her desk drawers, rummaged around in it, and came up with a magnifying glass. She placed it over the nearest photo and leaned in close.

I couldn't see much of anything over her shoulder. As she studied the second photo, I spoke. "See anything?"

"Not much," she said as she moved onto the third. "There's only a sliver of mirror captured in each of these. I can make out what looks to be a human form in the reflection, but its hard to tell. Based on the angle of the photographs, I'm guessing the photographer was tall and had the camera pointed downward toward the bed. That means none of these are going to show the photographer's face."

"Do they show any part of him?"

Moss wheeled her chair to the side. "I mean... a part."

I squinted as I got close to the photo in question. In the reflection of the mirror over Stella's head, I could just make out what looked to be a slice of forearm framed by a patterned shirt behind it.

I deflated. "That's it? We've got a forearm?"

Moss pulled the magnifying glass back her way. "It's part of it. As I said, based on the angle of the photo, we can guess the photographer was tall. And the picture quality isn't great, but if I had to guess, I'd say that forearm belongs to someone with skin on the darker side of the color spectrum. It's not a ton, but it's something. Although..."

Moss put the magnifying glass down and held one of the photographs to the lights above.

"What is it?" I asked.

Moss squinted as she looked at the picture. "Most professional photoshoots have tons of light on the subject so the photographer can get a clear shot. This was anything but professional, though. The photos are too dark, too grainy. My bet is the photographer only had a single light on in the room and a weak one at that. Not good for picture quality, but it might be a boon for us nonetheless. Take a look and tell me what you see."

Moss handed me the photo and pointed to Stella's side. To the left of the nightstand was a window. The shades were drawn of course—even an amateur photographer wouldn't advertise a pornographic shoot to the world. They didn't look particularly notable, either.

"What am I supposed to be looking for?" I asked.

"The light," said Moss. "Is it just me, or is something bleeding through from outside?"

I looked closer and held the photo to the light, same as Moss. Now that she mentioned it, I did see something. "I think it's part of a word, maybe from an illuminated sign. I see a pair of capital O's, or maybe they're Q's or D's. It's hard to tell. And part of another letter. Something with angled lines. An X or a Y would be my guess."

"I thought they might be C's instead of O's, but I'm with you." Moss took the photograph back. "How many hotels do you think there are in this city with names that fit those combinations of letters?"

"Ones with Q's and X's? Probably not any," I said. "O's and C's and D's? Maybe a few. Still not many."

Moss smiled. "Exactly. Time to make some phone calls."

CHAPTER TWENTY-FOUR

Moss parked her Howardson Hornet along the barren stretch of sidewalk in front of the Brody Hotel, a place with as much charm as the makeup crusted faces of the prostitutes who stood on the nearest street corner. A vertical sign hung from the facade at a worrisome angle, as if it might pull free of its anchors and crash to the street at any moment. Half of the letters in the word Hotel had burned out, but the O, D, and Y in Brody burned bright orangish red, in plain view of the third and fourth story windows. Though the sign had seen better days, I wasn't sure the rest of the hotel ever had. Graffiti sprawled across the concrete walls at ground level, cracks laced the exposed foundation, and the emergency fire escape that zigzagged to the top floor was more rust than metal.

As I stepped from the Hornet, I nearly fell into a crack in the sidewalk that could've swallowed me whole. Though Moss had parked a good twenty feet from the sign, I could nonetheless hear its incessant mosquito-like buzzing.

I eyed the place with distaste. "I know they say not to judge a book by its cover, but this sure looks like the kind of hotel a sleazeball would pick for a porno shoot."

The Hornet clanged as Moss closed her door behind her. "I think it's the type of flophouse in which *every* kind of illegal activity has taken place at one point or another." She nodded toward the women standing by the roadside, all of whom had taken a few paces from the street and were now laboriously engaged in pretending we didn't exist.

"Speaking of," I said, "you want to do anything about that?"

"Not really," said Moss as she came around the car. "Even on my meanest days, I'm not keen on criminalizing sex work. Besides, we haven't caught them doing anything but loitering, which I doubt the owners of the Brody would want to prosecute given how much business those ladies provide. Come on."

Moss nodded toward the front door. No shop bell sounded as she pulled it open, though the hinges squealed in despair. The room that greeted couldn't be called a lobby. It was more of a pass through to the stairs in back. There wasn't anywhere for guests to sit and little more to stand, though it appeared the rail-thin guy working the check-in counter had a stool on which to rest his bony behind. He sat behind an iron grate, staring at a magazine while a radio blared out a tune with a bluesy flair.

The guy didn't look up from his glossy pages as we approached the counter. When he spoke, it was with a voice that was rough and tired. "You want to rent for the night or by the hour?"

"Neither." Moss slid her badge onto the counter through the pass through at the bottom.

"Great." The guy looked up, revealing himself to be at least two decades younger than his voice. He had a few wrinkles on his forehead, and his cheeks sagged underneath a layer of salt and pepper scruff, but it was the deadness of his eyes that both-ered me. "What happened this time?"

"This time?" I said. "Are you really that jaded?"

The guy stared at me, silently judging me and answering me at the same time.

"We have reason to believe one of your rooms was used for a pornographic shoot," said Moss as she slid the badge back inside her jacket.

One of the guy's eyebrows inched up. "You don't say."

"You shouldn't be so cavalier," said Moss. "It's illegal."

"Oh, we don't condone that behavior. In fact..." The atten-dant pointed to the side of his enclosure. A sign hung on the wall outside it. It proclaimed, in faded red letters, that harass-ment and threats against staff or customers, solicitation, prostitu-tion, indecent exposure, public intoxication, distribution and or consumption of narcotics, begging, gambling, distribution and production of pornography, and cruelty against animals were all strictly prohibited at the Brody Hotel.

I blinked at the last one. *"Cruelty against animals?"*

"Just covering our bases," said the attendant.

I snorted. "You forgot apostasy and payola."

The guy lifted an eyebrow. "Don't make me tap the first offense on the sign."

"You and I both know that notice is for liability purposes," said Moss. "Frankly, I don't care what happens in these rooms so long as it doesn't affect someone else. Unfortunately, the porno-graphic shoot I mentioned *has* affected someone else, to the tune of blackmail and murder. You follow me, Slim?"

The guy sighed and closed his magazine. "You've got my attention."

"Do you keep track of who rents the rooms?"

"We have a ledger," said the guy. "But I don't check ID's. People can write down whatever name they want, if you catch my drift."

"I want to see it anyway," said Moss.

The attendant sighed and hopped off his stool. He bent over and came up with a tome that might've survived the last theological inquisition. It scraped against the bottom of the iron grate as he shoved it through the pass-through. "Knock yourselves out."

Moss grunted as she slid it across the counter to me. "Vernon said the photos arrived a month ago. Add a few days for the photos to develop and a couple more for everything to work through the mail. See if any names sound familiar. Even an alias would be something."

I nodded and cracked open the leather-bound doorstop while Moss kept talking. "Do you work nights?"

"Sometimes," said Slim.

"Were you here four to five weeks ago?"

"Hmm. Let's see. The night of August twelfth to twenty-sixth-ish? Yes, I remember that vague two week period well."

"Don't be a dick," said Moss. "Were you working or not?"

The guy sighed. "It's fifty-fifty. I'm here about half the nights."

"Did you see a guy with a camera come in? Perhaps with a petite blonde on his arm? Mid-thirties?"

"Does it look like I pay a lot of attention to who walks in and out?" Slim picked up his magazine and dropped it on the counter for emphasis.

I found the final page of entries and worked my way back as Moss continued her interrogation. "Answer the question, Jack."

The attendant shook his head. "I didn't see anyone with a

camera, but a guy coming to shoot nudie pics isn't going to make a production of what he's up to. Our patrons tend to value their privacy. People come in, they get their key, they head to their rooms, and I ask as few questions as possible."

Moss scowled. "Don't hold out on me, Slim. You see who comes in and out. Have you got cameras hidden in the rooms? 'Cause if you do, I'll drag your ass to jail so fast and hard that you'll wish the guys you bunk with overnight are half as nice as me."

"*What?*" said the attendant. "No. This isn't some peeping tom operation. We're just a shitty hotel. We cater to desperate middle-aged guys and drunks and working girls. Most of the time, I barely look at the folks who check in. I swear!"

Moss gave me a nod. "Phair?"

I shook my head as I scanned the pages. "I'm not seeing anything. No Vernon. No Stella. No names of anyone we bumped into at the circus. Maybe if we knew Stella better, we might able to decipher some hidden message from this jumble of names, but I doubt it. The entries are mostly John and Jane Smiths."

Moss's lips flapped as she blew her breath out forcefully. "To be clear then, Slim, you don't know anything about a boyfriend or some sleazeball scammer who came in a month ago and took nude pictures of a slim blonde woman?"

"Can't say I do," he said.

Moss shrugged. "It was worth a shot."

Moss gave me a nod. It seemed as it the whole building shook as I shut the ledger.

"That said," continued the attendant, "if you're looking for a sleazeball photographer, there are a couple who do shoots for the working girls for their promo materials."

Moss planted her hands on her hips. "Are you kidding me? Why do you think I've been standing here grilling you for the past five minutes?"

"You asked if a guy came in with a camera and a blonde woman on his arm. You never specifically asked about photographers."

Moss pressed her face into her palm for a moment before bringing it back up. "The names, Slim. Give me the names!"

The attendant put his hands up. "Alright, cool it. You want the short dumpy guy or the tall dark elf?"

Moss and I shared a look. "I think the latter will do just fine."

CHAPTER TWENTY-FIVE

Moss pushed into the interrogation room on the first floor of the precinct, and I followed. A tall dark elf in a paisley silk shirt and grey slacks sat at the steel table in the middle of the space. He had his chair angled to the side, his legs crossed at the knee, and was stroking his pencil mustache as we entered.

"Finally," he said, flicking a hand into the air. "I've been in here for hours. Am I finally free to leave?"

There were two empty chairs opposite the dark elf. Moss settled into one, and I settled into the other.

I glanced at the rap sheet in my hands. "Gunter Illuvar?"

The dark elf gave his head a bob. "Yes? Can I go?"

A couple of patrol officers had dropped by his place and brought him in. This was the first time I'd set eyes on him. "Not yet. And for the record, you've been here forty-five minutes. We can keep you for forty-eight hours without charging you."

"Forty-eight hours?" said Illuvar. "You've got to be joking! I haven't done anything!"

"Maybe not recently," I said, glancing at the sheet. "But

you've done plenty wrong. Violation of censorship, distribution of obscene materials, multiple instances of fraud. You served ten months of a two year sentence before being let out on parole."

"And?" said the elf. "I served my time. That doesn't justify my perpetual harassment on behalf of the city's bluecoats, you know."

"No one's harassing you, Mr. Illuvar," said Moss. "We just brought you in to ask a few questions."

"For two days?" said Illuvar. "That doesn't sound like harassment to you?"

"We'll happily release you as soon as you give us the answers we're looking for."

Gunter shook his head. "You could've at least brought me a glass of water."

I ignored the man's request. "What do you do for a living, Mr. Illuvar?"

It seemed like the guy wasn't too into eye contact, as he gazed idly at an imaginary spot on the wall. "I'm a freelancer."

"Meaning what exactly?"

He shrugged. "I write. Paint. Do a little consulting."

"Any photography?" I asked.

The spot on the wall must've been very interesting. "Sometimes."

I pulled the envelope with the nude photographs of Stella Vernon from under my rap sheet and dumped them onto the tabletop, spreading them out so they were easy to see. "Do these photographs look familiar to you?"

"They do not."

The elf hadn't pulled his eyes from his preferred wall. "You didn't look at them."

Gunter wrinkled his lips as he took a glance at the photos,

dedicating less than a second of his time to the task before returning to the wall. "Never seen them."

"You might want to take a closer look," said Moss. "There's a mirror visible in each of those photos. In that mirror, you can make out part of the photographer. Tall. Slender. Dark skin. Sound familiar?"

Illuvar bypassed the table entirely and fixed his gaze on Moss. "Lots of dark elves in the city, Officer."

"It's detective," said Moss. "And while there might be plenty of dark elves in New Welwic, there are fewer who frequent the Brody Hotel to snap dirty pics of prostitutes for their pimp's flyers. Even fewer who have darkrooms in their apartments. I wonder how many might have the negatives to these photos hanging in said rooms."

The officers who'd picked Illuvar up hadn't mentioned anything about a film studio or negatives, but apparently Moss decided to take a shot based on the guy's history.

Based on Gunter's reaction, it was a miss. He raised an eyebrow and sneered. "You want to get a warrant to search my apartment? Go for it. You won't find any negatives for those. No prints. Nothing."

If Moss was willing to take a shot in the dark, I figured I was allowed to as well. "Maybe we won't find the negatives to *these* photos, but what do you wager we'll find others? Or perhaps we might find a patterned shirt that resembles the one in these photos?" I picked one up and held it to Moss. "What do you think? His style?"

Moss smiled. "Could be. And could be some of the undeveloped film in his apartment features subjects who haven't reached adulthood either."

That got Illuvar's attention. "Hey! I do *not* take pictures of kids. Never have, never will."

"Implying you *do* take nude photographs of adults."

Illuvar sighed. "Look. Even if I *had* taken these photos—which I didn't—there's nothing illegal about it. These photos are clearly part of a private collection. Creation of pornography isn't a crime, only distribution and sale of it is."

I snorted. "He seems to know the law on pornography pretty well for a guy who doesn't snap nudes for a living."

"Going to prison for it once will do that to a guy," said Moss. "Look, Illuvar, since we finally seem to be making a modicum of progress, let's cut the fat and get to the meat. We know you took the photos, and while you're correct that taking obscene images isn't a crime so long as you keep them to yourself, even you would have to admit that blackmail is a form of distribution."

The dark elf blinked. "Blackmail?"

"You know," said Moss. "Where you demand money in exchange for your silence? It's often accomplished using embarrassing photographs such as these."

"I'm not blackmailing anyone," said Illuvar. "I don't know anything about blackmail!"

I turned to Moss. "I wonder if his bank statements would agree. Fifty thousand crowns are hard to hide."

Gunter's eyes widened. "Fifty thousand crowns? Look, I promise you, I've never blackmailed anyone in my life. I took those photos, yes, but on commission. They were supposed to be for private use."

"Aren't they always?" said Moss. "So who hired you? And who drugged the girl?"

Gunter grew more confused. "Drugged what girl?"

"The woman in the photos, genius," said Moss. "Or are you going to claim she took part in these of her own free will?"

"Well, of course she did," said Illuvar. "She's the one who hired me, after all."

I paused with my mouth open. "Wait... come again?"

"The woman in the photos," said Illuvar. "Her name was... Vernon, I think. She hired me to take the photos. We met once to hash out the details and a few nights later for the shoot. I guarantee you, she was completely lucid the whole time. I don't think she'd even been drinking. If she had, I wouldn't have taken her money. That's not how I operate."

Moss's furrowed brow suggested she was as confused as me. "Was there anyone with her? A boyfriend? Someone coercing her into doing this?"

"Not that I met," said Illuvar. "It was just her. She hired me, and when it was over, I gave her the negatives. Said she could develop the photos herself. For what it's worth, her behavior didn't suggest to me that she was scared or under stress. If anything, she was... *into it*. I assumed the photos were for her husband."

Moss and I locked eyes, but it was Moss who spoke. "Well, they were for her husband... in a way. The question is why?"

CHAPTER TWENTY-SIX

M y desk chair groaned as I leaned into it. Stella Vernon's diary lay open before me, one of many pieces of evidence Moss and Justice had bagged and brought with them from their visit to Vernon's. When I'd found it was among the pieces recovered, I'd lost my mind, but Moss had quickly beaten out my nascent flame. Apparently, she'd reacted similarly when she and Justice found it, but a quick perusal of it at Vernon's had revealed it wouldn't answer any of our most pressing questions. Indeed, Stella had mostly stopped adding entries about a year ago.

Of course, mostly wasn't the same as completely. There were a handful of entries penned onto the cream-colored pages during the past twelve months, including one dated three and a half weeks ago. Said entry didn't address Stella's drug use, her trips to the circus, her marital infidelities, nor any new friends she'd been spending time with, though it did address the nude photographs. In the entry, a seemingly distraught Stella wondered how JT could ever believe she'd posed nude, much less in such sexually suggestive poses. She wondered how he could think she would've done anything to smear him, especially when the photographs appeared to be an attack on her rather than him, and she lamented the fact that JT had turned into a callous, mean-spirited shell of the man she'd once loved.

Unless Stella was a master at weaving nuance into passages where there appeared to be none, the painful and intensely personal diatribe didn't contain any clues to her murder. What it did was add to the picture painted by the last three years worth of filled pages. As expected based on Dean's discovery of benzedrine in her bathroom, Stella Vernon was not a happy woman. The diary didn't reach back to when Stella met JT, nor even to their marriage, but it nonetheless revealed their relationship hadn't always been strained. At the start of the diary, Stella wrote of her husband in loving terms. She wrote of gifts he'd purchased for her or compliments he'd bestowed upon her. Over time, though, their relationship soured. I couldn't find any particular inciting incident that caused it, but as the months covered in the pages passed, Stella wrote less and less of her husband. When she did, the descriptions were no longer so glowing. She no longer mentioned his kind words or his smile, instead noting how he'd been brusque or short-tempered with her, how he'd brushed her off and how it made her feel unwanted and ugly. Her entries became more listless and disinterested, which perhaps explained why there were fewer and fewer of them as time went on.

For our investigative purposes, the most important thing about the diary was what it lacked: details. Stella didn't mention why she'd moved out of a shared bedroom into private quarters. She didn't mention many friends or acquaintances, and those she did seemed to become less present in her life over time. She didn't mention any particular fights with her husband, certainly not physical altercations, though there were passages going back well over a year that indicated he abused her mentally and emotionally. Most notably, she never suggested she was romantically involved with anyone else. If anything, I'd guess the opposite from reading her words: that Stella had lost not only her love for her husband, but her love of life itself.

All in all, if someone had handed me the diary and told me it belonged to a woman who was addicted to drugs and recently died, I might've assumed her death to be a suicide. That would fit her pattern of depression and disinterest. Of course, if she *had* committed suicide, she would've needed an accomplice. One committed to turning her death into the most bizarre, convoluted goose chase imaginable.

At the desk next to me, Moss spoke into her telephone. "No, of course not. I understand. I do sincerely appreciate your time, Mr. Vernon."

I heard a click as Moss returned the phone to its base, and she sighed.

I pushed back from my desk, peering around the partition. "I'm guessing Vernon is as pleasant over the phone as in real life."

Moss pushed her chair back, too. "Less of a creep, but more of a jerk."

"What did he have to say about Stella?"

Moss shrugged. "The same as before. He's adamant Stella wasn't involved in the extortion scheme. Says she was beside herself when he showed her the photos. That she swore up and down she'd never been a party to such a thing. He still thinks she didn't remember the ordeal because she was on drugs."

"Well, *she* says it wasn't because of drugs." I picked up the diary. "According to her, she never did it at all."

"All I know for sure is someone is lying," said Moss. "Either Illuvar is lying that Stella was lucid and clear-headed when he photographed her, JT Vernon is lying that he thought she wasn't a part of the extortion scheme, or Stella was lying in her diary about not having participated willingly in the photoshoot."

"Why would she lie in her diary?"

Moss rubber her brow. "I don't know. She'd only do so if she was planning something illegal and was setting up supporting evidence for herself in the event she got caught. It seems crazy, but everything about this case comes across as nuts. At first I thought the murder and cremation was the puzzling part, but the blackmail doesn't make sense either. If we take that scuzzy porn photographer at his word, then we have to ask why Stella would participate in a blackmail scheme against her own husband? Was she not getting enough of an allowance from the man for her shopping sprees? Did she have a personal vendetta against him?"

"I still think someone else was involved," I said. "Illuvar said Stella didn't specify who the photos were for. If they were for a boyfriend, perhaps he's responsible for the blackmail. It would explain why Stella refused to admit to her husband that she'd taken them."

"But she went to the trouble of reinforcing that lie in her diary, in which she'd barely written for the past year?" said Moss. "Why?"

I shrugged "I don't know. And none of our theories explain why Stella got murdered."

Moss sighed again. "Tell me about it."

The way Moss hung her head suggested she was more frustrated by the state of the case than I'd realized. I didn't know if any of it was my fault, but I tried to brighten her mood, regardless. "I think this is all going to come together once we figure out who Stella intended those photos for. That person has to be behind the blackmail and most likely the murder. And there's definitely someone involved beyond Stella. I mean, look at the letter Vernon got." I picked it up off the pile of evidence on my desk and held it alongside the diary. "It's not in Stella's hand."

Moss didn't brighten the way I'd hoped. "Even if she was behind the blackmail, she wouldn't pen the letter herself. Her husband would recognize her handwriting. If she was involved —a big if, still—she had an accomplice. Maybe a lover, but I'm not convinced. Nothing in her diary makes me think she was seeing anyone. Besides, call me crazy, but that blackmail letter, while not in Stella's hand, nonetheless looks to have been penned by a woman."

I frowned as I turned my eyes back to it. The penmanship was perhaps a bit on the loopy side, but feminine? "You think?"

"It's a hunch. I don't have any evidence, and honestly, I'm reaching the point where the more I think about it, the more I'm going to end up guessing rather than inferring." Moss stood and grabbed her jacket. "I think I'm going to head home. Get some rest. You should, too."

I glanced at my wristwatch. So much had been going on that I hadn't realized it was past six. "I will eventually. I just want to sort through a few things first."

Moss slipped into her coat, flicking her blonde hair out from under the collar as she did so. "You realize there's no overtime pay, right? I know Dean's been on your case to prove yourself and take charge, but there's layers to that. Standing up to thugs and asking hard hitting questions is great, but you have to be willing to stand up for yourself, too. Knowing when to pack it in for the night is part of that."

I nodded. "Sure. But I'm not staying late because I'm trying to prove myself to Dean. He's not even here. It's that... How should I put this? I feel as if there are a thousand fish swimming around my brain, and if I can just get the right angle on them, I'll be able to see the whole school together at once. It's weird. I've never felt this way before."

Moss gave me a knowing smile. "That's a danger, too. Can lead to sleepless nights. The good news is if you're in need of a support group for your particular neurosis, you're in the right place. Just give Dean a ring." She gave me a nod. "See you tomorrow, Phair."

"Yeah. See you."

I wheeled back into my desk, setting the diary down but not the blackmail letter. I eyed the flowing script, wondering if Moss was right about who'd penned it. On the one hand, I didn't want to believe her. I didn't think there was any concrete science tying handwriting style to gender, but the bigger reason I refused to believe it was that it threw my theory of marital infidelity out the window.

Or did it? Who was to say Stella's accomplice, and possibly her lover, wasn't a woman? It wasn't that rare of a thing to like the same sex. Heck, if my interpretation of the events I'd witnessed this morning at the bank were any indication, one such individual might have a desk across from me. Besides, it might explain some of Stella's behavior. Someone who struggled with their sexuality might suffer from depression, same as she did, and it might explain her secrecy. Having an affair while her husband ran for office would be bad enough, but for her to have an affair with a woman? I could see how JT Vernon might want to hide that. So did that mean he was responsible for her murder after all...?

Behind me, Dean's phone rang. I turned in my chair and eyed it, wondering what the protocol was. Dean hadn't asked me to answer it when he wasn't around. Then again, he hadn't told me not to.

I figured a lead being lost to Dean's absence would be worse than me breaking some unspoken decorum. I stood and picked up the receiver. "Detective Dean's desk. Officer Phair speaking."

The voice that responded was surprised and a bit flustered. "Oh. Officer Phair. It's Emmett Jowynn. From the morgue?"

"Oh. Hey Emmett. How are you?"

"Uh... good," he said. "Is Detective Dean around?"

"Been gone most of the afternoon," I said. "You want to leave a message?"

"Sure," he said. "It's about the black silicate glass I found in the sample from the crematorium. I was hoping I could show him something before I headed home for the evening."

"Show him what exactly?"

The guy might've been a coroner, but he knew how to set a trap. "Well, you're part of the investigative team now, aren't you? Why don't you come down, and I'll show you instead?"

Why not, indeed?

CHAPTER TWENTY-SEVEN

E mmett was at his desk with the typewriter as I entered the morgue, though his fingers weren't clacking at the keys. He sat with his foot crossed over his knee, a folder in his lap. He'd already taken off his lab coat, revealing the rumpled green shirt and khaki slacks he wore underneath, confirming he was waiting on me before he clocked out.

I hailed him. "Hey, Emmett. Sorry to keep you waiting."

He set the folder down and stood. "Not a problem. I called you, after all. Well, technically I called Dean and you answered, but still. Even if Dean had answered, he would've had to descend the stairs to get here, same as you, and given that you're both tall and have legs that are comparable in length, I can't imagine it would've taken him any less time that it took you. At least I would assume so without taking into account motivation or other outside factors." He smiled nervously. "The point is, it's okay. I don't mind staying a few extra minutes."

I smiled back, figuring the gesture was an easier response than trying to decipher what the heck he was going on about.

"You said you'd discovered something about that chip of obsidian from the Fogel and Sons sample?"

Emmett lifted a finger. "Well, it's not obsidian, as it turns out. And it's not a chip, either. More of a globule. But it is a form of silicate glass."

My brow furrowed. "Is there *non*-silicate glass?"

I might as well have punched Emmett in the face. His eyes widened, and his mouth flattened. "Of course there is! Glass refers to any non-crystalline, amorphous solid. You can make glass of any number of base elements. Phosphates, borates, germanates, antimonates, nitrates, fluorides. Even metal can form glass, at least in theory. I've read papers that suggest metallic glass could be the next big technological breakthrough, if anyone can figure out the engineering side of it. But to answer the question I think you were getting at, most *common* glasses are in fact silicates."

"So how is the fact that it's silicate glass important?"

"Well, it's not. I mean, it is, in a way. But that's not the focal point I was trying to get at." Emmett swallowed air. "You know, I think it might be easier if I show you."

I didn't know if Emmett's proclivity to qualify every statement he made had anything to do with me or if was just the way he was, but either way I got the impression that if I asked too many questions, neither Emmett nor I would ever make it home. "Sure. Take the lead."

Emmett nodded, and it seemed to me there was a hint of relief in his eyes. He waved me toward a far table, the one near the light board. "Right. As I mentioned, it's about the pieces of silicate glass. I couldn't stop thinking about their presence in the sample. If it were regular soda-lime glass like you find in windows and bottles, there could be all sorts of explanations for how it might've worked itself into the remains. From a watch whose face burst during the cremation process, for example. But as you saw, it wasn't soda-lime glass, or at least the color suggested it wasn't. In addition, the glass isn't in shards or chips, as you stated. The edges are rounded. Smooth. That suggests the glass was formed in the furnace or at the very least heated enough that it lost its structure and became malleable enough for gravity to mold. That in turn suggests something about the heat of the furnace, as I alluded to this morning, but what formed the glass in the first place? Sand? That's the primary ingredient in silicate glass, but it requires much higher tempera-tures to melt than what you typically obtain in a furnace designed for cremation. So what was it and how did it form?"

I shrugged as we stopped at the table. "I have no idea."

Emmett smiled again. "Oh, I wasn't asking you. I was simply framing the question. Anyway, I took a closer look at the sample to see if I could find any glass precursors among the ash, and, well... see for yourself."

Emmett waved to a microscope upon the desk. I didn't know what I was supposed to be looking for, but I placed my eyeball to the eyepiece regardless. Though the image was fuzzier than I would've hoped for, I could nonetheless get a general sense of what I was looking at. I just had no idea what the hell it was.

I pulled away. "I see a bunch of squiggly lines."

Emmett's smile grew and he leaned in, as if he had juicy gossip to share. "Those squiggly lines are *fibers*."

I frowned. "Fibers? What kind of clothes could withstand a furnace without burning?"

"None that I know of," said Jowynn. "But those aren't plant fibers. They're silicate fibers."

I still wasn't getting it. "Silicate fibers?"

Emmett nodded. "Specifically, asbestos fibers."

I didn't know a lot about asbestos, but I knew it was toxic. I pushed back from the desk. "Whoa. Should we even be here?"

"You can relax," said Emmett. "While asbestos is carcinogenic, the amount present under the microscope wouldn't be dangerous, even it wasn't immobilized between two glass slides. The rest of the sample you obtained from Fogel and Sons, on the other hand, could be dangerous. I've sealed it in an airtight container for now."

"Didn't this stuff get banned?" I asked. "What is it doing here? I thought asbestos was used as a fire-retardant."

"It was banned," said Emmett. "Six years ago, after medical research proved its deadly effects upon the lungs. Before then it was present in all sorts of things. Construction materials, including walls, insulation, and tiles. Clothing. Brake pads. You name it. Often as a fire retardant, but not always. As to what it's doing in the ash, your guess is as good as mine, but it explains the presence of the silicate glass. I had to look it up, but asbestos fibers melt between four hundred and eleven hundred degrees, well within the range of a cremation furnace. It's these fibers that melted together and coalesced into the black pea-sized piece of glass I showed you earlier."

I blinked, trying to process the implications of what Emmett was telling me. "Are we talking about a little asbestos or a lot of asbestos mixed with the ashes?"

The coroner's eyebrows rose. "In terms of mass? Maybe not much, but from an occupational health and safety standpoint? A lot. Enough that consistent exposure to it could lead to real health problems. I think we need to contact the crematorium."

I nodded. "Definitely. But why would there be asbestos fibers in the ashes?"

Emmett shrugged. "I couldn't say. My best guess is the bodies are wrapped in an asbestos-laden shroud while burned, but I couldn't tell you why. If I'm right though, we need to put a stop to it. The exhaust from that crematorium is quite literally toxic."

I sighed, feeling the weight of responsibility on my chest. "Alright. I'll update the team first thing in the morning."

"Please do," said Emmett as he grabbed his jacket off a nearby coat rack. "I know your team investigates murders, but this? It could be far worse..."

I nodded. Jowynn slid into his jacket and grabbed his brief-case from the desk with the typewriter, but as he turned my way, I stopped him with a finger. "One more thing, Emmett. The fibers. Did you find them in the remains from the circus *and* the mortuary?"

The coroner shook his head. "I didn't. Which implies—"

"That Stella Vernon wasn't cremated at Fogel and Sons," I finished for him. "I figured as much."

Emmett smiled glumly. "Sorry."

"Not your fault. I appreciate your efforts, even if they don't clear anything up."

"Any time." Emmett glanced at the door, but he didn't move toward it. "Well, I guess I should be going. Enjoy the rest of your evening, Penelope. I mean, uh... Officer Phair."

"You, too, Emmett."

The elf's cheeks reddened, and he bobbed his head before shuffling toward the door. It was only as he headed into the hall that I put the pieces together. Emmett's occasional stammering.

His awkward smiles. The fact that he'd called me by my first name, as if it were an accident, but the red cheeks that followed suggesting otherwise.

Was Coroner Jowynn... sweet on me?

CHAPTER TWENTY-EIGHT

I sat at the small round eat-in that served as Cliff's and my dining table. Once again, I'd failed to think ahead and pick up food on my way home, but Cliff hadn't been so absent minded. As I'd walked through the front door to our apartment, I'd found him hard at work in the kitchen, short brown hair tousled and his broad shoulders filling out a plain white tee. Bacon sizzled in a pan while flapjacks from a store-bought box of Aunt Mae's mix fluffed up in another. He'd even cut up some apples and oranges and tossed them in a bowl with berries, all of which sat upon the eat-in waiting to be consumed.

A more persnickety individual might've complained that the meal was breakfast and not dinner, but given the last time I'd cooked I not only infused our home with meat smoke but also accidentally invented a risotto soup, I figured I could over-look the food choices. Besides, I was hungry enough to eat anything, freshly-cooked or not. I'd thanked Cliff and poured a couple of glasses of iced tea, and within minutes of taking off my shoes, I was seated at the table, stuffing my face with syrup-slathered hotcakes and slabs of crispy bacon.

Cliff spoke as I ate, telling me about his day, but I wasn't giving him my full attention. All through my subway ride and resulting walk home, I'd kept thinking about the case, and as much as I hated to admit it, the host of fresh smells in the kitchen hadn't turned off my brain. If anything, the addition of fuel to my belly was helping me develop new ideas.

First, there was the asbestos problem. I wasn't willing to accept that the lack of fibers in Stella's remains meant she hadn't been cremated at Fogel and Sons. Perhaps I just *wanted* there to be a connection because it made sense that Stella's body had been cremated in a furnace rather than a backyard bonfire or a steel trashcan someone had converted into a forge in their garage. Fogel and Sons was the only crematorium we'd visited where the furnaces might've been used after hours, though Fogel's gas bill suggested they'd been used that way for weeks. Still, there might be a connection with the asbestos and Stella's murder. Asbestos was used as a fire retardant and an insulator, so perhaps asbestos gloves had been used to transfer Stella's hot remains to the aviary. Afterwards, the murderer could've returned to the crematorium and burned the protective gear to get rid of the evidence. It was a convoluted scheme, and there was little chance of incriminating evidence being left on the gloves, but a criminal who'd never committed murder might not know that.

Cliff spoke as I chewed, both on the bacon and my thoughts. "So as we pulled up to this house, I had a bad feeling, you know? It wasn't that the place was run down or that the lawn was hidden by more junk than at a scrapyard. I've made plenty of house calls to shacks, and though I don't like clutter, I can deal with it on someone else's property. But there was something about this place I couldn't put my finger on. Maybe it was that the blinds were cinched tight or that the windows had enough grime on them so you couldn't have seen through them even if the blind were drawn. Anyway, my TO had the same gut feeling, so we were on guard as we headed toward the door."

I nodded, trying to act as if I was paying attention even though I wasn't. Maybe the asbestos was a red herring. What I needed to focus on was Stella's involvement in the blackmail scheme. I'd been too keen on figuring out why Stella might've taken part in the nude photoshoot without trying to understand who might've benefitted from her death. As Moss had said, rage and jealousy alone usually weren't strong enough motivators for someone to commit murder. So why kill Stella? Had she agreed to take part in the blackmail at a lover's behest and later scrapped it for fear of being caught? Or because she couldn't bring herself to extort a man she'd once loved? Did that cause her partner to double-cross and murder her? Or was the individual blackmailing JT Vernon also forcing Stella into actions against her will? Did they have blackmail on her that they used to create blackmail against JT? If Stella had reached a breaking point and refused to cooperate further, they might've killed her, especially now that they had dirt on her husband, but who would do such a thing? Maximillian Bumblefoot? The man came across as conniving and shrewd, but he wasn't a murderer, was he?

"...and while we're talking to Mr. Hammond at the door, we hear a muffled thump from the back. So we ask him, is everything okay? And that's when this guy gets *really* cagey. Because of the noise, my TO asks if we can come in. Hammond flat out refuses, but you don't need a warrant to enter under exigent circumstances, and let me tell you, the guy who lurched out from the back hallway with his arms tied behind his back and a gag in his mouth was about as exigent as it gets. My TO reached for his sidearm, but damn if that Hammond wasn't quicker than he looked. He..."

As I thought about Bumblefoot, my mind drifted to Dean's actions outside his office. He'd pushed me to speak up and take charge, which he'd claimed was driven by his desire to make me valuable in the eyes of the captain, but why was Dean so keen on keeping me around? Was it that he saw me as a valuable addition to the team, as he claimed, or was there an ulterior motive? Did Dean... *like me?* He'd treated me kindly and encouraged me, but it seemed to me that he treated most people with courtesy. He had opened up to me about his dead fiance, though, which was most certainly *not* something most people did with new colleagues, regardless of circumstance. Of course, I might be projecting my feelings onto him. I'd found him striking from the first moment I saw him, so calm and collected and full of confidence, though if I was being honest, there was more to him that I liked. He filled out a pair of tight slacks nicely, too. Still, beyond being kind and open, he hadn't done anything to suggest he was romantically interested in me, not like Coroner Jowynn. I still couldn't believe how nervous he'd seemed around me. Did I cut that striking of a figure? I might in a low-cut dress, but not in a police uniform, surely. And yet, there was no question in my mind that Emmett liked me. I might not be great at reading men, but I wasn't blind either. And if Emmett could find me attractive, why not Dean?

"...and so I've got Hammond in a chokehold, but he's fighting me tooth and nail. We stumble into the kitchen when I hear another person barreling around the corner. It's Hammond's partner. He's got a wicked looking spear point knife in hand, probably eight inches in length. He lunges, but he doesn't notice the guy with the gag on the floor. He stumbles over him, hitting the ground like a sack of bricks, and by this point my TO is flying in to get my back. His uniform is stained with his own vomit from when Hammond kicked him in the stomach, but... hey, Nell? *Nell!*"

I looked up from my pancakes, blinking away thoughts of Dean and Emmett and the case. "Huh?"

Cliff looked at me with those dark brown eyes of his, the thicker than normal stubble on his cheeks failing to hide the square jaw underneath. He wasn't frowning, but he wasn't smiling either. "Are you listening to anything I'm saying, Nell?"

"Uh... of course I am. House call. Guy. Knife. Vomit."

Cliff lifted a suspicious eyebrow. "Are you sure? Because here I am telling you about my most exciting day on the force *by far*, and I feel like I'm talking to a brick wall. You've looked at the bacon more than you have me."

"I'm paying attention."

"But not interacting," said Cliff. "Not asking me anything as I go, not even to see if I'm okay. I'm fine by the way. Didn't get knifed."

"Not to ruin your story, but I kind of figured."

Cliff snorted and shook his head. He grabbed the bowl of fruit and spooned some onto his plate. "Right. Maybe you can tell me about your day since clearly mine wasn't interesting enough."

As the slightly longer hair on top of Cliff's head bobbed, it struck me that it was more mussed than usual. From the tussle at Hammond's? Maybe I should've asked... "Trust me, my day was not that interesting."

Cliff looked up. I thought he might be relieved, but he

looked even more annoyed. "So you have a boring day, yet that's *still* more engaging than what I went through?"

I frowned. "What? No. I mean, I had a lot going on. The case I'm working on is super weird, and there are a lot of pieces I'm trying to fit together. I'm not ignoring you, I just have a lot on my mind."

Cliff snorted again. "Yeah, well you might not be *trying* to ignore me..."

I set my fork down. "What's that supposed to mean?"

Cliff sighed as he returned the bowl to the middle of the table. "It means that since you've embarked on this adventure with your detective friends, I've barely seen you, much less talked to you. For crying out loud, Nell, a few days ago you were questioning whether police work was right for you. Now it's all you think about? Don't get me wrong, I think you were right to stick it out. I told you as much, but it's a big shift from being ready to give it up to caring about nothing else."

"That's not a fair comparison," I said. "A few days ago, I was stuck in a partnership from hell with no way out. The way out arrived, and now I'm getting to use my brain and work on murder cases instead of being stuck on the beat."

"Like me?" said Cliff.

"I thought you liked patrol. I mean, the day you had today sounds like a thrill ride. Isn't that enough?"

"It wasn't enough for you," said Cliff. "Not when you decided to jump to the front of the line and become a detective."

"I'm not a detective," I said. "I never claimed to be. I'm an officer, same as you. And who said I jumped to the front of the line? Dean demanded my transfer, if you'll recall. I didn't have a say."

Cliff shook his head. "That's not the way you phrased it the first night. You made it seem as if you transferred of your own free will."

It's possible I had, but I was starting to get annoyed under Cliff's negative barrage. "Is this an envy thing? Are you annoyed a detective took me under his wing instead of you?"

Cliff threw his hands into the air. "No! The *thing* is that you're not interested in my life, and I'm trying to figure out why."

"I told you, I'm busy," I said. "I just started with a new team. There's a lot of pressure with this move to the Fifth. My focus needs to be on my work."

Cliff averted his gaze. "Yeah. Maybe it does."

I felt rage rising up in my throat, but there might've been a spoonful of nervous bile in it, too. "And what is *that* supposed to mean?"

Cliff sighed. He tilted his head to meet mine, his eyes dark pools. "It means you didn't seem that interested in what was going on in my life when we were both at the Williams Street precinct. I attributed it to you being stuck with a TO from hell and to hating your job. I thought maybe police work wasn't for you, but now you've switched to a new team and you're invigorated and engaged. It's all you think about, where all your focus is. And yet despite everything that's changed, there's one constant. You're still not interested in my day."

The bile in my throat rose higher. "Cliff..."

He rose from his chair, eyes downturned and lips pursed. "I need to take a shower and get to bed. I have first shift in the morning. Sorry, Nell."

Cliff swept past me en route to our bedroom. He closed the door gently, which was far worse than slamming it behind him. It showed he wasn't acting irrationally out of anger. That he'd given his actions the requisite thought they required. And if I was honest with myself, I didn't think Cliff was wrong. I hadn't paid attention to him throughout dinner. I'd vacillated between thinking about the case and thinking about Emmett and Dean. While one subject was understandable, the other wasn't.

I sighed as I stood, gathering plates to take to the kitchen. I didn't have any answers, and I didn't think I'd come across any before I went to bed. The one thing I did know was that I didn't wanted to venture into our bedroom until after Cliff had fallen asleep, and that alone seemed to me like a bad sign.

CHAPTER TWENTY-NINE

Ogden was the only one at his desk when I arrived at our third floor cluster, same as the morning before. I gave him a nod even though his back was to me. "Morning, Justice."

He flicked a wave at me over his shoulder, pen in hand. "Morning, Phair."

Between the sheaf of papers on his desk and the pen, I'd figured out his game. "Already stuck filling out forms? It's not even nine, you know."

He turned my way. "Technically, I'm writing a report. Didn't get a chance to do it last night. Or rather, I chose to go to sleep at a reasonable hour rather than do it."

I paused outside my desk's partition. "A report on the Tarot Card Killer lead?"

Justice rolled his eyes. "Calling it a lead would be like calling a leashed possum a dog. More like an attention-starved wannabe celebrity looking to launch themselves into a spotlight."

"That bad, huh?"

Justice snorted. "I hate when we get a tips on cases with public notoriety. Not only do they bring out the crazies, they bring out the self-dealers, the attention whores, the folks who'd do anything for ten seconds of fame. Drives me nuts. I wish we could ignore every tip that comes over the phone, but you've got to do your due diligence. And since this one was about the Tarot Card Killer, of course Dean's going to go the extra mile."

I glanced at Dean's empty desk. "Is he still checking out the lead?"

Justice leveled a judgmental finger in my direction. "I told you, it's not a lead. It's a waste of time, but yes. Normally, he's excellent at separating bogus tips from ones that have the scent of truth on them, but not so much this time. He's too focused on catching this guy. Can't allow anything to slip by him, even if it means humoring the nutcases. He's—"

"Obsessed?" I said.

Justice frowned. "You said it, not me. And it's not a bad thing. I mean, it might be for his personal well-being and mental health, but not for catching the killer."

The good thing about Dean keeping his desk so organized was that it was evident when someone left something there for him to peruse. This time it was a grey folder with CSU stamped across the front.

I picked it up and showed it to Justice. "Is this on the Vernon murder?"

Justice nodded. "You can take a look. I already did. It's from their sweep of Stella's car. Unfortunately, they didn't find any blood in the trunk, nor did they find any hairs that don't seem to have belonged to Stella herself."

I quickly scanned the report. The lack of blood or other

tissues surprised me, but not as much as what they *did* find. "She had a suitcase in the trunk?"

Justice nodded. "She'd packed clothes. Toiletries. Everything a woman would need to survive on her own for a few weeks, other than food."

"She was planning to run away," I said. "The question is whether she planned on having anyone join her."

Justice shrugged. "Your guess is as good as mine, but if so, it would appear that extra someone was taking their own car. That or Stella got murdered before they got a chance to slide their luggage into the trunk alongside hers."

I slapped the folder against my hand a couple times, thinking about the implications of the suitcase, but I didn't want to let myself get carried away, either with Stella's car or any of my lingering personal thoughts. There were other more pressing matters to attend to.

I dropped the file on Dean's desk. "Well, we can worry about that later. Right now we need to visit Fogel and Sons."

Justice lifted a brow. "We do?"

I nodded. "Coroner Jowynn found traces of asbestos in the sample we scraped out of Fogel's furnaces."

Justice blinked a few times. *"Asbestos?"*

"I think you'd agree we need to figure out what the hell is going on."

Justice did agree. We headed to the parking garage and piled into his Phantom before hitting the road. Justice asked me a few questions about the asbestos as we drove, all of which I answered to the best of my ability, but apparently I was either too tight-lipped or too focused on buildings in the far distance for Justice's tastes.

As the ogre slowed for a red light, he gave me a nod. "You okay?"

I brought my attention back inside the vehicle. "I'm fine. Why?"

Justice shrugged. "Moss made it seem like you were more of a talker. You didn't say much when we were driving around yesterday morning, either."

The biggest reason I hadn't opened my trap was that I thought Justice might eat me if I mentioned the encounter with the flamboyantly dressed man at the bank, but to his credit, I don't think I'd spoken much before that either. In my defense, I'd been slightly hung over from our trip to the Jjade Palace, and beyond that, I hadn't accepted that I should take a prominent role in our investigations. I still hadn't, but I was trying, hence my suggestion to visit Fogel.

I shook my head. "I'm not trying to be antisocial. I've just had a lot on my mind."

The light turned green. Justice grimaced as he gave the Phantom some gas. "It's the tarot murders, isn't it? I shouldn't have told Dean to include you. It's tough when you're so close to a case. In some ways, Dean is, too."

"It's not that." And that was the truth. Though having been in the proximity of the killer had given me the willies, I'd mostly gotten over it. As a member of a homicide team, I'd probably end up spending lots of time in the vicinity of murderers without knowing it.

Justice gave me some side eye. "You sure?"

I wasn't sure how much I wanted to open up to Justice, but he seemed genuinely concerned. Besides, I didn't want him to ask Dean to pull me off a case because of a misunderstanding. "Have you been in many serious relationship, Justice?"

That caught the big guy off guard. "What?"

I sighed. "I think my boyfriend and I might've broken up last night."

Justice's brow furrowed. "What do you mean, *you think?* Did you or didn't you?"

"That's the thing. I don't know. I mean, I've broken up with guys before. Normally there's yelling or insults thrown around, and in one instance punches, but this time... there wasn't. Just a sense of sadness that lingered. We even slept in the same bed afterwards, but nonetheless, I have a feeling it's over."

Justice's eyebrows shot up. "You think you broke up, but you still spent the night at his place?"

"We share an apartment."

Justice's mouth made a little 'o', or as little as it was capable of. *"Okay.* For future reference, I shouldn't be your go to target for relationship advice, but even I can tell you that you need to find a new place to stay. Like, today."

I snorted. "Gee, thanks. I hadn't thought of that while staring through the windshield listlessly. You want to forget the case and drive me to some listings?"

The ogre shook his head. "I'm just saying..."

I turned my attention back out the windshield, feeling a bit miffed, but I only needed a moment to recover. Justice hadn't meant any ill. "Sorry. That was uncalled for. It hit me out of nowhere, that's all."

Justice shook his head, eyes on the road. "No apology necessary. I get it. Break ups are complicated at the best of times." He paused for a moment. "Do you love him?"

I thought about that, and about the note Cliff left me over chicken stir fry. "I don't know. I like him a lot, though."

Justice nodded, as if that was all I needed to say. "That's what makes it hard."

We both rode in silence for the rest of the trip, though it only took us a few minutes before we rolled into the Fogel and Sons parking lot. Justice asked me if I was ready as he killed the engine, but I assured him I was fine. I might let my personal life loose in the car, but I was professional enough to leave it hidden from everyone else.

Justice and I pushed into the storefront. The shopkeeper's bell rang, but unlike a couple days prior, there wasn't anyone at the desk on the far side to help us.

Justice stepped into the middle of the displays, looking over them. "Hello? Anyone home?"

The walls failed to answer him, so I suggested we try the back. I headed down the hall and punched through the heavy steel door into the cavernous room behind. Luckily, it was more heavily populated than the front. Fogel stood on the concrete floor in front of a body on a gurney as three goblins circled him: one taking notes on a clipboard, another cataloging personal belongings, and third standing idly by with a mangled push broom in hand.

Fogel swiveled about at the steel door's clang. He looked tired. "Officers. Sorry. I must not have heard the bell."

Justice descended the steps to the main floor. "Not a problem. We found you. We're resourceful like that."

Fogel nodded, the dim light reflecting off the bags under his eyes. "What can I help you with? Don't suppose you've come to shed light on my gas bill problem."

Justice waved for me to take over, given I'd been the one to talk to Jowynn the night before. Good thing I was becoming more comfortable in the role. "Not exactly, Mr. Fogel. Do you remember the sample we scraped out of your furnaces a couple days ago? We analyzed it and found something odd amidst the ash. Asbestos."

Fogel's eyes widened. "Come again?"

Justice had split off toward the furnaces, his massive hands stuffed into his pockets. A scowl spread across his face, as if he disapproved of something. I don't know if it was an act, but it seemed to be working if Fogel's nervous look was any indication.

"Asbestos," I said. "It's a silicate mineral, banned for use in consumer products due to its toxicity. It's particularly dangerous to breath it in. Can I ask where the flue gas for these furnaces goes?"

Fogel was running a few steps behind. "Hold on. *Asbestos?* Why would there be asbestos in my furnaces?"

"That's what we're trying to figure out," I said. "You mentioned your dad built them from scratch. Do you know what materials went into their construction?"

Fogel's eyes remained wide. Between that and the bags, he looked a little wild, but he wasn't the only one. The two goblins near the cart looked up at him in confusion, but the one with the broom had backed a foot away. I kept an eye on him.

"No way," said Fogel. "There's no chance my dad put toxic materials in the furnaces. They're made of fire bricks. Besides, if there was asbestos in them wouldn't it have burned up decades ago?"

"I couldn't say. I'm not an expert. What about attire? Might any of the deceased you cremate have been wearing fire-resistant clothing?"

Fogel shook his head. "We strip everyone down. That's what we're doing with this individual. All part of the process."

"What about other stuff?" I asked. "Have you ever burned

waste materials in your furnaces? Drywall, plaster, insulation, roofing shingles?"

The goblin with the broom took another step back, suggesting I might've hit on something even if Fogel hadn't realized it. "Of course not. Why in the world would I burn construction materials in my furnaces?"

I pointed to the goblin with the broom. "You might want to ask that guy."

"Urzz? Why would he know?" Fogel did a double take before turning back to the goblin. "Actually... doesn't your uncle work in construction, Urzz?"

Urzz hesitated for a fraction of a second before throwing his broom at us and darting toward the rolling shutters on the far wall. Fogel cursed and batted down the broom. Under better circumstances, Urzz's quick-thinking might've allowed him to reach the door before us, but the little guy forgot about Justice. The huge ogre lunged and scooped Urzz up as he might a feral cat, holding him by the back of the shirt as he struggled and cursed in some foreign tongue.

Justice pulled handcuffs from his back pocket and smiled. "Looks like you could've been an exterminator, Phair. You couldn't have flushed this rodent out any easier if you had a telescoping pole."

"Flushing him was the easy part," I said, as the little guy continued to spit and sputter. "Getting him to explain to us what the heck is going on might be a whole lot harder."

CHAPTER THIRTY

A couple officers slurped their coffee in the Fifth Street precinct lobby as Justice and I entered. A guy who was about seven and a half feet tall loomed over the duty officer at the welcome desk, inquiring about a parking violation, but what drew my eye was Detective Dean, who stood by the entrance to the pit as he spoke with Captain Ellison.

Dean noticed us, giving us a nod and saying something to the captain that made him take notice as well. The captain patted Dean on the shoulder, meeting my eyes before he turned toward his office. There wasn't malice in his gaze, just a knowing glance, as if to say he was keeping an eye on Dean and me both.

Dean met us near the welcome desk as we pushed our charge into the station. He nodded toward the goblin at our knees, his hands cuffed before him. "This is?"

"Yoiks Glamfist," said Justice. "Owner and operator of Glamfist Remediation. We're booking him on conspiracy, breaking and entering, and multiple counts of violating the Clean Air and Asbestos Elimination acts."

Dean lifted an eyebrow. "We do that now? I thought we were in homicide. Did I miss a memo?"

"Yoiks is the uncle of a goblin by the name of Urzz, who until this morning worked at Fogel and Sons Crematorium," I said. "As it turns out, Mr. Glamfist's remediation business isn't on the up and up. He's been skirting health and occupational safety guidelines while ripping out asbestos insulation and drywall from people's homes, but he's been putting more than his own workers' health at risk. Instead of disposing of the asbestos properly, he's been having Urzz let him into the crematorium and burning the materials in the furnaces overnight, which, I shouldn't have to tell you, is super dangerous."

Dean's face grew tight as he glared at the goblin. "You've got to be kidding me, Glamfist. So instead of paying a fee to properly dispose of that stuff, you incinerated it and spewed the toxins all over the city? All to save yourself a few crowns?"

Glamfist didn't say a thing, keeping his eyeballs glued to the floor.

Justice snorted and shook his head. "You're not going to get a confession out of him. Glamfist is exercising his right to remain silent. Either that or he doesn't speak our language."

"Oh, he speaks it," I said. "He didn't seem to have any problem understanding our commands when we rolled up to his place of business."

Dean scowled as he shot a thumb over his shoulder. "Unbelievable. Get him booked, Justice."

"You got it." Justice shoved the goblin forward.

Dean watched the pair walk toward the pit, shaking his head as they left. "Guys like that disgust me."

"More so than the killers you normally pursue?" I asked.

"I think you'll find most of the folks we put behind bars

aren't particularly vicious or cruel," said Dean. "They just get themselves into emotionally charged situations and make split-second decisions that snuff out another person's life. Even career criminals who commit murder usually don't do it on purpose. They panic when a robbery or an extortion attempt goes wrong, and before they know it, someone's dead. There are of course those with screws loose. The ones who get a sick pleasure from killing. I'll never understand them, but arguably worse are those who put others at risk and don't even care. That's Glamfist. He'd let hundreds die so he could afford a slightly nicer car. Think about that."

"You really think he's on the same level as someone like the Tarot Card Killer?"

Dean shot an admonishing eyebrow my way. "That might be taking it too far. There are those who kill for sport and those who torture their victims as they go. Those who make them suffer even as they're dying. I don't think there's any worse group."

I swallowed hard, not wanting to think about it. "Well, we nailed Glamfist, but the bad news is we hit a dead end on our crematorium lead. Fogel and Sons was being used after hours all right, but not to cremate Stella Vernon."

"I surmised as much," said Dean. "I suspected it once I saw Jowynn's report."

"He left you one?"

"On my desk. Just saw it, along with the report from CSU about Stella's car."

"Any thoughts as to who she might've been running away with?" I asked.

The duty officer at the welcome desk had extracted himself from the giant's grasp and was on the phone. He held the receiver to his shoulder as he called out. "Detective Dean? Call for you!"

Dean lifted a finger. "Give me a moment."

He headed over and took the phone. The hum of activity from the pit prevented me from hearing everything Dean said into the mouthpiece, but I caught a snippet or two.

Dean nodded and replaced the phone, heading back to me with his brow furrowed and lips twisted into a frown.

I put the only snippet I'd overheard to good use. "Was that Mr. Vernon?"

Dean nodded. "Yeah. And you'll never guess what he just received in the mail."

CHAPTER THIRTY-ONE

JT Vernon paced behind the desk in his idiosyncratic study, his face flushed. "This is outrageous, detectives! To think of everything I've gone through these past few days. Finding out my wife has been murdered, her remains dumped in one of the animal pens at my own circus like so much garbage. To learn it was her from dental x-rays, of all things. To not be afforded the chance to gaze upon her and say one last goodbye. But *this*? How can this hellish nightmare refuse to recede even after my wife is dead? What kind of callous, despicable rogue would do this? To keep blackmailing me after my wife has been reduced to so much ash and dust? *Who, I ask?*"

I sat with Dean in one of the chairs before Vernon's desk. It struck me as pertinent that Vernon's self-aggrieved whining was about the effects of his wife's murder on *him*, not on the pain and suffering she might've endured, but I pushed that to the side as I focused on the new blackmail letter in front of me.

Dean focused on the letter, too. "To be honest, Mr. Vernon,

I'm not sure it's accurate to say someone has *kept* blackmailing you after your wife's death."

Vernon scowled, his cheeks red. "You're an expert on linguistics now, are you? How would you put it?"

"You're missing my point," said Dean. "There are differences between this letter and the first two that suggest a new blackmailer might be behind this."

Vernon's eyes widened. "What? *You've got to be joking!*"

"I wish I was," said Dean, "as it would make this case easier to unravel, but no. As you've no doubt noticed, the blackmailer has demanded to switch the drop site. The first two letters instructed you to deposit the cash under a bridge. This one requests you leave it underneath the bleachers in the tent at your circus, tonight no less. Do you have a show going on this evening?"

"Of course," said Vernon. "Three times a week, like clockwork."

Dean rubbed his chin. "I imagine the blackmailer knew that. Instead of demanding you leave the money in an isolated location, they've gone in the opposite direction, now choosing a crowded locale. The shift in tactics suggests one of two things. The first is that they suspect the police are now involved. A remote drop location served well when it was you or your butler dropping cash, but the same location is a liability when you have people watching the bag. The other possibility is that we're dealing with a new criminal who employs a different strategy."

Vernon snarled, his nostrils wide. "That's ludicrous! What are the chances that not one but two lowlifes are extorting me at the same time!"

"Perhaps not as slim as you might think," said Dean. "The key element of an extortion attempt is the blackmail, in this case the photos you don't want getting out. It's entirely possible the individual who first blackmailed you was working with a partner, one who's decided to take another dip into the honey pot. Or it could be the blackmailer sold their operation to another enterprising law-breaker. That's why we recommend that people who are being extorted only pay off their blackmailers once we're tracking the money, because if you pay them and they suffer no consequences, they're going to keep coming back. There's no incentive for them to ever stop."

Vernon wiped a hand across his face. "You don't understand. I had to pay them! My campaign was ramping up. We'd been getting positive press, radio interviews, newspaper features. The polls were tipping in my favor. I couldn't have those photos of my wife leak. Everything would've been ruined!"

Dean cocked his head in acknowledgement. "And your blackmailers surely knew that. They target people at their weakest. Their most vulnerable. That's how they succeed."

"Well, they succeeded with me, that's for damned sure." Vernon threw an angry hand at the letter. "You said there were multiple differences between this letter and the last. Do you really think we're dealing with someone new?"

Dean peered at the letter. "Well, in addition to the drop location having changed, the instructions for the drop are more detailed. That could be due to the logistics of dropping off cash during a live show, or it could be an indicator of a new party at the helm. They're also asking for double what the previous two letters did. There's something else, though." Dean pursed his lips. "Phair, do you see it?"

Perhaps Dean didn't want to mention what *it* was as a way to avoid influencing my thinking, but something had stood out to me from the first sentence I'd read. "The handwriting. This letter is in another person's hand."

Vernon frowned. "Are you sure?"

Dean nodded, but his focus wasn't on Vernon. He looked at me with a measure of satisfaction. "It's definitely not the same handwriting as in the first two letters, which doesn't definitively mean this is the work of another party. We could be dealing with a crew working together, but someone else wrote the letter, that much is plain."

It was the question of who wrote it that bothered me. As Moss had noted, the first two blackmail letters were written in a looping script, something Moss interpreted as a woman's hand. I wasn't so sure, but this wasn't the same penmanship. Nonetheless, there was something about it that looked familiar. In fact, if I knew it wasn't impossible, I might've thought it was *Stella Vernon's handwriting*. It reminded me of her diary, but it was shaky, strained, perhaps rushed. Could it be possible she'd written it before her death, perhaps under threat of harm from her eventual murderer?

Vernon placed his hands on his desk. He sighed, and his shoulders slumped. "Whoever wrote it, it's blackmail nonetheless. I suppose it doesn't matter. What's imperative is that we catch the criminals behind this and destroy the photos. The viability of my campaign is going to hang by a thread once word of my wife's murder leaks to the press. Perhaps I can spin it as a positive, get a bit of sympathy from voters as a result, but I won't be able to if these photos get out. If that happens, it's over."

Once again, it struck me how Vernon expressed far more sympathy for himself and his image than he did for his deceased wife, but I didn't think it prudent to bring it up.

Neither, apparently, did Dean. "It'll be tricky to catch the perpetrators in the act on such short notice, but I'm open to trying if you are. We'll need to scout the circus. Speak to your staff, so they understand they'll be a police presence there tonight. Study the points of entry for the bleachers. Set up a perimeter with plainclothes officers and detectives at the exits. It'll be a balancing act baiting the blackmailer to take the drop. If we're too close, they'll spot us and flee, which risks them releasing the blackmail, but if we're not close enough, we risk them getting away. I'd suggest we leave a fake drop. A duffel, as listed in the letter, but filled with blank sheafs rather than bills."

Vernon chopped his hand through the air. "Absolutely not. I can't risk having this thief escape with fake cash. Can you imagine their anger? That would ensure they'd ruin me! I'll deliver the money. I can get it from my bank on short order, but what I can't do is risk the lot of you bungling the trap and tipping this person off. That would be even worse! Promise me you'll only move in if you're certain you can arrest this person. I won't go along with it otherwise!"

Dean leaned back in his chair. "Mr. Vernon, when it comes to volatile situations like this one, it's impossible to make promises. Any number of events can—"

Vernon leaned forward, his scowl taking over his face. "Promise me, Detective, or I will be withdrawing my assistance in this investigation, effective immediately."

Luckily for us, it was Dean who'd led the interview, as I would've told Vernon exactly where he could stuff his assistance. "We'll do our absolute best, Mr. Vernon. I can't promise you we'll catch this extortionist, or even your wife's killer, but I can promise you that we won't rest until we do."

CHAPTER THIRTY-TWO

I sat on the bleachers inside the tent at the Vernon and Daly Circus as crowds filled in around me. Underneath me, on the cold concrete hiding amidst the steel jungle of the bleacher supports, was a black canvas bag stuffed with a hundred thousand crowns of unmarked bills. I wasn't supposed to stare at it lest I give away that I was a police officer, but if I didn't stare at it, how would I know if someone was about to steal it? Just thinking about it was giving me heartburn.

After leaving Vernon's, Dean and I drove to the Fifth where Dean immediately met with Captain Ellison and requisitioned a team to help us. With Moss and Justice and a few other officers in tow, we'd headed to Vernon and Daly's and started to set up a stakeout.

It wasn't as easy as I'd hoped. For one thing, the circus's main tent was more architecturally intricate than it appeared. As I'd noticed while interviewing the contortionists, the main stages and surrounding bleachers sat on poured concrete, and as I'd suspected, there was more to the floor than met the eye. A series of tunnels crisscrossed underneath the stages, allowing magicians and animal handlers to sneak in and out unnoticed, but the tunnels also extended to underneath each of the bleachers and to hatches outside the tent altogether.

Dean wasn't pleased when he discovered that, but it did solidify his thinking that we were dealing with a new black-mailer, one with a sharper mind than whoever initially mailed the dirty pictures to Vernon. I spent the next couple hours sweeping the tunnels underneath the tent alongside the rest of the officers, making sure no one was hiding in them and mapping them so we knew which exits to place officers at once the show started. Meanwhile, Dean, Moss, and Justice developed a plan of action alongside a lieutenant by the name of Oglethorpe, who apparently was an expert in blackmail drops.

As the afternoon bled into the evening, it was time to get into position. I'd changed out of my police uniform into plain clothes, as had the other officers on duty. Dean and Oglethorpe ran through the plan, giving us instructions on how we'd be distributed, what to look for, and how to act. As Dean mentioned at Vernon's, the evening would be a balancing act. If we acted too suspicious, the blackmailer might spot us and choose not to pick up the package. Act too lackadaisical and we might not notice when the criminal struck. We also didn't know when the blackmailer intended to make the pickup. They'd demanded the package be in place by six, but the show wouldn't start until seven. That would make it hard to hide our presence at the beginning of the window, but Oglethorpe didn't think anyone would move on the package until crowds had moved in for the show.

As Dean wrapped up, he listed where each officer and detective would be stationed. Unsurprisingly, he placed Justice above the bleachers where the bag was to be stashed, on the end near a side hatch where someone might sneak in. I didn't, however, expect Dean to place me on the opposite side of the same bleachers. Perhaps he chose me for my broad shoulders and quick feet. I'd never tackled anyone outside of the academy, but I was athletic enough that I felt confident I could catch most folks in a footrace. Then again, perhaps he chose me as another way to build my confidence. It seemed to be a focus of his, although given the stakes, I thought it made sense to give the position to someone more experienced. The third option was that he trusted me. He'd placed Moss in the underground tunnels, and he himself was going to hide in the upper portions of the scaffolding intended for performers. There, he'd use a flag to signal us if he saw any suspicious activity those of us on the ground missed.

If it was the latter option, I appreciated the trust, but it didn't settle the butterflies in my stomach one iota.

I eyed the folks filling in around me, trying to judge if any of them looked suspicious or out of place, all while keeping eye on the isle at my side where someone might slip underneath the bleachers to grab the duffel. In general, the folks didn't seem threatening. Most were couples, some families with older children, and only a few who appeared to be on their own: an older gentleman with a thick gray beard, a teen boy with his jacket wrapped tight around his thin frame, and a fae girl in her twenties who'd never before been to a circus if her doe eyes and eager expression meant anything. I cast a glance at Justice, who'd changed into a pair of jeans and a plain grey coat, but the ogre was too busy keeping tabs on his end of the bleachers to shoot me any non-verbal signs.

A loud bang startled me. I jumped in my seat, reaching for

the pistol I wasn't wearing, but music blared through the loud-speakers even as I noticed smoke from the pyrotechnics that had erupted on stage. A line of dancing girls streamed out of the main tunnel across from me, arm in arm and wearing bright red and gold tutus. As they did so, gymnasts back-sprung their way from the side aisles onto the main floor, though not the one next to our bleachers. As the ladies danced and the gymnasts spun and twirled, more pyrotechnics fired from the cannons, and the show was off and running.

After the initial dancing number, the gymnasts took over, standing upon each other, flipping in the air, forming pyramids, and performing feats of balance and strength that made me think I should spend the next year or twelve in a gym. After-wards came the trapeze show and the trampolinists, then following a brief session of silly antics from a cadre of clowns, the animal trainers took to the stage with their trained dogs and apes and eventually the big cats. I caught a general sense of the action, but I didn't pay close attention, instead keeping my focus on the bleachers and the aisle to my left. I didn't catch anyone shimmying their way through the slats or skulking about, and though I cast my glance into the scaffolding more than once, I never caught sight of Dean's flag. As the first hour of the show stretched into the second, I started to wonder if our crew of offi-cers had been made by the blackmailer or if the drop had been a ruse to keep us busy while someone robbed Vernon's home or cleaned out a safe elsewhere on the grounds. Maybe someone had already swapped out the duffel while we set everything into place, or they'd do so later in the evening, stealing the cash as we delivered it back to Vernon.

I banished the thoughts as the big cats were herded back

into their cages and wheeled off the floor. All I could do was my best. To maintain my vigilance and make sure the cash didn't go missing on my watch, and I intended to do just that. Besides, if the throng of performers streaming onto the floor was any indication, the show was nearly over. The dancing girls came back out and pranced about, showing off their long lean legs while the clowns juggled, the gymnasts flipped, and the trampolinists bounced. Music blared throughout the tent, the pyrotechnics burst with light and burped acrid smoke, and the loudspeakers warbled as the performers took a bow: "Ladies and gentleman, the world's greatest spectacle! Thank you, and good night!"

The audience rose from their seats, all except the skinny kid with his jacket collar turned up. He took a quick glance over his shoulder, flipped himself around, slid his feet between his bleacher seat and the footboard, and wiggled through the gap into the space underneath, as fluid as a fish through water.

I shot to my feet, shocked at how quick it happened. Through the slats, I could see flashes of the kid's jacket as he headed toward the far side of the bleachers.

I took a deep breath and yelled as loud as I could, hoping my voice would carry. "Justice!"

The big detective heard me. He saw my wild gesturing toward his side of the bleachers, too. He leaped the railing and dropped over his side in hopes of intercepting the kid at the hatch. I pushed my way through the people getting to their feet, ignoring their indignant cries as I climbed to the top of the bleachers and ran along them toward Justice's side. Once there, I leapfrogged the railing and dropped to the ground below, excusing myself as the exiting circus goers backed away in horror.

Justice was bent over the hatch. As I got to my feet, I instructed people to step back. Justice pulled back out, bringing with him the young man who'd sat near me the whole show. The kid's eyes were stretched wide, and his face had gone pale.

Justice slammed him against the side of the bleachers, snarling. "NWPD, kid. No sudden moves."

The kid shook like a leaf, shrinking under Justice's fury. "P..P...Please. I don't want any trouble!"

I glanced at the kid's hands. They were empty. "Justice. He doesn't have the duffel."

"I caught that," he said. "Start flapping those gums, kid. NOW. What's going on? Where's the rest of your crew?"

Even more blood drained from the youth's cheeks. "I... I don't have a crew. Some lady bought me a circus ticket and paid me a couple crowns. Told me she'd give me a couple more if I snuck out underneath the bleachers at the end of the show. That's all I know! I swear!"

"A woman?" I said. "What did she look like?"

The kid's voice shook, just as he did. "I don't know. Medium height. She was wearing a floppy hat, a dress, and dark glasses."

I glanced at the hatch Justice couldn't quite fit through. This time, I took charge without thinking about it. "Justice. Head out. See if you can find her in the crowd. I'll check on the duffel."

I dove underneath the bleachers, not waiting for Justice's response. I ducked and weaved around poles and under supports, almost too big to spelunk through the darkened space, but I moved as quickly as I could, fueled by my worst fears. Fears that came true as soon as I reached the drop site.

Where once the duffel had rested, I found nothing but popcorn and peanut shells.

I cursed and ran back to my side of the bleachers, my heart

beating hard in my chest. I smacked my head on a low hanging support, but I pushed forth, forcing myself on as fast as I could. As I reached the hatch, I found it hanging open by an inch. I pushed my way out, surprising circus goers who were shuffling through the aisle to the grounds. On the scaffolding above the main floor, Dean was nowhere to be seen.

I cursed again, apologizing as I shoved people on my way out of the tent. I was tall but not tall enough to properly survey the scene, so I worked my way to the nearest lamppost and shimmied up it, holding it for support while I stood atop a raised ridge three feet off the ground. Ignoring the alarmed whispers from those around me, I cast my gaze across the crowd, looking for any sign of a woman in a floppy hat.

Perhaps during the day, my task might've been easier, but with night having arrived, vast stretches of darkness shrouded the crowds. I looked at the yellow cones lit by the lampposts, hoping I might get lucky, but I saw nothing.

My heart rose into my throat, a sense of panic burbling alongside it. My fingers tingled, and I feared I might vomit. This couldn't be happening. The bleachers were my responsibility. If I'd kept my post, I could've stopped the heist, but I hadn't. Now a hundred thousand crowns had been hauled off, all of it on my head. All because of me! My heart beat like a drum, blood rushed through my ears, and visions of my failed career flashed before me.

And then I saw her.

In the glow of the lights near the exit, I spotted a hat, wide-brimmed with edges hanging low. Almost as if by fate, the crowd opened up, and the slight woman in the hat cast one last look over her shoulder toward the circus. She was at quite a distance from me, and much of her face was covered by a pair of dark glasses, but there was nonetheless a sense of familiarity to her, as if I'd seen her before. Not in person, but in photos.

It was Stella Vernon.

I hopped off the lamppost and raced toward the exit as fast as I could, but by the time I arrived, she was gone. She'd disappeared without a trace, leaving not even ash in her wake.

CHAPTER THIRTY-THREE

M oss frowned, her arms crossed in front of her. "Are you *absolutely* sure?"

I stood outside the tent in one of the lamp-post's cones of light. Justice, Moss, and Dean stood around me, but the circus patrons had long since left. The performers were still around, changing and cleaning and decompressing, as were the other officers, many of whom continued to sweep the grounds and the surrounding blocks in a futile attempt to find the woman in the floppy hat.

I sighed. "No, I'm not absolutely sure. How could I be? I saw her from afar, and only for a moment. Even then, I never met Stella Vernon. I've only seen photos of her—some of them showing far more than I needed to see. But if you're asking me my impression from where I stood? Yeah. It looked like Stella."

Dean warmed his hands in his pockets, his lips pursed. "For what it's worth, that was my reaction when I saw her enter the bleachers. Admittedly, my vantage in the scaffolding didn't allow me to get up close and personal, and I only got a quick glance, but if it wasn't Stella Vernon, it was someone who'd gone to a lot of trouble to look like her."

Justice shook his head. "It has to have been someone dressed as her. She's dead, after all. We identified her remains."

Dean lifted a finger. "The most *likely* explanation is someone was impersonating her, I'll give you that. Take a woman of her build, color her hair, give her the right makeup, then hide what you can't change behind a hat and glasses and it wouldn't be hard to fool someone, especially from a distance. But I don't want to exclude the possibility, however minor, that Stella isn't dead. Identifying remains is a tricky business. Jowynn matched her skull to her x-rays, true, but it could be possible to fake it. To take someone else's skull and mandible and damage them in a way that they could pass as her own."

Moss scoffed. "You've got to be kidding me, Dean. Are you suggesting not only that Stella Vernon faked her own death, but that she had the wherewithal to disfigure another woman's remains in a way such that they might be misconstrued as her own? What sort of criminal mastermind do you think this woman is?"

"I don't know that I'd call this the work of a criminal master-mind," said Justice. "More like the work of someone whose motives we can't fathom. We've been struggling to make sense of this case from the start. From the placement of the remains to the cremation to the blackmail. It all seems haphazard rather than meticulously planned."

"All except this heist," I said.

Dean regarded me with cool eyes, his lips still puckered. "What are you getting at, Phair?"

"As Justice said, nothing about this case makes sense. It's all random and weird. None of it seems planned—until tonight.

And of all the crimes we've investigated—the murder, the black-mail, the asbestos—it seems to me this heist is the one crime Stella could've pulled off. Whoever recovered that duffel and slipped away must've had an intricate knowledge of the grounds, as well as have known precisely when the show was about to end. We know Stella visited the circus frequently. Her husband confirmed it, as have several of the hands. If anyone could've set herself up to steal the hundred thousand crowns, Stella could've."

Moss's brow furrowed, and she shook her head. "I'm not buying it. Even if Stella had the know-how to properly fake her death, which she didn't, how does she pull it off? Where does she get a body? Where does she cremate it? How does she tamper with the skull to make it look like hers? Why does she leave her car behind? And what's driving her to do this in the first place? Because she hates her husband? Fine. Get a divorce. But fake her own death? Come on."

Dean took a deep breath. "I don't know. Normally I'd agree with you, Ginger, but Stella pulling this off herself makes about as much sense as does Vernon's blackmailer impersonating Stella while swiping his cash out from under our noses. I'll tell you what I do know for certain, though: that there was more to Stella Vernon than meets the eye. And one way or another, we need to figure out what it was."

CHAPTER THIRTY-FOUR

I sat at my desk, staring at the blackmail photographs of Stella Vernon, when I heard Detective Dean's voice behind me.

"Phair. You're early."

I turned around in my chair and gave the detective a nod. As usual, he looked fetching; today in an olive green sports coat and well-tailored grey slacks. "Good morning, Dean."

Dean checked his wristwatch, his brow slightly furrowed. "In fact, you're *very* early. I did tell you to arrive at nine, didn't I? Or is my wristwatch running behind?"

I shook my head. "It's as early as you think it is. I couldn't sleep, so I figured I'd come in."

Dean stripped off his jacket and draped it across his chair, revealing a crisp white shirt underneath that was as form-fitting as his pants. "Mind stuck on the case, is it? Seems you and I have something in common."

"Something like that."

"Oh." Dean's face fell as he seated himself, and I realized

the thought of someone else being as devoted to the work as he was had cheered him. "Something else bothering you?"

I waved my hand, hoping to veer him off. "It's a personal matter. Nothing that's appropriate for work hours."

Dean glanced at his watch again and gave me a sly smile. "Once again, you're not supposed to be here this early, and though I don't have a set schedule, strictly speaking, neither am I. Neither one of us is technically on duty yet."

Part of me wanted to open up to him—he'd shared with me the painful story of his fiancée's overdose, after all—but the dynamic was different. Dean was my supervisor, and he'd shared a story that was pertinent to the case. I wasn't sure if it was the right call to bring my problems to him, even if he'd asked.

In addition to his other impressive qualities, Dean might've been a psychic. "You know, Phair, when I brought you onto this team, I intended for you to be a part of it. Teammates help and support each other, on and off the field. You don't have to share anything you're uncomfortable with, but it's okay to do so if you want."

Dean flashed a brilliant white smile, and it crossed my mind that one of the reasons I might not want to open up to him was his role in my predicament. But gosh darn it if that smile of his didn't make me want to be honest with him.

"My boyfriend and I are breaking up, I think. The complicated part is that we live together."

"You *think?*" Dean lifted an eyebrow. "You haven't talked it over with him?"

"You sound like Justice. And yes, we did. A couple nights ago. I think we both know it's over, but neither of us wants to say it out loud because of our living situation."

"Penelope, you realize ignoring problems doesn't make them go away."

It was the first time he'd called me by my first name. He probably didn't even know I preferred to go by Nell, but he was making an attempt to be personable. I appreciated that. "I know. I have plenty of experience ignoring problems only to have them get worse. It's just... ending things can be hard, even if you know it's the right path forward."

Dean nodded. "Accepting the truth is challenging sometimes, even when you don't have a choice in the matter. I've been there."

We sat in silence for a moment. Dean didn't try to convince me everything would be okay, which I appreciated as much as his company.

Dean clapped his hands on his thighs. "Well, the good news is, we can help you get back on your feet. I know an apartment hunter. There's got to be something close to the precinct, if location matters to you. And if you need a place to crash until you find something permanent..."

My heart fluttered a beat. "Yes?"

"Well, I imagine Moss could host you. She's got a pretty nice place."

I swallowed back a lump. I might've thought Dean was handsome, but jumping out of one office romance only to dive into another, with a superior no less, was a terrible idea. Perhaps I should try to learn from my mistakes rather than endlessly repeat them.

"Thanks, Dean. I'll talk to Moss. I appreciate the support."

"Any time." He nodded to my desk. "Although clearly I wasn't *completely* wrong about the Vernon case being on your mind."

I spread the nude photographs across my workspace. "Guilty as charged."

Dean eyed the photos with a raised eyebrow. I thought he might crack a joke about him or Justice being better suited to spending long hours poring over them, but I should've known he wasn't that crude. "What are you trying to parse from those? You already tracked down the photographer."

I sighed. "Have you ever had a criminal get away from you? And I don't mean in the sense that you failed to catch the perpetrator of a crime. I mean have you literally chased someone and had them escape?"

"A couple times, actually," said Dean. "Believe it or not, I wasn't a track athlete before I joined the academy. We ultimately caught both of those criminals, though one committed another murder before we did so. Why do you ask?"

I took a moment to gather my thoughts. "It's weird. I kept tossing and turning last night, seeing the woman who got away with Vernon's cash through my closed eyelids. It's as if the image burned itself into my retinas. Dean, I feel as if it's my fault. I abandoned my post on that side of the bleachers when I saw the kid slide underneath them. She got away because of me."

Dean reached out and lay a hand on my knee, his touch soft but firm. "It's not your fault. We had an entire team there, all of us working together. The woman who stole that money eluded capture by outsmarting us, not because of your actions. I know it might be hard for you to accept that, but you need to hear it all the same."

I nodded. "Thanks."

"That said, it's not uncommon to feel the way you do, or to have the image of that woman seared into your memory. I was the same way both times murderers slipped my grasp, one more so than the other. Roberts was the guy's name. I couldn't forget his face, no matter how hard I tried. I remembered every pore, every scar. He was always there, taunting me. It was a tough few weeks until we apprehended him."

"Right. That's the thing." I picked up the photographs. "Even though I wasn't that close to her, her face imprinted itself upon me. When I close my eyes, I see her there, as if I'd stood no more than ten feet away. And when I look at these photos... I don't see the same woman."

Dean took the blackmail photographs from my hand. "You've changed your mind? Now you think it was an imposter after all?"

I pointed to the evidence. "It's her face. These are the most recent photographs we have of Stella Vernon. You can see her cheeks are drawn. Her face is gaunt. She looks tired, for lack of a better word. The woman I saw in the crowd had the same features, but her face was fuller. Her cheeks redder. She was more vibrant and full of life." I shook my head. Now that I said it out loud, it didn't sound as convincing. "I don't know. Maybe I'm imagining things."

Dean chewed on his lip while he eyed the photographs. "She might've been wearing blush, or the cool night air could've brought some color to her cheeks. Or perhaps you're right. Perhaps the woman we saw wasn't Stella. That's the logical conclusion, anyway. Either way, I've learned over the years to follow my instincts. You should stick with this."

Dean handed the photos back, and I tossed them onto my desk. "While I appreciate the vote of confidence, I'm not sure staring at these photos any longer is going to help me come to new conclusions."

"No, but getting the image in your mind on paper might. Come on. Let me introduce you to our department's sketch artist team."

Dean stood and led me to the second floor. In a set of cubicles in the back, he introduced me to the only member of the team currently at her desk, a young woman by the name of Feoris with pointed ears and a complexion that was more green than olive. Like so many others in the city, she was almost assuredly of mixed parentage, but she was quite nice regardless of her species. After Dean made the introductions, Feoris sat me down, pulled out her sketch pad, and started asking questions. Not all of them were about my encounter at Vernon and Daly's. She asked about me and shared a little of her own journey to being employed by the police, which not only put me at ease but gave her pencil an opportunity to catch up with my mouth. She'd take breaks to check reference books with sample features, then ask me whether the cheekbones she'd sketched should be higher or lower, the forehead broader or narrower. I'd answer those, and we'd drift back into conversation. A story about one of her professors in art school stretched on for so long that I wondered if I should check back in with Dean, but as the thought crossed my mind, Feoris turned her pad around and showed me the final drawing.

I was gobsmacked. I no longer had to close my eyes to see the woman from the circus. Now all I had to do was glance at Feoris's drawing.

I thanked her and wished her well before skipping back to the third floor. Dean looked over his shoulder at the sound of my footsteps. I gave him a beaming smile as I showed off the sketch, almost as if I'd drawn it myself.

"Check it out. Its Stella Vernon, but it isn't at the same time.

It's Strella Dernon, if you will."

Dean snorted, but he smiled too. "Maybe we can call her Jane Doe. But I'm with you. After having looked at those photos some more, I don't think that sketch shows Stella. Seems like our impostor theory is on firmer legs than our faked death theory."

Justice's smooth bass tickled the back of my earlobe. "You can say that again."

I turned to find Justice and Moss coming around the edge of the partitions. "Morning, guys. Where have you been? Dean and I have been on the clock for—" I glanced at my watch. "—almost an hour. Jeez, didn't realize I'd been talking to Feoris that long."

Moss pushed past Justice. "Your insistence on getting up early is your problem, not ours. But for the record, Justice and I were up catching the worms, too. You want to show them, big guy?"

Today, Justice wore a black pinstripe suit that slimmed him down from four bills to a clean three and a half. He pulled a manilla envelope from under his arm and held it to Dean. "You were saying you thought the woman we saw last night was impersonating Stella Vernon? If Moss and I are right, that's only the half of it."

Dean's eyebrow rose as he accepted the envelope. "What's this?"

Moss sat on the edge of her desk. "Stella Vernon's birth records, among other things. Justice and I dropped by public records first thing this morning. Figured if we were going to ferret out who Stella Vernon was, we might as well start at the beginning. As it turns out, Stella's maiden name was Stella Middleton, but her real name was Stella Cross."

Dean pulled the papers from the envelope. "What do you

mean her real name?"

"Stella was adopted," said Justice. "Given up at birth by her mother and taken in by the Middletons when Stella was less than a year old. Her sister, on the other hand, wasn't so lucky."

Dean looked up from the documents. "Sister?"

"Twin sister," said Justice. "Gillian Cross. Her birth records are in your hands, too. She was never adopted. Bounced around in foster care before running off at age fourteen, as far as we can tell."

"And when you say *twin...*" said Dean.

Moss smiled. "The birth records don't say whether they're fraternal or identical, but as you can see from the photo in the file, regardless of which, Gillian and Stella look a *hell* of a lot alike."

I blinked, trying to put it all together. "Are you saying the woman I saw last night walking off with Vernon's money was Stella's sister?"

Moss cast a quick glance at Justice before turning back to Dean and me. "Here's our theory. Stella and Gillian weren't separated at birth, but they were nonetheless split apart young enough to have no memory of each other. There's no reason anyone at the adoption agency would've told Gillian she had a sister, or vice versa. Adoption records are usually sealed tight, after all. So the two led their lives blissfully unaware the other existed—until Stella appears in the news following the announcement of JT Vernon's congressional campaign. Gillian probably cracks open a newspaper and sees, for all intents and purposes, herself hanging on JT Vernon's arm. She's dumbfounded, but she digs a little deeper. Pulls her own birth records and finds out she has a sister. Most people would be overjoyed. They'd reach out, try and connect with their long-lost sibling, but not a career criminal like Gillian. You see, after running away she fell in with some bad people. She has debts. Obligations. So instead of contacting Stella, she impersonates her. Takes photos of herself nude and passes them off as Stella in order to blackmail JT. And why stop at one successful extortion attempt when three is such a nice round number?"

Dean flipped through the documents. "That *is* a nice theory, but do the facts support it?"

"You can see the photo for yourself," said Justice. "As for the rest? We pulled Gillian's criminal record. She's been arrested multiple times for solicitation and drug possession. Once for burglary. Plus, someone pulled her and Stella's birth records before we did. Seven weeks ago, to be precise. About the same time Vernon's campaign began to blitz the papers and airwaves, and only a couple weeks before the first blackmail letter arrived."

I blinked, still confused. Ginger's theory about Stella's long-lost sister made total sense. It would explain Stella's insistence that she never took the nude photographs. It would explain the motive behind the blackmail, as well as last night's incident at the circus. It explained just about everything—except for why the woman I saw at the circus, who I now presumed to be Gillian, did *not* appear to be the same woman as the one in the nude photographs, who we also presumed to be Gillian.

If Dean was similarly confused, he didn't show it. "Do you have a current address on Miss Cross?"

"I don't know about current," said Justice with a smile, "but we have *an* address. A quick trip would prove it one way or another."

Dean stood and grabbed his jacket. "Well, what are we waiting for? Let's pay Miss Cross a visit."

CHAPTER THIRTY-FIVE

D ean knocked on the door again, louder this time. "Gillian Cross, this is the NWPD. We have a warrant for your arrest. This is your last chance to comply!"

I stood beside the door, pistol drawn, while Justice hunched at the other side, sidearm similarly in hand. I strained my ears, but I didn't hear any response from within, nor even the sound of footsteps.

Dean took a step back from the apartment door. "Justice?"

The big detective nodded. He squared himself, planted one foot on the ground, and slammed the other into the door, level with the lock. The door groaned and cracked. Upon the second kick it flew inward, rattling as it bounced off the backstop. Justice surged inside with his pistol in front of him, and I followed.

The apartment was, quite frankly, a dump. The living room into which I stepped looked as if it had been trashed by a group of fraternity pledges. Cigarette butts overflowed from an ashtray, spilling onto the warped veneer of the coffee table underneath. A couch sagged beside the latter, its back broken and its cushions worn thin from use. Empty bottles of liquor were everywhere, on the kitchen counter, the coffee table, even window sills, and a stale funk hung in the air, one part body odor, two parts tobacco smoke, and three parts skunky beer.

I tried to ignore the odor as I swept through the living space, my pistol always leading me. I checked behind the couch before sidestepping into the attached kitchen, making sure both were empty. "Living space clear."

Justice replied from the next room over. "Found her."

His lack of screams for Gillian to get on the ground or put down her weapon suggested she wasn't an immediate threat, but I didn't realize how right I was until I followed Justice into the bedroom. On a bed that was dressed with a stained fitted sheet and nothing else lay a woman who until recently I would've assumed was Stella Vernon. She was nude except for a pair of skin-tone underpants, her arms wrapped around a completely nude gentleman whose eyes were as glazed as her own.

I coughed at the smell, which was worse than in the living room. "Good gods. Are they dead?"

Justice stood by the bed, index and middle finger held against Gillian's throat while he gripped his pistol in his other hand. "Pulse is weak, but no. They're high as kites, though."

Dean walked into the room, his nose wrinkling. "Smack, unless my nostrils deceive me, although who knows what they've mixed with it. Alcohol, if nothing else." Dean picked up a hypodermic needle from a nightstand and scowled. "We need to call the EMTs. Just because they're alive now doesn't mean they will be for long. Moss?"

Ginger called from the living room. "On it. Headed to the car now."

Dean shook his head as he regarded Gillian and her lover. Color blossomed in his cheeks, but he held his anger better than he had at Vernon's. "Justice, get them cuffed. I doubt they'll be able to move under their own power, but I don't want to take any chances. I'm going to see if I can find anything that confirms Miss Cross's identity. Phair, search the rest of the apartment. See if you can find anything more incriminating than these narcotics."

"Got it." I holstered my pistol and headed back to the living room. I hadn't done much more than give the space a quick glance to make sure there weren't armed thugs lurking in the shadows, but I hadn't seen sacks of cash or firearms laying about either. Instead of turning over the couch cushions in search of weapons, I started with the coat closet by the front door.

My instincts paid off. Underneath the coats, a mix of ratty cotton affairs with frayed edges and thick furs that still had department store perfume on them, sat a duffel, brown in color to last night's black. The top was unzipped, so I pushed the fabric to the side and took stock of the contents. I wasn't the best at estimating, but there seemed to be far less than fifty thousand crowns inside, something the brand new furs might've been able to confirm could they speak.

"I found some cash," I called. "From one of the initial black-mail drops, I'd guess. Looks like some of it's been spent."

Dean's voice echoed around the corner. "Good. Leave it be for now. We'll have CSU see what they can pull off it."

I stood and took stock of the rest of the living room. Now that I looked closer, most of the liquor bottles were of expensive brands, Glendale whiskey, Black Swan vodka, and Jimmy Dunworth bourbon, red label no less. Had Gillian Cross blown most of her ill-gotten blackmail gains on booze, drugs, and furs?

There was only one other door beside the one to the bedroom. A hint of dirty tile suggested its purpose as I entered, but the bathtub and toilet further confirmed it. The bathroom was as disorderly as the rest of the apartment: the mirrored medicine cabinet hung ajar, clumps of bluish-white paste stuck to the sides of the washbasin, and a wastebasket next to it overflowed with tissues, as well as from bottles of solvent and other chemicals. Those would've seemed out of place if not for the string hanging between eye hooks in the walls. There weren't any wet, glossy photographs affixed to the string, but as I opened the medicine cabinet, I found what I was looking for. Hiding amidst pill bottles that didn't look as if they'd been administered by a pharmacist I found a half dozen clothespins and two strips of negatives. I pulled a glove from a uniform pocket. Once I had it on, I picked up a strip and held it to the light. Sure enough, there was Gillian in all her glory, small though she might be.

I replaced the negative and my glove and headed back into the living room, mentally preparing myself for the prospect of digging through filth in search of more incriminating evidence. It didn't have much storage space, so I got to work on the kitchen, pulling open drawers and cabinets in search of additional contraband. I'd gotten about two-thirds of the way through, finding little more than pots, pans, and empty boxes of cereal, before I heard a clamor at the door.

Moss pushed through the front, and close behind her followed two EMTs wearing white shirts, navy pants, and matching caps. They carried a collapsible gurney between them as they wormed into the bedroom.

I followed them in, moving to the side as they expanded the gurney. Justice offered to help, but the medical techs waved him off, saying they worked better together. With a couple grunts, they shifted the man onto the gurney and draped his lower half with a blanket, all while the man muttered something unintelligible and fluttered his eyes.

I didn't pay much attention to him. I kept my gaze on Gillian. On her gaunt face, her hollow cheeks. There was no question she was the one in the blackmail photos, and yet the rosy color I remembered in the thief's face at Vernon and Daly's was nowhere to be seen. Maybe it was the way she lay there, barely breathing, her face pale, but I couldn't square her image with the one that burned in my memory from the night before.

The EMT's pushed the man out of the room, and Moss and Justice followed them. Meanwhile, Dean sidled up to me. "Find anything else?"

I nodded, watching Gillian's chest rise and fall from weak breaths. "She turned her bathroom into a makeshift darkroom, and I found the negatives. She's responsible for the blackmail."

"Or at least some of it," said Dean.

I met Dean's ice blue eyes. From them I could tell he'd noticed the same things I had. "There's no black duffel here, Dean. No hundred thousand crowns in cash. And perhaps most importantly, no floppy hat and no sunglasses."

Dean nodded glumly. "No murder weapon either, so far as I can tell. It's possible CSU will find traces of blood or ash or other remains, but I doubt it."

"What does it all mean?" I asked.

Dean pursed his lips. "It means this case isn't solved yet, and that Gillian's testimony, if we can get it, might be our best bet for understanding what the hell really happened."

CHAPTER THIRTY-SIX

I headed out of the break room with a mug of coffee warming my hands. The aroma of the beverage was more reminiscent of how an empty mug might smell rather than one filled with fresh brew, but beggars couldn't be choosers. Unless I brought my own beans from home, whereupon the coffee I brewed would promptly be consumed by everyone on the third floor, then the tepid tea-like concoction was the best I would get.

My ears perked as I headed back to my desk, tickled as they were not only by Justice's smooth, deep rumble but also Moss's sultry mezzo-soprano and Dean's even baritone. I found the three of them in their chairs as I turned the corner.

"You're back." I smiled. "So soon, too."

Moss, still in her leather jacket, snorted. "Yeah. Those last six hours really flew by."

As we'd finished at Gillian's dumpster of an apartment, Dean snagged Moss and followed the ambulance to the hospital, leaving Justice and me to oversee the CSU team and bag the remainder of the evidence, as well as to ensure that none of the remaining blackmail cash mysteriously disappeared. That was a lunch and several coffee breaks ago. I'd started to wonder if they'd make it back to the precinct at all.

I crossed to my desk, ignoring Moss's glances at my steaming mug. "I take it from the lack of sullen faces that Gillian and her beau pulled through."

Dean had already hung his coat. He leaned back in his chair, foot crossed over his knee. "It's too early to make that proclamation, but it's looking better for them, Miss Cross especially. She's in a bad way and will be for the next forty-eight to seventy-two hours—the vomiting has already started, and the shakes will only get worse—but she was able to open her eyes, nod in comprehension when spoken to, and even answer a few questions, albeit it with one or two word responses."

"So you were able to interrogate her after all?" I asked.

Moss cocked an eyebrow at me. "You know how when you talk to a dog they tilt their head and look confused and occasionally whine? More like that."

"While not inaccurate," said Dean, "it's not the best metaphor. The dog doesn't speak because he can't, not because he chooses not to."

Justice's chair sagged under his weight. "She was holding out on you, huh?"

Dean shrugged. "I've seen enough people clam up in response to questioning to know what it looks like, even though a veil of heroin. She wasn't lucid by any means, but she made her choice."

"So much for her shedding light on the past twenty-four hours, then." I took a sip of my coffee. It was warm but tasted sour and lemony.

"Time's on our side," said Dean. "Once she sobers up and

realizes how deep of a hole she's in, she might change her tune. The same goes for her boyfriend, or whoever it is we found her with. Where do we stand on the evidence?"

Justice sat up. "We've got her dead to rights on extortion. We checked with Vernon. That's his duffel we found in her apartment, and though the bills weren't marked, it's safe to say she was blowing though his cash. We can also charge her with numerous drug offenses, but as far as murder?" He shook his head. "The most dangerous item we turned up from her home was a chef's knife, and although CSU still has some materials to process, there's no reason to believe we're going to find physical evidence of Stella Vernon's murder. We can't pin it on her, not with what we have."

Dean sighed. "I didn't expect you'd turn anything else up, but I could hope." He rubbed his chin, upon which the barest layer of stubble had cropped up. "I hate cases where we can't find a weapon. In this one, we don't even know *where* Stella Vernon was murdered. One step forward, two steps backward it seems."

"Maybe we should focus on motive instead of means," I said. "As I see it, Gillian might've had quite a motive to murder her sister."

"How so?" asked Justice.

"We know Gillian was behind the blackmail of JT Vernon," I said. "She used nude photographs of herself, but Vernon blamed Stella for them. Obviously, Stella knew they weren't photos she'd taken, unless she too thought she'd taken them in a drug-induced stupor, but she defended herself of the charges to her husband and wrote the same in her diary. If I were her, I wouldn't let an attack like that fall by the wayside. I would've tried to figure out who'd taken the photos, and who's to say

Gillian is the only one who investigated her past? Perhaps Stella found out about Gillian and realized she was behind the photographs. She might've confronted her sister, threatened to turn her into the police if she didn't explain everything to JT, return the money, and destroy the photos. Gillian, being the unsavory sort, wouldn't have gone along with it. Perhaps she killed Stella to keep her quiet."

"That's a lot of mights and perhapses," said Moss. "While it's a decent story, we don't have any evidence to prove it. Besides, it doesn't explain crucial elements of the murder, like why Stella's remains were left in the aviary."

Justice cleared his throat. "I know this is going to sound crazy, but are we *sure* Stella is dead and not Gillian? Or rather that Gillian *isn't Stella?*"

All of us turned to stare at him.

"What do you mean?" asked Dean.

"We got a positive identification on Stella's remains, but because of the fact that the remains were cremated, we're not entirely sure how old they are. What if Stella died a while ago and Gillian stole her identity? Consider Stella's drug addiction. That she was often gone from her home, that she'd isolated herself from her friends. Those all could've been results of her worsening depression, but they might've also been because she quite literally was no longer herself. Because Gillian had taken over her life."

Moss frowned. "You know I love you big guy, but we have literally zero reason to believe any of that. You're pulling theories straight from your keister."

"I'm willing to entertain any theory," said Dean, "but I'll admit, that one's far fetched. I'd be more willing to believe the most simple theory that everyone is ignoring, which is that JT

Vernon killed his wife. They were in a loveless marriage, after all. He believed Stella was cheating on him, taking lewd photographs she'd leaked to someone who in turn was blackmailing him. He admitted he was furious about it. He believed the presence of the photos imperiled his campaign, which as far as I can tell is more important to him than his relationship with his wife was. Heck, from our most recent discussion with him, it seemed as if he was already trying to figure out how to spin his wife's death into a sob story. If we're going to throw about baseless accusations, that's the one to toss."

"And it is indeed baseless," said Moss, "because the evidence doesn't support that theory either, even if it doesn't specifically refute it."

Dean sighed. "Don't I know it."

"Excuse me? Detectives?"

We looked up to find a heavy-set officer with a thick mustache standing at the edge of the cubicle cluster.

Either Justice knew him, or he read his name tag. "Yes, Officer Reed?"

"There's a man in the lobby here to see you," said Reed. "Says his name is Radoslaw?"

"The zookeeper?" I said. "What does he want?"

The officer shrugged. "Said he had some information he needed to share, but he wouldn't tell the duty officer in charge what. Said he needed to speak to you. Mentioned Officer Phair by name."

The other detectives all looked at me, but I shrugged. "I've spoken to him a couple times. I guess he remembered me."

Dean nodded, as if that answered it. "Let's go see what he has to say, then."

All of us got to our feet and followed Reed down the stairs.

We found Krzysztof Radoslaw seated on one of the benches in the lobby, dressed in the same tattered canvas jacket I'd always seen him in. His skin was even yellower in the artificial lights than it was outdoors, and the bags under his eyes seemed to have grown, making it look as if he'd lost a fight.

We all stopped a couple feet shy of him. "Mr. Radoslaw? I'm Detective Alton Dean. I understand you're here to speak to us."

Radoslaw gave a glum nod as he stood. "That is correct." He coughed as he finished his short sentence, but luckily it only lasted a few short bursts instead of devolving into the long, hacking stretches I'd endured at the circus. "I am here to turn myself in."

Dean cocked his head. "Turn yourself in for what?"

Radoslaw's eyes were sad, but he spoke without hesitation. "For the murder of Mrs. Stella Vernon."

CHAPTER THIRTY-SEVEN

I sat in the same interrogation room in which I'd helped question the lewd photographer, instead this time it was Dean who sat next to me and Radoslaw on the other side of the table. The zookeeper hunched in his chair, shoulders slumped and head bowed. I don't think he was afraid to meet our eyes but rather too tired to do so.

"I'd like you to walk me through the night of Mrs. Vernon's murder, Mr. Radoslaw," said Dean. "What exactly happened that evening?"

"Mrs. Vernon arrived after dark." Radoslaw tapped his wrist. "I do not wear a watch, so I do not know what time. Late. After midnight, I think. She would drop by the circus to spend time with the animals, as have I told Officer Phair. I could not sleep that night, due to my cough, which is how I was awake when I saw her enter the aviary. She was quiet. Did not look at me, or say a word, though I think she noticed me as I followed her. She sat in the middle of the aviary in a single beam of moonlight that filtered through the leaves overhead. I stood there, watching her as I listened to the trill of the cotingas, and after a while... I snapped."

"What do you mean, you snapped?" I asked.

Radoslaw stared at the table. "I killed her. I cannot explain why. Perhaps I developed a fascination for her. Seeing her there, skin so pale, so quiet, such sadness in her face. I could not take it. I ended it for her. The suffering." He shook his head. "She will be better now. At peace."

"How did you murder her?" asked Dean.

"I put my arm around her neck, and I squeezed," said Radoslaw. "I strangled her."

"She didn't cry out?" said Dean. "Or fight back?"

"She was lost in her own world at first," said Radoslaw. "Once she realized what was happening, she tried to cry for help, but could not. I had too tight of a grip on her neck. She kicked and swatted at me but could not do much. I am strong, even if I do not look it."

Dean gave a slow nod, his eyebrows furrowed. "Then what?"

"There is a fire pit on the grounds, behind the main tent. The hands gather there for beers sometimes. Mostly we use it to burn refuse. That is where I burned her body."

One of my eyebrows crept up. "On a wood fire?"

"Yes. We had a number of pallets to burn. I stacked several, then placed her on top."

"It takes a large funeral pyre to cremate a body, Mr. Radoslaw," I said.

The man shrugged. "There were many pallets."

Dean cracked one of his knuckles. "Let's back up a bit. How did you get Mrs. Vernon's body to the pit?"

"I carried her," said Radoslaw.

"All by yourself?" said Dean.

Radoslaw coughed, hacking four or five times before getting his breath back. "As I said, there is still strength in my bones. I have spent my whole life laboring."

"No one saw you carry Mrs. Vernon's body to this fire pit?"

Radoslaw shook his head. "I guess not."

"Did you use any accelerants to get the fire going?" asked Dean. "Anything from the pyrotechnicians' pen?"

"Just matches," said Radoslaw.

"How long did it take for the body to burn?"

"A few hours, I suppose. Again, I do not wear a watch."

"And no one stopped by during that time?"

Again, Radoslaw shook his head.

"Did you strip her down before you set her on the pallets?" I asked.

Radoslaw lifted an eyebrow. "Why would I do that?"

"Just curious. You said you'd developed a fascination with her. Was it sexual?"

"No," said Radoslaw.

"Did you rape her?"

Radoslaw's cheeks darkened, and genuine anger crossed his face. "Absolutely not."

Dean rapped his fingers on the bare metal of the table. "So you stayed by the fire throughout the night. No one saw you. As the wood burned to coals and Mrs. Vernon was reduced to ash, what then?"

Radoslaw swallowed and stared at the table. "I gathered her remains and took them to the aviary. It seemed fitting I should leave them there given her fondness for the birds."

"How did you get the remains there?" asked Dean.

"I carried them," said Radoslaw. "They did not weigh much."

Dean snorted. "That's not what I meant. Surely they were hot, having roasted in a fire for hours."

"Oh." Radoslaw nodded. "I used a shovel. Put them in a wheelbarrow."

"You just said you carried them," I said.

Radoslaw stared at his hands. "I misspoke. You have to understand, I am flustered. None of this is easy for me to admit."

"Speaking of," said Dean, "why *are* you admitting to it? You told a different story to Officer Phair and Detective Moss previously. Why change your mind?"

Radoslaw sighed. "It is the guilt. I cannot sleep. I have barely eaten in days. And I—" Another round of explosive coughs cut the man short. This batch wasn't as easily dissuaded as the last, causing Radoslaw to double over the table and hack and sputter, each of his coughs resonating like drumbeats.

"Do you need a glass of water, Mr. Radoslaw?" asked Dean.

He waved Dean off as he straightened, taking a few deep breaths to still a tremor going through him. "I fear I have little time left to make amends. That is why I am here. I killed Stella Vernon. Please take me away, or give me a notepad to write down my story. Whatever the process. Please. I want it to be done with."

Dean pursed his lips. He was quiet for a moment before nodding. "Very well. We'll get you that notepad. Phair?"

He gestured to the door, and we both got up and headed into the adjoining hall.

Dean had barely closed up behind him before I opened my mouth. "He's full of crap. He didn't murder Stella Vernon."

Dean smiled. "What gave it away? The wheelbarrow flub, or the uncanny strength that allowed a dying man to carry a woman and stack pallets one atop another as they were cordwood?"

"Or maybe the fact that we didn't find any wheelbarrow tracks heading into or out of the aviary," I said. "Or the minuscule probability of none of the other people who live at the circus inquiring about the massive bonfire he claimed burned all night, or the similarly tiny probability of him scooping the melted glob of Stella's engagement ring into the *wheelbarrow* alongside the rest of her remains."

"Or even that said bonfire wouldn't have been hot enough to melt the ring in the first place," said Dean. "Trust me, I agree with you. Radoslaw is lying. The question is why."

"To protect someone?"

"Possibly. Or there could be a more nefarious reason."

Despite the fact that we'd had a good day—we'd identified Gillian Cross, captured her, and had someone confess to the murder of Stella Vernon—I felt defeated. "So what now?"

Dean stared down the hallway, his eyes distant. "We'll keep digging. Keep pulling at the threads until the whole things unravels—even if someone instructs us not to."

My brow furrowed. "What do you mean?"

"I need to take Radoslaw's confession to the captain," said Dean. "I'll make clear my suspicions, but if Ellison thinks Radoslaw's admission is good enough, that may mark the end of the investigation."

I blinked, not believing what I'd heard. "You're kidding. Why would the captain do that?"

Dean flashed a glum smile as stuffed his hands in his pockets. "You remember JT Vernon is running for congress, right?

Sometimes the proper resolution in the cleanest, or so people at the top would have us believe. Don't worry about it. That's my problem. You have others to deal with."

"I do?"

"The one we talked about this morning?" said Dean. "With your boyfriend? It's about time to head home, after all."

My heart sunk. I'd been so focused on the case I'd forgotten what awaited me at home. But Dean was right. My problems wouldn't solve themselves, and it was time to make a change.

CHAPTER THIRTY-EIGHT

I closed the apartment door behind me as I slipped off my shoes. "Cliff? You home?"

A bit of noise from the back alerted me before his response did. "In the bedroom. Getting ready for duty. Working third shift tonight."

I hung my coat on the rack by the door before heading toward his voice. As I walked, I noticed a brown paper baggie on the kitchen counter. Though it was faint, I detected an aroma of grilled onions and charred meat. It would be like Cliff to make peace with food, but I ignored the smell and the rumbling in my belly as I headed into the bedchambers.

I found Cliff in front of the mirror, working his way up the buttons on his shirt. He only had three left, but he usually left the one at the collar unbuttoned.

He gave me a quick glance. "I left a burger from Phat's on the counter. I didn't feel like heading any further before work, but something's better than nothing, right?"

"I appreciate the food as much as the gesture, Cliff. You know that."

Cliff moved onto his cuffs. "Anyway, Sergeant Willows asked if I could get in early tonight. I don't pull a lot of nights, so I don't know him as well as I do Zaxby or Anderson." He grabbed his watch and slapped it on his wrist. "How was your day? Catch any criminals?"

"I did. Maybe two, though one of them turned himself in. I don't think he did it, but that's neither here nor there. Cliff, can we talk?"

Cliff glanced at the watch he'd put on. "Can it wait until tomorrow? Like I said, I promised Willows I'd be there by eight."

"Five minutes, Cliff. This is important."

He sighed. He turned away from the mirror, resting a brawny arm on the dresser as he regarded me with his warm brown eyes. "I'm listening."

I took a deep breath to still my nerves. He really was a handsome guy, but lust alone did not a relationship make. I needed to be honest with him. "I've been thinking about what you said the other night. About me not paying enough attention to you. About me investing too much of myself in my work and not enough into our relationship. About me not being emotionally available, for lack of a better term."

"Nell, I think I know where this is going, and—"

I held up a hand. "Please, Cliff. I need to get this out."

Cliff pressed his lips together and nodded.

"I've thought about it," I said. "And you're right. I haven't been there for you, certainly not to the degree you deserve. It was simpler when we were both in the academy. We'd spend all day training, go home at the same time, share the same experiences. It was easy to connect. With our conflicting schedules and being at different precincts now, it's worlds harder, but that isn't the biggest problem. It's that I have a different focus than I did at the academy. At the time I thought establishing a career as a police officer would be a steady ascent, with trials along the way, sure, but a linear path. It's been anything but. A chaotic jumble. I feel like a marionette with all the directions I'm being pulled. If I'm going to navigate it, I need to put my focus into my career."

"You mean, that's where you *want* it to be."

I deflated a little. "Cliff..."

"Don't take that the wrong way. It's not a dig. Just an observation." He lifted his hand to his chin, rubbing his beard scruff as he stared out the window. "You know, when you were struggling with your TO and told me you were thinking about quitting, I supported you. I told you not to give up because I believed you could be a great officer. I'd seen your potential in the academy, and yet there was this voice in the back of my mind telling me it might be better if you jumped ship. That it would be easier if I was the only one on the force. Now that you've joined Dean's team, I realize I was right, even if I also realize I was being selfish. It wouldn't have been better for you, just for me. Because it's clear you're finally doing what you're meant to, even if you haven't fully accepted it."

As strained as the situation was, the compliment brought a smile to my face. "Thanks, Cliff."

Cliff sighed. "I just wish you'd be honest with me. Because the fact of the matter is, your job, your time, your focus. We could work through all of it if the will to do so was there. But will isn't the problem, is it?" He brought his soulful eyes back to meet mine. "Do you love me, Nell?"

I opened my mouth, then closed it again as I thought of how to respond. "I think you're a great guy. I like you a lot."

Cliff smiled. "*That's* the problem. Don't worry. It's how relationships work sometimes—or don't. I know because I'm the kind of person who falls fast and hard, just like you are. Sometimes when you fall, you land on your face."

I wrung my hands. "I wish I could tell you something different."

"Same here." He glanced at his watch. "I should be going. I know we've got a lot to hash out. The apartment, for one. Maybe we can get a foldaway bed for the living room until we figure out something more permanent. Or we can talk to the landlord. He might have another apartment available. I don't know about rent, but—"

"Cliff. It's okay. I'll pack my most important possessions tonight. I think I have someone I can stay with tomorrow. You can keep the apartment."

He lifted an eyebrow. "You sure?"

"It's within walking distance of the Williams Street precinct. I have to take the subway to get to the Fifth. Only makes sense I find something closer. I'll make it work."

"Okay, then." Cliff patted his pockets to make sure he had what he needed. "I guess I'll see you in the morning?"

"If I'm still around. Depends on the hour."

Cliff came over. His eyes weren't teary, but they had a sadness to them, nonetheless. "It was nice while it lasted, Nell. I'll miss what we had."

I eked out a smile. "Me, too."

Cliff nodded and headed for the door. I watched him go, feeling an ache in my chest that reflected Cliff's eyes. A voice inside me wanted to cry out, to tell him I'd made a horrible mistake, but I swatted it down. I'd made the right choice, even though it hurt. Hopefully I'd learn something from the pain.

Maybe the next time, I'd catch myself before I fell. Or if Dean's and my conversation this morning was any indication, perhaps I already had.

CHAPTER THIRTY-NINE

As it turned out, Captain Ellison either found Radoslaw's testimony convincing, or he was unwilling to stir the political pot. When I arrived at the Fifth, Dean conveyed to me he'd officially closed the murder and blackmail investigations, citing our suspects in custody for each. I didn't have to remind Dean that we'd failed to fully solve either case or that Radoslaw's story had more holes in it than a pair of fishnet stockings. He acknowledged as much himself, and in defiance of the captain's orders, he'd made a few calls prior to my arrival.

One of those had been to Vernon's residence. During the call, Dean hadn't spoken to JT Vernon. Mossbottom had stonewalled him, but the butler hadn't been completely opaque. He'd related his master's concerns about Radoslaw, that the man had always been surly, antisocial, and a bit of a sociopath, and he mustered up a fair bit of anger at our department's inability to identify Radoslaw earlier, anger Dean described as 'perfunctory' and 'forced.' Mossbottom also informed Dean that if he wanted to know more about Mr. Vernon's thoughts on the matter, he was welcome to listen to his press conference regarding his wife's death and the arrest of her killer, which would be occurring on live radio in the afternoon.

The news of Vernon's press conference came as a surprise but not a shock. During our last meeting, it already seemed he was scheming to use his wife's death to bolster his campaign, though it struck me as fortuitous that he'd managed to set up a broadcast press conference to discuss Radoslaw so soon after the man came forward. In fact, I wasn't sure how he knew he'd confessed, although I suppose Captain Ellison might've leaked him the news, which would then explain the captain's stance on our investigation.

For what it was worth, Dean shared my concerns. He found it too convenient that Radoslaw had reared his head just in time for Vernon to lay blame of his wife's death at his feet, not to mention that her death would engender more sympathy if it were at the hands of a supposed sociopath like Radoslaw instead of a disgruntled drug dealer or her long-lost prostitute of a sister.

When I asked what our next move was, Dean responded that we had none. The investigation was closed, and he'd been shuffled to existing open cases. That said, if we *were* to have a next move, it would be to investigate Radoslaw and figure out why he'd admitted to a murder he'd never committed. Dean also mentioned that while he'd be busy on new cases, he didn't antic-ipate there would be much for me to do today, and if I wanted to pick him up a coffee from Sangellies' Brew Stand on the far, *far* side of town, I was welcome to do so. The keys to his Viper were on the desk if I wanted them. But he made sure I understood the choice was mine.

I thought about Captain Ellison's warning for about two seconds before I grabbed the keys and headed out.

There were a number of places I could've visited, but I started with the obvious one. After parking at the Vernon and Daly's entrance, I followed the same path I'd taken when I'd first visited the circus, along the painted white fence hung with campaign posters, right at the covered wagon, and past the trailers and the cat pen. I slowed as I reached the aviary, searching the exterior for signs of workers. I didn't find any, but the exterior enclosure door was cracked an inch. I heard whooping sounds from within that sounded as if they belonged to the monkeys as well as a voice telling them to settle down, so I took a chance and pushed my way inside.

Morning sunlight filtered lazily through the branches as I passed through the interior drape. In the distance, a brown and green blur resolved itself into a monkey with a cabbage leaf in its mouth as it settled on a branch and munched away. On the path, not far from where Stella's remains had been recovered, stood a young man with a crate of produce. He was throwing it to the monkeys as much as they were taking it from him by force, but by the tone of his voice, he was having a good time.

"Come on, you scamps," he said. "Settle down. I'll make sure you all get some."

I spoke up as I got close. "Excuse me?"

The young man startled and spun, which the macaques took as an opening. One of them jumped and grabbed the side of his crate, ripping it from his hands and causing the contents to spill across the forest floor.

"Dang it, Gerard! I was going to give it to you soon enough. Fine. Take it." He turned to me, wiping his shaggy hair out of his face. "Sorry about that. I didn't hear you coming."

"And I didn't mean to startle you. I'm Officer Phair, with the NWPD. Do you work here?"

"Yeah. The name's Willard." He stuck out a hand, which I shook. "You here about Mrs. Vernon? Seems like we've had police around for days."

I nodded as I took my hand back. "Yeah. Do you work here in the aviary?"

The young man shrugged. "Sometimes. Guess I'll be doing more of it now that Krzysztof's gone. Still can't believe he murdered Mr. Vernon's wife."

Apparently, news travelled fast. I guess it was to be expected given Vernon's press conference on the subject this coming afternoon. "That's actually why I was here. I was hoping I could ask you a few questions about Radoslaw. How well did you know him?"

Willard shrugged again as he glanced at the macaques, who were dispersing with the last of the vegetables. "Not that well, if I'm being honest. Kept to himself for the most part. He only opened up when he was telling me about the animals. Some people are like that I guess. Only comfortable in certain environments. This one was his, I think."

I didn't like that Willard's summary of Radoslaw fit the sociopath profile he'd laid out for himself, but I pressed on. "So you probably couldn't tell me if he had any sort of relationship with Mrs. Vernon?"

The young man lifted an eyebrow. "Like... *relations* kind of relationship?"

"No. Just if he spoke to her often. Had a rapport."

Willard shook his head. "I couldn't tell you."

"Don't suppose you were out and about several nights ago? The night before Mrs. Vernon's remains were found? Radoslaw supposedly had a fire burning in the pit out back in the wee hours of the morning."

"If he did, I wouldn't have known about it. I'm a sound sleeper. Try not to get up before eight if I can avoid it."

I could commiserate, even if my career aspirations had made that close to impossible. "What about Radoslaw's illness? Has he always had that cough?"

"I don't think so." Willard leaned down to pick up his crate. "Seemed like a chronic thing. He didn't like to talk about it, but it was clearly getting worse. If it's his health you're curious about, I'm not the one you should be asking, though."

"Yeah. He mentioned he had a nephew that works here. Mateusz?"

"Sure, him. But I was talking about Krzysztof's wife."

I blinked. "Radoslaw is married?"

Willard nodded. "Yeah. His wife's name is Zuzanna. She was one of our unicyclists and jugglers."

"What do you mean, *was?*"

"Uh..." Willard's mouth dropped open, and I could tell he hadn't meant to drop that tidbit.

I tapped my badge. "You're not under oath, but you'd better tell the truth, otherwise we might have to continue this conversation at the station."

Willard swallowed hard. "Look, nobody tells me anything. I just hear rumors."

"What rumors?"

Willard looked around, as if the macaques were listening. "Apparently, Zuzanna took off last night. So did Mateusz. Nobody knows where they went."

"Before or after Krzysztof turned himself in?"

"I don't know. When was that?"

I gave him an approximate time.

"After, I guess."

"And what does the rumor mill suggest as the reason they left?"

The young zookeeper shrugged again. "Your guess is as good as mine. But if Krzysztof did murder Stella Vernon... well, I can't imagine Mr. Vernon would keep either of them around long, if you catch my drift."

I couldn't either, although firing them was only one of the routes he might've taken...

As I considered the implications of the Radoslaws' flight, I felt a rush of wind and a rustle of feathers, followed by a powerful avian cry.

Willard's eyes widened as he looked over my shoulder. "Well, I'll be damned..."

I turned to look at what had drawn his attention. On the branch above me perched a bird, similar in size to a macaw but with brilliant red and gold feathers and a tail close to two feet in length. It tilted its head back and forth, regarding us with eyes as golden as its plumes. "Who is this majestic little guy?"

"Girl, actually," said Willard. "She's an Orellian scarlet aracanga, also known as a firebird. I can't believe she's back. She's one of the birds that disappeared when the enclosure was left open the night of the murder. We were able to wrangle some of the birds that got out, but not her. I wonder how she made her way back in?"

"Back up a sec," I said. "A *firebird?*"

"It's because of their plumage," said Willard. "Catch them in the right light and it looks like they're on fire. Supposedly, early settlers to the continent scared some of them at sunset, and they shot into the sky, like streams of golden flame. Helped inspire the legend of the phoenix, or so the history books would have us believe. They're beautiful birds, aren't they?"

I glanced at Willard, then at the bird, then back at Willard. "Radoslaw mentioned this bird. You're sure it went missing in the aftermath of Mrs. Vernon's death?"

The young man snorted. "I mean, she's hard to miss. I think I would've seen her over the past few days if she'd been here. I still don't know how she got back in. Maybe there's a tear in the netting?"

His brow furrowed as he stared at the radiant bird, probably wondering at the bird's recent journey. I did, too, but I suspected the theory I was putting together was very, *very* different that his.

CHAPTER FORTY

D ean and Justice weren't at their desks when I returned to the precinct, but Moss was. She twirled a finger around a curl of her long blonde hair as I crossed to my desk. "Look who finally showed up. Where have you been all morning?"

"Fetching coffee for Dean."

She looked at my empty hands and snorted. "Okay. And what are you doing now? Mowing his lawn?"

I ignored the jab. "Actually, I was hoping to catch JT Vernon's press conference. There's a radio in the break room, isn't there?"

Moss lifted a hand. "Hold on there, cowgirl. Haven't you heard? The press briefing was cancelled."

I blinked, confused. "Cancelled? Why?"

Moss plucked a newspaper off her desk and handed it to me. "Apparently, Vernon planned his conference before the morning paper made it to his mailbox. Check out the top story."

I glanced at the headline, which read: *Circus Showman and Congressional Hopeful JT Vernon Cheats Investors and*

Employees Alike, Exposé Discovers. My eyes widened, and I whistled.

"To be fair, most businessmen as wealthy as Vernon have lied and cheated to get where they are," said Moss. "Still, it's not likely to help his poll numbers. I'd guess he cancelled his conference because he figured he'd get more questions about his business dealings than about his dead wife."

I unfolded the paper. "Are there teeth to the allegations?"

Moss shrugged. "The article says they received documents from an anonymous source, but the *New Welwic Statesman* wouldn't publish the story if they couldn't back it up. There are three pages devoted to it, with a treasure trove of details to back up the thesis. Tens of thousands of crowns in outstanding backpay for his carnies. Overestimating his assets to banks to secure loans. Potential tax and mail fraud. If it checks out, he could be facing significant financial as well as criminal liability."

I scanned the text, getting a better sense of the details. "Who'd be in charge of investigating this?"

"The fraud guys, I guess," said Moss. "Though if you're asking which precinct, could be us or Old Town depending if the team gets assigned based on Vernon's address or the newspaper's. Why?"

"I think this may affect our investigation, too," I said. "You want to take a trip to the *New Welwic Statesman* offices?"

Moss smirked, a twinkle in her eye. "What investigation? You still need to get Dean's coffee."

I smiled. "You're right. I do." I lifted the newspaper. "Mind if I keep this?"

"Be my guest."

I headed out, but I stopped as I reached the end of the cubicles. "One more thing, Moss. Would it be possible for me to, ah... crash at your place for a few days?"

The twinkle disappeared, and Moss's brow furrowed. "Say what?"

"I broke up with my boyfriend, and I need a place to stay until I lock down a new apartment. Dean said you might be able to help."

Moss's eyes widened. "Dean knows and I don't?"

I shrunk into my neck. "Justice, too."

Moss snorted and threw up her hands. "What's the point of having another lady on the squad if I get left out of all the gossip? Just when you think you've made a connection."

"Sorry. It's recent. And the reason I'm asking is because of our connection. Pretty please?"

Moss sighed. "Of course. But next time tell me first! And I demand a thorough explanation of what happened tonight, perhaps over drinks."

"I can do that. You're a life-saver."

I shot her a finger gun before heading down the stairs to the first floor. I'd made it most of the way across the edge of the pit when a voice cracked at me like a whip. "Officer Phair!"

I screeched to a halt at the sound of Captain Ellison's voice, turning to pop my head into his open office door. "Yes, Captain?"

The grey fox looked at me from his desk, the expression on his face either one of curiosity or disapproval. Maybe both. "Did you hear the news?"

He didn't give me a lot of context, but given Moss had asked much the same question, I took a guess. I lifted the newspaper. "That JT Vernon might be in hot water? Yes, sir."

Ellison clicked his tongue. "Shame, that. He'd made overtures to the department that suggested he'd be a staunch ally of the police. Not that Congressman Bumblefoot has been an enemy of ours, but still. I have to imagine Vernon's campaign is dead in the water now, wouldn't you?"

I shrugged. "I couldn't say, sir. I'm not much of a political person."

One of Ellison's eyebrows rose, giving him a more devious air. "Of course not. You're just an officer. Politics are above your head. But you have spent your short stint here assigned to the Vernon case. Who do you suppose might've handed Vernon's dirty laundry to the *New Welwic Statesman?* That woman we arrested for blackmail?"

The curve of Ellison's eyebrow and the pucker to his lips told me he wasn't entirely interested in my answer, just as they told me not to inform him of my planned trip to the *Statesman.* "Someone who wanted to hurt Mr. Vernon or his family, I suppose. No shortage of those around, it seems."

Ellison snorted. "Indeed." The captain brought his eyes back to the file in front of him, but his tone didn't change. If anything, it grew icier. "Regardless, I'm glad we were able to wrap up the investigation into his blackmailer, as well as the murder of his wife. We wouldn't want a man like that holding a grudge against us, congressman or not."

I probably should've shut my mouth, but I wasn't wired that way. "And the allegations of fraud in the paper, sir?"

Ellison's head slowly rose. "Something for the fraud boys to take a look at, Officer."

I nodded, wishing I'd simply left. "Yes, sir."

Ellison intertwined his fingers before him on his desk, his eyelids narrowing. "Since you're here, Officer, how is Detective

Dean doing? Not distracted from his caseload by this Vernon news, I hope?"

Fact of the matter was I had no idea if Dean knew, but the truth was worse. Dean knew Captain Ellison wanted him to dust his hands of the case, and instead here I was, newspaper in hand with every intention of continuing to investigate Stella's murder and the sundry blackmail and smear campaigns against JT Vernon. I might not have been under orders from Dean, but I hadn't needed a lot of coaxing, either.

As I stood in the door frame, I was reminded of something my toxic former training officer told me. In a red-cheeked, frothy rage he'd hammered into me that even more important than our duty to the citizens of the city was our duty to each other. To protect and serve. That was the police motto. To him it meant the men and women in blue protected each other from violent criminals and thugs as readily as from lawsuits and prosecution, that we protected each other from the consequence of our actions and from the system of justice we purveyed as much as from actual danger. I'd thought it as vile, toxic, and deranged a stance then as I did now, but as I heard the slight intonation in the captain's voice, I realized there was truth in it, too. We did have to stick by one another. Protect each other by any means necessary, by hook or by crook, but not the bad apples.

We had to protect the good ones.

No one would do it for me. It was up to me to stand on the side of right, to do what I could to make sure justice and honesty and truth were served, regardless of who stood in the way. Dean and Justice and Moss were the ones on my side, the right side, and I'd stand by them. I'd put myself at risk to protect them if it meant furthering our shared ideals. The path might be difficult to navigate, and it might require me to play a game with Captain

Ellison that I wasn't particularly adept at, but I'd do it to stay true to myself and my beliefs.

I straightened my back as I answered, feeling as confident as I ever had as an officer. "Detective Dean's hard at work on the new caseload, sir. I'm doing my best to help ease the burden."

Captain Ellison smiled, but there was something about it that made me suspect he didn't put full faith in my answer. "Glad to hear it, Officer. As you were."

I nodded as I headed out, feeling as if a weight had been lifted from my shoulders. It wasn't the act of defiance that had done it. More the knowledge that I'd broken the glass from the box and could now use the tool within when the circumstances demanded it: in defense of myself and the people who shared my sense of virtue.

CHAPTER FORTY-ONE

I t was near the end of the day when I arrived back at our cluster on the third floor. Moss and Justice were missing, but Dean was at his desk, with an aroma of smoke clinging to him that suggested he'd just stepped inside from a cigarette break. Normally, the scent might turn me off, but I was too amped to care.

Dean turned at the sound of my feet. "You know, when I said you could borrow my car, I didn't expect you'd be gone the entire damn day."

I dug his keys out of my pocket and tossed them onto his desk. "Sorry about that. I've been busy. Much more so than I expected."

Dean eyed the folder in my left hand. "So it would appear. Is that a CSU report?"

The color gave it away, as well as the stamp that was partially legible through my fingers. "Guilty as charged. I'm assuming you read the newspaper story about JT Vernon?"

"I'm not sure anyone around here hasn't," said Dean. "I also didn't find any of it surprising. What about it?"

"That's why I've been gone so long," I said. "Although, technically, I've been back for a while. I've been hanging out downstairs talking to Emmett, and before that with Ben. He's one of the CSU techs. So I suppose I could've come and dropped your keys off, but I had a bit of a flirtatious rapport going on with Ben that I was hoping would pay dividends, which it did. Sorry. I'm getting ahead of myself."

Dean smiled. I think he got a sense of my enthusiasm from the speed at which I was talking. "Do you want to have a seat?"

"Sure." I grabbed my dilapidated chair and wheeled it over, plopping down in front of Dean. "So after Moss showed me the story on Vernon, I headed to the *New Welwic Statesman* to take a look at the materials on which the story was based. There was a lot of stuff, by the way. A thick stack of paper that, as expected, had been mailed to the newspaper anonymously. I didn't want to ruffle any feathers, so I didn't take the materials myself. Instead, I waited for a fraud team to get assigned. Eventually they arrived. Watts and Lajoie, from the second floor? I met them today. They were surprised I was on the scene, but I gave them a summary of our blackmail case and told them I needed to confirm it was the same person and they understood. Hopefully, they won't leak that detail to the captain. Anyway, I stayed on the sidelines as they gathered the papers, but I was of help when we learned the envelope the materials had been sent in had already been thrown out, which meant I got to go dumpster diving. That endeared me even more to Watts and Lajoie, because Watts apparently has a bad back and Lajoie was wearing a dapper suit that I'm pretty sure he didn't want to get dirty, which probably means they'll be less likely to rat me out to the captain now that I think about it."

Dean nodded, though his furrowed brow suggested I was losing him. "I see. And where does Ben from CSU come in?"

"Right," I said. "With the detectives' blessing, I hand carried the envelope to our CSU lab, which is where I met Ben. As I'm sure you know, CSU doesn't normally prepare reports on the spot, certainly not when an officer such as myself asks, but I dropped your name and was quite friendly with Ben, resulting in... this." I opened the folder and held it out.

Dean took it and studied the contents. "He was able to pull fingerprints off the envelope?"

"There were several—from mail carriers, probably the journalist who opened the thing—so it was a bit of a mess. But we eventually found a partial of the one I was looking for. This is it." I tapped the image for emphasis. "See how it matches the full print on the right? That's one we pulled off Stella Vernon's diary."

Dean chewed on his lip as he stared at the results. "You're saying Stella sent the incriminating data to the newspaper."

"Precisely."

Dean closed the folder, keeping it in his lap. "That suggests Stella mailed the documents to the newspaper before her death, which potentially implicates her husband. At least, it does if we assume Stella mailed the documents because she feared for her safety. The fact that she'd mailed them might be motive for JT to kill her."

"That's one possibility," I said.

Dean pursed his lips. "The other is that Stella is still alive, and the documents were mailed recently."

I leaned in. "I have a theory."

Dean tossed the folder onto his desk. "I'm listening."

A nervous energy burbled inside me, but fear crept beside it, too. Now that I was about to share it with someone else—not just anyone, but Alton Dean—I wondered if it was better left to simmer. "It's going to sound crazy. It did to me, at least until I spoke to Emmett."

"Your theory will only sound crazy if it's not supported by facts."

Dean smiled, and that was the only encouragement I needed. I took a deep breath. "We tossed around the idea that Stella faked her death, and to be fair, it makes a lot of sense. We know Stella was depressed. She was taking benzedrine, which is commonly used as an anti-depressant, and her diary chronicles her deteriorating relationship with her husband. JT only admitted to becoming angry and nearly hitting her after finding out about the nude photographs, but that sort of behavior doesn't come out of nowhere. It suggests he might've abused her regularly. Maybe he didn't beat her, but he might've berated her. Harassed her. Gaslit her. All of which is supported by Stella's diary. So she had a strong motive to leave Vernon behind, but what if she didn't see a way out? It could be that they had an ironclad prenup, making Stella think she'd get away with nothing in a divorce, or perhaps it was worse than that. Maybe Vernon threatened her, convinced her he'd never let her leave. It could've led Stella to consider another way out."

"By faking her death," said Dean.

"Not exactly," I said. "But I'll get back to that. First I want to discuss the evidence. We know Stella's sister Gillian was behind the nude photographs, which she used to trick JT into providing blackmail money. Stella knew the whole time it wasn't her, but the blackmail gave her an idea. That was her way out. Perhaps she couldn't escape Vernon through divorce, but if she disappeared and used the blackmail to get a hundred thousand crown payout..."

"Vernon would never know he'd been had," said Dean. "And the evidence suggests you might be right. We didn't find the hundred thousand crowns at Gillian's apartment, nor the pieces of the outfit the woman who picked up the duffel from the circus was wearing. Not to mention the woman you and I saw, the woman in the sketch Feoris drew, does not appear to be Gillian."

"Don't forget the suitcase CSU found in the trunk of Stella's car, which also suggests Stella was ready to run. And the final blackmail letter to JT? You stared at it, same as I did. Tell me it wasn't in Stella's handwriting."

Dean rubbed his chin. "Okay. I buy the premise. My problem is with the execution. Faking a death isn't easy. It's not as if she simply went missing. We found *someone's* remains, remains a coroner I trust identified as Stella's. If she faked her death, then whose remains did we find? Did she steal them? And how did she manage to doctor them to fool Jowynn?"

I took another breath and pushed it out forcefully. "I'm not suggesting Stella faked her death. I think she died, but I also think she's still alive."

Dean's mouth opened, then closed. He pressed his lips together, not saying a thing. "Okay. Now I see the crazy."

I leaned in. "Only if it's not supported by facts, you said. Hear me out. I spoke to the zookeeper who took over for Radoslaw. While there, a brilliant red and gold bird showed up in the aviary. The new hand was adamant the bird had flown away during the murder. Radoslaw told me the same thing, yet there it was, as if it never left. He claimed it was a scarlet aracanga, also known as a firebird. The same bird after which the legend of the phoenix is based."

Dean's brow furrowed, but I kept going. I was this far deep, after all. There was no point in pulling out.

"I know it's insane, but think about it. We found Stella's remains in the middle of the aviary, a place multiple carnies confirmed was a spot Stella liked to visit. And Jowynn confirmed they *were* Stella's remains! We also have reason to suspect a fire was set in the aviary. The ground underneath was scorched, after all. And let's not forget her engagement ring wasn't the only thing found melted. So was something else made of steel. Her car keys, perhaps. Steel doesn't melt easily. It takes a high temperature, one most furnaces can't reach. Remember how Jowynn said he thought the fire that cremated Stella burned hot and fast?"

Dean cocked his head. "I don't know, Phair..."

"Trust me, Dean, I'm not one for off-the-wall theories. Don't ask me how it happened. Maybe Stella lured the aracanga to her and it freaked out. Maybe she had a bond with it. Maybe the bird felt her sorrow and yearned to set her free, same as she yearned to be so. Let's say she held it and both of them somehow... *combusted.* Stella rose from the ashes. If we accept that impossibility as possible, then gosh darn it, *everything fits!* She would've been naked in the aftermath of her immolation, perhaps disoriented and afraid. But she had clothes in her car. A whole suitcase full. She ran out, only to remember she couldn't get back into her car because her keys were now a pile of molten steel hidden under ash. So she ran back to the circus, at which point a wine-soaked hobo spotted her and probably thought whatever drink he'd soaked himself in was the best he'd ever tasted. So what does Stella do? She breaks into one of the trailers that holds costumes, which we thought one of the macaques had done, dresses herself, and flees, giving herself time to set up the final blackmail drop against her husband."

Dean tapped his fingers against his armrest. "Phair, I'm still not seeing the facts you mentioned."

"Neither did I," I continued, "until I talked to Emmett. Dean, he found *feathers* in the morgue this morning. Red and gold ones, and the bowl that contained the ashes from the circus had been disturbed. He even called to have pest control come by because he thought an animal had gotten in, but isn't it obvious? The aracanga came back to life overnight! I don't know why it took so much longer than Stella—maybe its powers had been spent on her—but it must've found a way out of the station and flown back to the circus. It's the only explanation that makes sense!"

Dean was quiet for a while, perhaps considering turning me into the funny farm. "You realize the only way to prove any of this is to track down Stella Vernon, don't you?"

"Probably," I said. "But it should be easy enough to prove Radoslaw didn't murder her. He's terminally ill, and his wife and nephew mysteriously disappeared after he turned himself in. What do you want to bet that if we check Vernon's finances again we'll find another large withdrawal, one that went to Radoslaw's family in exchange for a fake plea of guilt?"

"Most likely," said Dean. "And it was probably a sweet deal for both parties, or at least it would've been for Vernon if this expose in the *Statesman* hadn't come out. Now, instead of garnering sympathy for his dead wife at the hands of a psychopath, he's stuck fending off criminal and civil suits alike. Hell of a turn."

I felt a massive smile come on. "So you're with me? All we have to do is find Stella and we can prove I'm right!"

"That's where things get tricky," said Dean. "Honestly, I think it might be better to let sleeping dogs lie."

My face fell. "You can't be serious? You're going to let this go when we're so close to cracking it? When we're so close to actually knowing for a fact what happened?"

"It's not that simple, Phair," said Dean. "For one thing, Captain Ellison closed the cases. If you'd unearthed ironclad evidence that pointed to someone having murdered Stella Vernon, you bet I'd take it to him, but you don't have evidence. You have a compelling story, one that suggests Stella took her own life—or didn't. Legally speaking, I have no idea if it could be classified a suicide or not. My point is, it's possible it's best that the people behind bars stay there."

"Gillian, yes," I said. "We have her cold on blackmail, but not Radoslaw. He didn't murder anyone."

"Maybe not," said Dean. "But filing false testimony is a crime, too, and how long does Radoslaw have to live? A few months? A year? Clearly he decided a hefty payment from Vernon was worth spending his last few gasps suffering in prison, at least for his family. And have you thought about what happens if we prosecute Vernon for paying him off? The money paid to Radoslaw's family gets taken away, and Radoslaw stays in jail."

I hadn't thought about that. "Okay. But at least Vernon gets what's coming to him."

"The wheels are already in motion for that," said Dean. "If you're right about Stella, she made sure of it. Everything we need to put Vernon away on fraud charges is downstairs with Watts and Lajoie. But I think you're missing the biggest reason to close the book and stop reading now. Because this way Stella goes free instead of getting ten to fifteen years for blackmail and falsifying her death. Doesn't she deserve better than that? To walk off into the sunset with her thieving husband's cash, forever free from their toxic relationship?"

My chair squealed as I leaned back in it. I brought a knuckle to my lips and chewed on it a little. I'd never considered what was best for everyone involved, just what the truth of the matter was. "What if I'm wrong though? What if Bumblefoot or someone else mailed the evidence to the *Statesman*? What if the feathers were planted? What if Stella really was murdered? Are we just going to leave it be?"

Dean smiled. "I've told you this before, and I'll tell you again. In this job, you never know the full truth. The closest you get is a vague approximation based on bits and pieces that never fully coalesce. That said, when the story makes sense, you can feel it. In here." He tapped his chest. "And either you're one hell of a storyteller, Penelope, or you already know the truth of what happened."

Dean's confidence buoyed me. Not a ton, but enough. "My friends call me Nell, actually."

"Nell it is, then." Dean's phone rang, and he glanced over his shoulder. "Give me a sec."

Dean grabbed the receiver and pulled it to his ear. "Alton Dean speaking."

I sank into my chair, wondering if Dean's praise was more for my story-telling ability or my deductive instincts. Both were compliments, but there was more to be proud of from the latter than the former. I momentarily lost focus as I thought it over, but when I regained my senses, I noticed Dean's face had turned to stone. The fingers with which he clutched the phone had gone white, and a vein in his neck pulsed.

"Who is this?" he said. "How did you get this number?"

My brow furrowed, but I didn't say a thing. At the edge of my hearing, I heard a processed voice leak from the phone's speaker.

Dean's face remained frozen until I too heard the click through the line. "Hello? Hello?"

"What is it?" I asked. "Who was that?"

Dean's arm dropped at his side, but he didn't let go of the phone. He stared past me, as if I'd disappeared. "If he was to be believed, that was the Tarot Card Killer." Dean blinked and met my gaze, his eyes hollow. "He said he's going to kill again, Phair. *Tonight.*"

ABOUT THE AUTHOR

Hi. I'm Alex P. Berg, author of *The Burnt Remains*. Phair may have flexed her investigative muscles in this novel, but she'll need more than her wits and gumption to survive the next case. Will Phair and Dean be able to stop the Tarot Card Killer before he paralyzes the city with fear? Find out in *Divination and Rot*.

Can't wait for the next Penelope Phair adventure? Well, have you read my Daggers & Steele series? It features Nell's great-grandparents and homicide detectives extraordinaire Jake Daggers and Shay Steele, back when New Welwic was just going through the industrial revolution. The complete ten book series is available now, so what are you waiting for! Read it today! You can even buy the complete series in a single low-priced omnibus volume.

Word of mouth is **critical** to my success. If you enjoyed this novel, please consider leaving a positive review on Amazon or your retailer of choice. Even if it's only a line or two, it would be a *huge* help. Thanks!

Want to connect? Visit me at www.alexpberg.com or contact me on social media.

For a complete list of my books, please visit: www.alexpberg.com/books/.